Amid the Noise and Haste

Written by Pamela Blair

The Gervais Family.

"We don't just meet people by accident; they are meant to cross our path for a reason." ~ Unknown

Hope you enjoy this book reading as much as I enjoyed writing it ! ♡

Pam

~Dedicated to Eli Pawliw~
Thank you for choosing me to be your mother!

Amid the Noise and Haste

~Prologue~

"What walks on four legs in the morning, two at mid-day and three at night?"
The Riddle of the Sphinx

The answer is **Man**; he crawls on all fours as a baby, and then walks on two feet for the majority of his life; then he gives way to the use of a cane as he reaches old age. Although there are many interpretations of the history behind the riddle, its purpose and its inventor, legend has most commonly credited it to Oedipus as a riddle that he enforced to provide security into the entrance of the great tombs of the pyramids. One needed to answer the question correctly or be slain. It was Hera, who knew the answer.

I was very fortunate throughout my life to have had the opportunity to travel and it was on one such adventure to Egypt where I was reminded about the complexities and the capabilities of the human spirit. I was in awe of the pyramids and the Sphinx and marveled at the construction of such eternal masterpieces because most particularly, they had been crafted so many centuries ago; but it made me realize that no matter how much we as humans have evolved, we are still plagued by the same riddles, suffer the same conditions and pay the same consequences as our human brethren did back then. We are the most evolutionary creatures on the planet. Yet we cannot seem to move beyond our own complexities and limitations. We are all united in our misery by what makes us divinely human.

My protagonist, naturally, is no different, she suffers the same human conditions; she lives, she loves and she dies. She is ever evolving moving from her morning to her noon then to her night of life, but she feels the need to go outside herself in order to seek what is really within all along, in order to find 'peace with her soul' as it says in *The Desiderata* and to find her 'home', whatever that is perceived to be. This then bares the question, is she actually meeting and seeing real people or merely incarnations of her self?

~~

Amid the Noise and Haste

BOOK ONE

Go placidly amid the noise and haste,
Remember what peace there may be in silence
As far as possible, without surrender
Be on good terms with all people;
Speak your truth clearly and listen to others
Even the dull and ignorant have their story.

Chapter One

Ever since I first laid eyes on her I have known some deeper connection, like we were an extension of each other and that our souls were one. And now it's time again we meet. She was going to move Heaven and Earth to get here.

The airport wasn't nearly as crowded as I was expecting but still, the sounds, the people, the hellos, the goodbyes, all seemed to add to my anticipation. I felt my chest tighten with the heat from the fireball that replaced what was once my stomach. My teeth clenched as they often did when I was anxious and a trickle of sweat began to drip down the back of my neck. *Lovely*! I thought. I'll be a sweaty mess by the time I get to see her. I remember telling her 'Don't be late!' in my playful way to emphasize to her just how much I wanted to spend every possible second with her, yet as luck would have it, it was I who was going to be late merely trying to negotiate the tunnels and passageways out of this chaotic frenzy.

And there she was!

She hopped towards me in a girlish burst of energy with her arms open wide yet not wider than her bright white smile that dimpled her face when she laughed. Her friendly embrace was what I had yearned for, for some months now when our long dormant relationship again took a more active and intimate path. She was taller and even prettier than I had remembered. As her grasp loosened with our greeting, my mouth grazed her ear. "I've missed you," I whispered, looking around in fear that I'd said it too loudly. She giggled and leaned back towards me. Her sweet breath and warmth surrounded me and so naturally guided me into the endearing caverns of her soul. "I am home", I thought. This was always the way it felt when I was with her.

~~

Piper was christened Patricia Jane Brown, shortly after her birth in 1965, the younger of two middle children in a family of four. In her earliest incarnations, Patricia Jane seemed to have only inherited her mother's wispy blonde hair; her other attributes from her deep blue eyes to her quick-temper, shouted loudly and clearly, that she was the daughter of an Irish man. From the outset, she was a passionate, compulsive, and imaginative spirit with a boundless curiosity that seemed to battle her logical powers, at every turn. She was known to move so quickly that she would already have journeyed well into the depths of the ocean before she ever considered that she might not be able to swim.

Her father, who was baptized Patrick James Bronwyn, came to Canada with his parents when he was just a boy in the 1930s. When he turned 18 and the threat of conscription and World War II loomed over him, he thought it would be safer to change his name to something less 'ethnic' and to become a true Canadian, so when he registered his citizenship and applied for his first passport, he became forever known as Patrick James Brown. That is until he graduated from medical school and became Dr. Patrick James Brown. And from what I remember being warned about him by Piper, keeping in mind 'the doctor' part of this address was as important, if not more so, than the 'Brown'.

Patrick, although having been somewhat of a ladies man and dating his share of women throughout university and med school, seemingly settled down early in his life with Emily Taylor, the daughter of a working class English man, 'a jack of all trades and master of none' as Piper would often reiterate from her mother's description of him. My only notions of the greatness of Piper's Grandpa Taylor came from watching Piper's eyes light up when she spoke of him. He died when she was 9 or 10; his death devastated and changed her. It was the first real experience she had with mortality and it marked her. It was a time of great upheaval for her. It also changed her father.

Although Stanley Taylor was his wife's dad, Patrick had a great deal of respect for him and held him in high regard. He had been his only living role model for the past two decades or so, after his own parents died in a single car crash. The blood alcohol level extracted from his father's blood stream at the time of the accident, was four times the legal limit. It was tragic but not surprising to him. He was an aggressive alcoholic and that's what pretty much kept Patrick on the straight and narrow, that and Patrick's admiration for Stanley. When Stan died unexpectedly from a sudden heart attack,

Patrick fell apart. He was always hot-tempered like a canon ready to go off, but this was the straw that broke the camel's back. Paddy-O, as the ladies loved to call him returned to his womanizing ways.

Many years later, Piper confided in me in how her father would terrorize the family in his drunken fits. He was a tall man and a prizefighter in his youth, as many Irish boys were trained to be. He'd throw punches and hurl insults. No one was left unscarred by his rage; so even as young as ten years old, PJ, as her schoolmates had called her then, wanted out. She often vowed that she needed to travel beyond her parentally instilled boundaries in order to truly know who she was or who she was to become. Consequently, this became the end of her idyllic childhood and the beginning of her journey.

When Patrick would become enraged and storm out of the house, a deafening silence always appeared amid the noise. Emily would assertively find her keys stashed away in her purse and would tiptoe out towards the interior garage door. She'd peak through the small crack made when she opened the door slightly to ensure that Patrick was gone, and then when she knew the coast was clear, she swiftly skirted to the driver's side, opened the car door and just as quietly closed it behind her. Within moments, she'd be barreling down the driveway out through the open roads that led away from the Brown's country estate.

PJ always thought that her mother went out to follow Patrick, as that's what she had been led to believe by her father himself. Emily was a suspicious person or so Patrick criticized, but Patrick had given her every reason to be, so the logic seemed to stick. However, Patricia had her doubts.

One day, after a thunderous threat from her father, to burn the house down, PJ managed to squeak out a, "Mum, where are you going? We're scared, please don't leave us;" the Brown children finally learned where Emily went and just how she coped in the dysfunction.

"C'mon kids, get in." Emily urged gently as her two youngest complied.

Ten-year-old Finola, the youngest of the Brown clan, and three years Patricia's junior, was always the first to speak. She shared the deep blue Irish eyes, like that of her sister, but had the dark brown hair and milky white complexion that went along with the authentic Irish stereotype. Although she was the youngest, Finola was most certainly going to be the tallest of the girls in the Brown family and that, and the fact that she was the youngest, seemed to give her the greatest strength to speak up when she felt there was an injustice going on, particularly if she believed the injustice revolved around her.

"Where are we going, Mum?" Finn asked.

Since they felt it a privilege to be sharing the ride this time, they moved quickly into the back seat and buckled themselves in without more than much of a whisper. About an hour later the girls could hear the sound of engines above that of the car's motor.

"Are we going to be flying somewhere? It sounds like we're at the airport." Finn concluded.

"We're near the airport, but we're not going anywhere," said Emily as she exited from the highway and onto a service road. She drove for another minute or two then stopped in front of a dead-end sign, pulled the car into the ditch, turned it off and asked the girls to follow her. They weren't out of the vehicle for more than a few seconds when nearby engines roared even louder, making them feel they had to duck to get out of the path of the oncoming plane. It vibrated the earth beneath their feet, distorting their vision.

"Look at that!" Finn screamed and pointed her finger in the air towards the overhead ground-seeking jetliner.

"Wow!" agreed Finn. "Amazing!"

The area where Emily parked was a popular spot, however off the beaten track, for aviation lovers to come and watch the planes as they took off and landed. They'd pull off to the side of the road and watch in awe. Some people, like Emily, even went so far as to find the hole in the fence. Emily led the girls through the hole, just large enough for them to squeeze through one at a time, to a flat grassy area just on the other side. They laid there for what seemed to be hours, just watching, listening and dreaming. The girls didn't ask for any explanation at that point; it was a defining moment. They knew that Emily was just going to put up with whatever Patrick was going to dish out and she'd find a way to keep strong.

PJ was hooked. She would forever find solace in the grassy fields near the runways and watch the airplanes as they took off and landed. She began imagining herself aboard a big jetliner headed to a far away place. She got so wrapped up in the imagery of being 'taken away' that when she turned 16 and could drive herself anywhere she wanted to go, she found that the car automatically took her to the airport. She extended the metaphor right into the parking lot and terminals. She'd watch the comings and goings of the many passengers and greeters and wonder what adventures would await them or had already graced their souls. She imagined herself to be a part of all the joyous reunions and the heart-wrenching departures, the kisses and hugs, the tears and the smiles. She'd walk back and forth through the main terminal, checking the flight statuses on the location boards. She'd close her eyes, twirl herself around and let her pointer finger land on the screen and whatever amazing city she pointed to, was going to be her next dream destination. Sometimes she wasn't too happy about the random selection, so she'd try it again, but usually, one pick would be enough to curb her hunger. PJ had wanderlust.

Despite the fact that it was her mother who showed her the pathway to this escapism, it was her father ironically, who shared with her his travel gene. Patrick had taken Emily and the kids on many adventures to both exotic and turbulent locations. Photos of PJ riding a camel around the pyramids in Egypt adorned the grand hallway of the Brown residence. Another family photo showed the children picking olives from an olive tree in Majorca, an island off the coast of Spain, and the pride of the pack, was a picture of Emily sitting on a chair in a circle with her two youngest on her lap amid a crowd of Tunisian children in a tiny, hospital room. Patrick had been working for a few months leading up to Christmas for Care Medico - an organization that sends physicians and surgeons to underprivileged countries around the world - and sent for Emily and the girls to join him. The photo had been taken while they were singing Christmas carols with the children in the pediatric ward. Of all the Brown children, it was PJ who appreciated this type of global connectedness the most. It gave her great insight as to the major issues of the world and what she could possibly do to help eradicate them. Unbeknownst to her at the time, this fascination with foreign cultures and her innate curiosity, both paved the pathway for her to a career as a reporter.

Patricia Jane had a great deal of Patrick James in her genetic make-up and that used to tear her up inside. She had his quick wit, his fiery temper and his curiosity and desire for a better life. However, due to his irrational side and his drinking, she only really saw how these traits could be so damaging. She rarely was able to see what goodness her father provided the world. Her fear of him and his intense rage pulled her further and further away.

Patricia Jane became PJ in her school days and then Piper arrived as her life rounded its first bend at 21 years of age, being handed the key to her career in journalism. Piper Brown had already been publishing her work for a few years: music and entertainment reviews, artist interviews, biographies, etc., in smaller, mostly community newspapers and trade magazines, when she arrived at my radio station fresh, wide-eyed, with a killer smile and eager for wanting 'to learn everything there was to learn', about becoming a broadcast journalist. She learned quickly and effortlessly. She was a sponge in the media world, and passionate about every story that landed on her desk.

Her years of vocal training and music lessons bode her well in learning how to turn a simple reading into an epic broadcast. She spoke with such clarity and sensitivity; she was a natural and she loved it! She fell in love with radio, in fact, seduced by all its wacky, weird and wonderful wizardries. The story of Piper Brown had just begun!

Chapter Two

I first met Piper upon hiring her for the small town
community radio station where we worked in the mid
80s. For a young person just newly establishing a
career, she already had a pretty extensive resume with
a varied journalistic portfolio, but had, had no on-air
experience; yet with a limited budget in radio, green is
all I could afford to hire. She seemed like a perfect
candidate for the job. I jumped at the chance to bring
her on board and felt like we'd hit a gold mine. She was
a great addition to the radio station, by all accounts. Not
only did she give us something to look at every day,
with that killer smile, but she gave us things to think
about too. She was never one to let any unfinished piece
of business go to the wayside. She was determined to tie
up all loose ends and get to the bottom of every story.
She was well known in 'making things happen'. If one
had a dream, all they'd have to do would be to let Piper
in on it and voila, the dream would come true. There's
nothing more she loved to do than to please others.

Her admirers were too numerous to mention right from
the outset. But this adoration was all for naught. We
soon realized that the more we loved her the quicker
her time with us would come to an end. My production
manager kept saying, "Don't get all wrapped up in her.
She won't be here long. What do we have to offer her?"
At the time I was thinking he meant financially.

It was all so bittersweet! I'll never forget the day, some
ten months after I hired her. She came bubbling down
the hallway towards my office, an occurrence that
happened regularly enough to leave me waiting daily in
anticipation. I always knew it was going to be Piper at

my door, her skipping gait, and her aura, that hint of patchouli – intoxicating! With a light tap on my open door to 'alert me without disturbing me' she'd say "Hey Mr. Anderson?"

"Call me Steve, Piper, and you don't need to knock. That's why I leave the door open. You're welcome in any time." I persuaded.

"Oh okay, thanks, but I think I still will. My mother raised me that way," she said courteously.

"What's up?" I said dreamily while visions of my fantasies of running away with her danced through my head.

"You'll never guess what," she burst. "Brad Stiller called me last night. You know him, right? The GM at CNDY?"

"Yep." My head was nodding yes but my heart was saying *'oh no'*.

"He's offered me a news job over there. Street beat, city hall reporter."

"Awesome kid. You done good. That's a great fit for you!" *Of all the radio stations in the metro area, why did it have to be that one?* I thought. CNDY meant 'indy', and indy at the time referred to independently owned and managed and it was right up Piper's alley. She was not a 'corporate' girl; she prided herself on never giving into the fat cats, preferring the company and the lifestyle of the starving artist. She had the 'stick it to the man' kind of mentality. In fact, her favourite band, at the time, was *Skinny Puppy*, a Vancouver-based electro-industrial group, aptly named for their distaste of the corporate world. I knew this because Piper would so proudly wear their t-shirt on the days they'd be in town for a concert. The guys around here would admiringly tease, that on Piper, "Skinny Puppy" across her chest, was probably more of a misnomer and not entirely appropriate. It was bordering on harassment but the industry was rampant with such innuendos. Not that I'm excusing it; it did bother me the way men seemingly treated women. I asked Piper what she thought about it and whether she felt comfortable with the 'joking' that went on, both on-air and off.

"God, don't worry about me. I'm a big girl," she returned the teasing. "Strong, like bull!" imitating the famous Rocky and Bullwinkle line. "In essence, it really IS harassment but humour and sarcasm is made up of the inappropriate, in language and behavior. That's really what makes things funny in the first place. And Lord knows I have a sense of humour. You've just got to in order to survive in this nasty world. But you've made a good point. It really depends on who's saying what. When you guys, people I love and respect, say these things, it's funny, but if someone I don't know very well or has an 'odd' air about them says it, it just creeps me out."

We've had this discussion a few times and I think I keep coming back to it because I get stuck on the 'people I love' part of her argument. I love hearing her say this. Every time she says it, I tingle. She *loves me. And I love her too*, I admitted to myself.

As hard as I tried to hold off hearing about what Brad Stiller had to say to her, the more painful it was going to be, so I gave in. "So...what did you tell him?" I asked.

"I told him I was excited about the opportunity and that I'd talk to you and my husband and get back to him."

"I'm so happy for you, Piper!" I lied, already plotting and scheming what I would do to try to win or lure her back to us again.

"Thanks Bud!" She said as she turned and twirled out. *'Bud?' That's all I was to her? Couldn't she have said Mr. Handsome, Mr. Man-of-My-Dreams?* I rationalized internally. This was not a good day.

I ran into her a few more times throughout the remainder of the day and as always, sat opposite from her in the news booth for our drive show news magazine. She had been particularly charming that day with her witty repartee in her role as co-host. She was the best radio sidekick I'd ever had and probably would ever know. She understood when to take charge and when to sit back and let me run the show. She was particularly strong as an interviewer. Her insight and research into the various people and topics we explored was unparalleled in my mind, especially from someone so fresh in the business and she had the most assertive and calming way to put the interviewee at ease in the studio. If they couldn't understand what they were being asked or how to respond to a question, or even if they just couldn't come up with an answer quickly enough, she would be there to support them and guide them through. And today, she was definitely at the top of her game. Approval was everything to her and since she was just offered a better position at a more powerful radio station, that gave her the confidence to come alive and be her best self. One would surely not have to use much imagination to believe that Piper had what it took to make it in the big leagues.

I came into the booth the next day minutes before the show with the script, some extra slips of paper and a calculator. Without making eye contact, I shoved a piece of paper in front of her.

"What's this?" she asked.

"That's the salary I can give you if you stay." I looked up at her gingerly, trying not to let her see how embarrassed I was for the offer of such a small wage increase. "It's all we've got. I'm sorry."

She assured me, "It's okay. They're not offering me that much more but I really feel like I need to do this. It's major market, a great beat and at my dream station." No matter how hard she tried to make me feel better, it just made me feel worse. She was a die-hard fan of the business now. There were no dollar signs in her eyes. One couldn't survive in this business with pure monetary interests or you'd never make it. She had passion and we were going to lose her.

Her last two weeks went by very uneventfully. I laid low because I didn't want her to see my disappointment and didn't want to interfere with her excitement. The station had just come out of ratings at the time and we'd been blessed with a good book; the managers organized a party for the staff that coincided with Piper's last few days with us so it was a great way to say all our goodbyes. A local hall was reserved, one of the overnight guys who worked part-time as a club DJ as well, was hired to spin the tunes and staff and significant others were invited for a night of drinking and debauchery.

Piper brought Tim, her very handsome and very athletic husband. They were quite the pair. Tim in fact, although a huskier version, looked a lot like Patrick Swayze and with him throwing Piper around the dance floor the way he was, just added to that 'Dirty Dancing' notion. It was a fun night. We all got pretty inebriated but not drunk enough to forget seeing our share of Piper's sweet little polka-dotted undies as she flipped cartwheels. This behavior executed by other women may have bordered on the seamier side, but with Piper it was different. She was just so natural and so much fun to be around. Needless to say, the next day at work, Piper's last day with us, was diametrically opposed in sentiment to that of the party. We were all so disheartened with the thought of letting her go but I had to face it at some point; I had to own up to my courage and give her a proper send-off.

Courage was something that I always wished I had more of and perhaps that's one of the reasons why I respected Piper so much. She just went for it. She had moxie and the shoes to match. It never seemed to dawn on her that she couldn't; she'd just do it, like the Nike advertisement. She embodied the fearlessness of the swoosh. I don't really know what was holding me back. I'd recently ended a long-term relationship and there was nobody standing in my way. What would it hurt if I just laid it all on the line to her and told her how I felt?

'Time is of the essence,' I thought to myself as I saw a possible opportunity.

She'd been loading up her car in the parking lot with all her interview notes and such, from her past year's experiences, her headphones, reel-to-reel tapes, even old carts from former newscasts, which we still used in the industry at the time, when I noticed that her laden arms contained her purse and jacket. I had to do it now because she was on her way out the door. I gathered up all my gumption and sprinted outside to her car.

"Hey Pipes!" as I teasingly nicknamed her. "Going now?"

"Yep!" She sighed. "I'm all ready."

"Just wanted to...wanted to..." I stammered, trying desperately to get the words out.

She leaned in and kissed me, sending a surprise shiver down my spine. "Wanted to... kiss me?" she giggled.

"Yah, but not like that. Like this." I had to retaliate, show her who was boss.

I reached my arms around her waist and drew her in. Then took my hand and wiped away a wisp of blonde hair that had fallen in front of her face. My other hand came up to join the first and cradled her jaw. Our eyes then met for the first time for what I had hoped was going to be many first times. I plunged my tongue deep between her parted lips and the moment became electric. Just like in those old-fashioned romance movies, the pyrotechnics blasted away all around us. It was all very magical.

For that moment, the world stood still for me; fantasy and reality became one. I had no idea what possessed me to make the move at that time; neither of us could ever have known what fate had in store for us; I just knew that I had to connect with her and that there was some reason why our spirits were so linked.

Chapter Three

Piper's first days at CNDY were a lesson in contrasts, a whirlwind and a little bit of a disappointment too. She had longed to be in this creative environment but having taken on the 'street' job as a reporter as a way in, she didn't really ever get much of a chance to be physically at the station. The powers-to-be gave her a small cubicle at city hall in a room shared with the other reporters that she utilized to set up her tape recorder. She'd file her reports through the microphone and telephone supplied and installed by the station. There was a large telex wire and reel-to-reel machine that systematically fed reports via the Broadcast News wire service. For CNDY she was also responsible for covering the police blotter. It was exciting because it was new but highly formatted thus didn't provide the creative aspect she had ultimately desired.

She was a welcome student down at city hall, though, befriending some key print and television reporters, which in turn, became an important asset and true testament to her character. She often recalled getting squeezed out of 'scrum' circles, as in a rugby scrum, the circle of reporters that pursue the interviewee following an important press conference; however, having become friends with a few more senior journalists, they would see her fall back, grab her microphone flag and tack it to theirs so she wouldn't miss out while her radio station would get the credit by being seen on TV. She soon learned that reporters, at least in Canada, were certainly not as cutthroat as she was led to believe. She also learned quickly that politics wasn't something she wanted to touch with a ten-foot pole.

Although a little uncertain at first about whether she'd made the right decision to leave the comfort of a community radio family, she forged on in these first few months. Her reporting in: the horrific Paul Bernardo/Karla Homolka case, in which a photo of her interviewing the prosecutor, made the front page of *The Toronto Star*, her day-to-day coverage in the Dubin Inquiry – into the use of steroids by athletes of which stripped Canadian Ben Johnson of his Olympic gold medal, and her exclusive interview with Peter Gabriel, an artist who wasn't known for his admiration of the media, made quite an impression, not only with her fellow street reporters but the personalities back at 'DY. The buzz was that Piper's interests and abilities were far more outreaching than that of a simple 'street' reporter. She also really just sounded good and for radio, that was pretty much everything. Her deep, docile tones from years of voice lessons encouraged by Emily were finally paying off and she recalled to me just how much she needed to appreciate her mother for 'gently persuading' her to stay committed to them.

It wasn't long before they brought her into the station full time. For now, she was deliriously happy. She seemingly had everything that her big heart desired. Piper was assigned the evening news anchor position and it was there where she was introduced to some of the most colourful and extraordinary people she'd ever meet. Due to her quick wit and obvious love and talent for music, she'd often become part of the banter between the disc jockeys as she awaited the stinger for her hourly newscasts. She wasn't your 'typical news lady' as one very prominent on-air personality used to say. She would always find an intelligent and interesting way to add to their talk while she waited for her moment in the spotlight, from her perch in the news booth. And it was said often enough and by many of the personalities at CNDY, that Piper became a permanent co-host for their evening music magazine shows. The days turned into weeks, the weeks into months and the months into years. She was imbedded into the fixtures of CNDY at a very pivotal time in radio history. But as everyone knows, nothing lasts forever; a pastoral landscape must endure the ever-changing forces of nature.

I too, was moving up in the world. I got offered an administrative position at a station in Regina and moved out there fairly soon after Piper had left for CNDY. There was no doubt in my mind that she was certainly courageous enough to have asked me to stay if she really had been interested in me and believed we had some kind of a future and thus, when I hadn't heard from her, I took the plunge and moved out west.

With the movement forward in her new career, Piper began to have growing issues with her husband, Tim. He was a very easy-going and likable man who seemed to just want what was best for her and he thought that her progression into a bigger market and finally getting paid more substantially for her efforts in a 'real' job, would be the sustenance she needed to sustain her desires. In fact, however, it did the opposite. It created more avenues for her to explore and ultimately, get herself into trouble. The more freedom he gave her in allowing her to seek out her passions, the more freedom she took.

Tim had, had the luxury, in the first few years of their relationship, of Piper's full attention. They had met when he was in first-year university and she was still in high school. Despite the fact they were only a year apart in school, Piper had skipped a grade in elementary, being part of the avid readers' acceleration program, so that made him almost three years her senior. To top it off, he was very mature for his age. He'd looked after his siblings from a very young age when his father was killed overseas and his mother was institutionalized after a nervous breakdown. He was the oldest male in a family of seven. Piper had looked up to him to give her the stability and comfort that an older and more responsible man could, since her lack of a father or a negative paternal force seemed to influence most of her decisions at the time. Her union with Tim was in essence, as she learned later in her life from all her therapy, to replace her volatile and undependable father. Once Piper got her feet wet and began to feel secure in her self and her abilities, and had set out on her own path in life, her needs in this kind of relationship became less and less and they began to grow apart. Not to mention all the exciting stimulation she was receiving in her new career. Who could pass up the seduction of a new love when it comes parading past your front door?

That playful, fun-loving part of Piper was being put to the test. She'd come home in those first few months at CNDY beaming from ear to ear. An eight-year-old fatherly relationship with Tim just couldn't compete with the constant flirtations, dares and creative games of radio and all its crazy characters. Simple disagreements turned into heated arguments moved into all-out war. Piper found more and more reasons to take on extra assignments at the station to avoid going home and facing him, while Tim wrapped himself up in his semi-pro hockey career. With Tim being on the road a fair bit for long periods of time, it was easy for Piper to stay out late and not come home some nights at all. And so it was easy for Piper to fall into the arms of another man.

Mike Gryphon was the evening and weekend features host. Mike had smiled a few times at Piper as she passed him in the hallways in her early days there but it wasn't until she went into the booth one evening for her final broadcast of the day some months into her initiation at 'DY that she had the opportunity for formal introductions. Mike was in early to edit a particularly interesting musical segment set to air that evening.

"Pat - " Mike said. Piper looked puzzled and nodded. She hadn't been called 'Pat' since her childhood.

"Chouli! Patchouli!" Mike clarified.

"Oh! Yes!" Piper extended her hand to shake. "It's Piper actually! And yes I notice that you like patchouli too!" Piper confessed. The intoxicating herbal oil preceded them; the familiarity made them both smile.

"There's no secret in this scent. I've always loved the smell; it's a throwback from my pot-smoking, hippie days and it gives away my age," Mike admitted. "But you're no hippie. You're a baby. How did you discover patchouli oil?"

Piper turned red. She realized she was younger than Mike but didn't want age to come between them. "I have a really cool older brother," hoping that this explanation would suffice in ending the topic of age difference.

Despite the fact that she was no longer in need of the 'father figure' in her life, she still was drawn to older men and still desired the feelings of having someone with more worldly experience to help navigate her path. "I'm not a pot smoker, too much into healthy living for that. My folks caught Jonny smoking up one day and he promised them he'd never do it again; but I think he just bought a big vat of patchouli instead." They both laughed.

She began, "It's funny about that essence. I splashed it on after my workout the other day because I didn't have time to shower and then jumped in the car. Shortly into my drive there was a police officer directing traffic at an intersection. There'd been an accident that blocked the road I needed to take and I rolled the window down to ask the cop for an alternate route. He bent down to my level to speak and then said, 'Have you been smoking up, ma'am?' 'No sir, just came from a workout and splashed on the patchouli.' He smiled and then assisted in my concerns. I felt insulted though, at the time but it really was funny." It was ironic, actually; people were mistaking the smell of patchouli for what it was trying to masque in the first place.

"You sound great, by the way," interrupted Mike. "It's about time we get a newscaster around here that fits our image. I'm sure you'll show them a thing or two."

Piper blushed again. "Well, thanks Mike! I hope I can."

It had become quite clear to Piper at that point in time, that she had made the right decision to expand her career at CNDY and to move away from her husband. She'd heard interesting things about Mike by putting her ear to the grindstone. She didn't want to make any waves by actually coming forth with her possible fancies of him. After all, she was the new kid and he was the veteran, pseudo-superstar. She would just do her thing for a while and see where their innocent flirtations would take them. She had been warned that it was often too easy to make enemies within the industry and she had no idea about his home life, let alone any possible suitors that were waiting on stand-by, so she thought she'd just lay low and see it how would all play out. In the meantime, she got a prime seat with first viewing options in creative radio. Mike was a master. He'd often splice his interviews with tracks that he'd actually cut himself. He used his own voice dubs and much of his newly produced material went live directly onto radio even before it received a passing grade from the music director and a staff of critics. Mike had a great deal of panache. If ever he got even close to being reprimanded for his creative risks, he'd just flash his pearly whites under his nicely fitted fedora and all was right in the world again. That was Mike Gryphon, or at least Piper's bleary-eyed, lovesick version of him.

Chapter Four

"How are you holding up, Steve?" Piper consoled, loosening her grip in our embrace, far too hastily in my estimation.

My mother had been battling breast cancer for just over a year now and I got word from sis that she'd taken a turn this past weekend, so I booked a flight back to the homestead, and then called Piper to greet me at the airport if she could. I knew she'd move 'Heaven and Earth' if she had to. Being responsible was another fundamental characteristic of her personality. She claimed to me that it was a quality instilled in her by her mother, at a very young age. It was a trait about her though, that made me feel that she may have just admired me or even loved me out of duty rather than in what had been true in her heart.

Although it had only been less than a year since I'd last seen her, the distance both emotionally and physically, made it feel like there was a wall between us where there was none before. I sighed, "I guess okay. I've never really been through something like this before. I've been pretty fortunate in my life so far. But wow! It's so good to see you and hold you." I changed the subject, trying to pick away at the invisible barricade we both detected.

Piper nodded seemingly noticing that I was hanging onto her for dear life. "Let's get outta here!", she urged pulling me along through the corridor of the terminal.

"When did you switch jobs and move away?" She asked me.

"It was pretty soon after you left. I got offered a PD job in Saskatchewan and I've been there for the past few months; it wasn't the same at the station without you so I figured I needed to change it up too. But enough about me," *'How do you feel about me?'* I thought to myself repeating that old and very worn out joke. "What do you have planned for us?" I said, knowing full well that she had concocted some grand scheme. She was always good at that.

There was a sort of contrived spontaneity that was so much a part of her, an oxymoronic character trait that often made anyone around her exceedingly frustrated. It made her unhappy at times too. But I think it just added to her charm. She was so much fun to be around and seemed so random when all along she had been plotting and planning for weeks to come up with the most perfect occasion. For her, the fun was all in the planning. Her brain and body moved so quickly that she never was able to take time to enjoy the moment while it was happening. She'd enjoyed it months before. She was always well into the next adventure by the time the first one took place. I felt like tackling her sometimes and pinning her to the ground. 'Slow down' would become a standard obsessive phrase I'd articulate if I could ever fortune a chance with her.

"Get in!", she shouted above the sound of the diesel engines around us. We hopped into the roofless jeep and took off out of the parking lot away from the airport noise and haste. The summer heat of July in Toronto was a welcome visitor while driving at top speed toward the lake. People always complained of the scorching heat of summers in the city but clearly they'd never been in a convertible driven by the speedster, Piper 'A.J Foyt' Brown.

"Whoa", I pleaded. "What's your hurry? You're going to be the death of me, Pipes."

"I'm so excited!" She beamed. "I've got this great little picnic all ready for us on the beach. I've picked the perfect spot. I don't want anyone to grab it before we can get there."

"Sounds great!" I said with less enthusiasm.

"Awww, what?" she asked, managing to peel her eyes away from the steering wheel long enough to catch my tone. She responded without awaiting my reply. "Oh I'm sorry sweetie. I wasn't thinking. You're probably in no mood to eat. How insensitive of me. I've just got all this planned and I knew we'd only have a few hours together before you have to hop on a train to see your Mom," she said intently. "You're not hungry?" she asked.

I nodded, really wanting to confess how ravenous I was but not for food. "Well that's okay," she agreed. "I can eat enough for both of us!" I chuckled. That was the truth! I've never seen any woman eat as much as Piper could. She could pack it in. Not sure exactly where she was putting it all because every time I saw her it seemed her body just got more beautiful, toned and fit. And legs, man, long and lean and so bloody defined. It was all that running and those fitness classes she taught. I used to watch people around her checking her out, men and women alike. I got tingly just thinking about it. "You okay?" she queried again after what seemed like just a moment had passed.

"Yea sure. Why?" I questioned.

"Because we've been sitting here for a few minutes now and you haven't budged. You look like you're somewhere else, that you're lost. Can I find you?"

"I'm right here with you, baby. Right where I want to be." I confessed and reached my arms out for her embrace. I wanted to stay in that moment forever.

Our two short hours together were made shorter due to the fact that we kept worrying about how brief our time together would be. I learned though, that after some very rough road, she had left Tim and had moved on in her life to put more emphasis on her own career. She didn't speak too much about the actual painful details in keeping with what Piper is all about, highly selfless in her tribulations; however, I did get the feeling that there was someone or something else waiting in the wings for her. Whether it was another man or an urbane ideal in her efforts to change the world for the better, Piper wasn't completely alone in this transitional time period. She offhandedly said something to the effect of perhaps her 'happily ever after' would best be served to the 'many' rather than the 'few'. It was the first time I'd actually heard her mention this desire and it was a bit of a paradox compared to her previous naïve beliefs in the archetypal fairytale. It sounded like something out of *Star Trek*, I realized, but rest assured this was all Piper Brown and not Gene Roddenberry.

Piper was a different person now or at least she seemed to be on a different path than the one I knew her to be on just a few short years earlier, when we first met. She appeared now prepared to want to conquer the world. I held her tightly to my chest, inhaling the sweetness of her wind whispered hair, my arms wrapped succinctly around her. The only imperfection to the moment was that I knew it must soon come to an end. With an all-encompassing sigh, she wriggled herself out of my grasp and made tentative plans to see me again once I had my own life settled.

As it turned out, my mom lived only long enough for me to say goodbye and to send her on her way, a true cherub. I know she's still watching over me to this day. Perhaps that is why Piper popped back into my life at this time. Piper embodied the spirit of everything good and honest for me; she was the most well-intentioned person I would ever come to meet; she helped me find my place of quiet amid the noise and haste.

~~

"You sure about this kid. You know that once we go all the way, there's no turning back?" She nodded however unconvincingly, or so that's the way I had remembered it.

"'I'm right where I want to be'," she repeated my favourite saying. "On top and in charge." She playfully grabbed the shaft of my penis circling her fingers around its circumference until it began to throb and bulge. With a quick and flexible movement she had completely positioned herself on top of me, maneuvering her body so that my hard and moistened erection rubbed along the crease of her labia. I had been ready to explode already for several minutes, probably as soon as she mentioned that she wanted to make love to me. I was both trying to hold off longer for her, to ensure that she got the pleasure she desired and for myself; but as Piper was Piper, always one step ahead, she didn't need to wait a moment longer. She pressed my tip into her now dampened clitoral lips while I plunged my tongue deep within her mouth. While we rocked and swayed I could feel her energy releasing its passion and her soul melting into the caverns of mine.

We made love several times over the course of the weekend. It was undeniably the best few days I'd ever experienced and I was sure it was unmatchable in anything I could possibly ever conjure in my imagination or dreams, but there was something so unreal about it. It's like it existed in another time, or in another place. We never talked about a future or our past, for that matter. It was just the present, a gift we were sharing.

On the third day, Piper rose quickly out of bed revealing again her beautiful sun-stroked body in the clarity of the morning light, the way she had done the previous mornings. In fact, we spent a good majority of the weekend enjoying each other's nakedness. She liked to cook and to eat and we'd spent time putting snack trays together to nibble on in bed, on the couch, on the table, on the staircase and in the bath. I loved taking a grape and resting it on her nipple then watching it as it rolled down into her navel. I'd swirl my tongue around her bellybutton to retrieve it only to do it again and again. Our hungry nibbling was satiated in every way. There wasn't a spot, a blemish, a curve, or a wrinkle that I didn't explore with my tongue and taste buds that weekend. But on this day, as the sunlight silhouetted her youthful softness she reached for a bed sheet for cover, in uncharacteristic modesty.

"I've got to go, baby. Get things done," she said.

"Okay?" I questioned, with a mixture of shock and dismay, and really not crazy about the idea. I certainly could have made a habit of spending my days pampering and enjoying the sweetness of all her pleasures.

"I've got a life; you've got a life. We've got to get on with it." She confirmed. As much as I hated hearing the words, I knew she was right. I didn't say anything just nodded in agreement. Where was my courage when I needed it the most?

Our parting was short and sweet. At the time I'm not sure whether she believed she'd ever see me again or not, because she never revealed her intentions and I'm not sure I gave her any indication about mine either. But I can admit that if she had given me the word or even a sign, I would've pulled the ring out of my pocket.

Life continued. I felt deeply disappointed in myself that I couldn't drum up the gumption to offer her more at the time, but I was never really sure that, that's what she wanted and I was not one to take the chance or risk being hurt; otherwise, I'm sure I would've jumped at the chance. I had no idea how long it would be before she'd reach out to me again, if ever, but I did feel great pride in believing that there was a certain purpose for our union, a connection that seemed to repeat itself at the most poignant times in both our lives. As much as we had in common, I always wished I had more of her moxie. That was Piper; she was fearless or so she always wanted us to believe. She was now poised to conquer the world.

Chapter Five

It was a feverish six-month introduction for Piper and Mike at CNDY; they seemed to have two circuits, hot and red hot; they became inseparable. She had become a regular fixture as co-host on his evening show and then helped produce and edit interviews for his weekend features. Despite the fact that Mike insisted they try to keep their physical relationship a secret at work, it was pretty clear to everyone around that they were a 'hot and heavy' item. Mike was a bit of an enigma to most people, not revealing much about his personal side but that seemed to work well for Piper at the time. She didn't think it was wise to advertise this new relationship either, so hot off the heels of her broken marriage.

Show upon show they gained momentum in their chemistry. They'd go back to Mike's office to finish laughing off the funny quips that occurred spontaneously during the evening 'live' shows. The laughter would move them to touching, embracing and petting. It was after one particularly steamy session where the pair got caught with their pants down, literally. Mike had pinned Piper up against the wall in his office and was driving himself hard into her when his normally locked door came flying open. "Oh my god, so sorry so sorry!" they heard as their technician exited as quickly as he arrived. They both shrugged knowing that the incident wouldn't really get much further and if it did, so be it; they weren't going to concern themselves with such trivialities. Coupling off was maybe not a regular occurrence but common enough not to be highly gossip-worthy.

Regardless of the laissez-faire attitude, Mike whispered. "I think we need to take this somewhere more comfortable. You deserve more than this, Pipes," and she agreed.

"We can't go to my place. Tim hasn't officially moved out yet. How about yours?" This was the first time that Piper opened the door for Mike to talk about his current status.

"We could go to my sister's place." He diverted. Piper noticed that he hadn't taken the bait.

"I'm game," she said. "Take me to bed or lose me forever," she continued, using the very endearing Meg Ryan line from *Top Gun*.

"Here are my keys, meet ya in the car. Gotta make a quick call," Mike replied. Within moments, the pair was squeezed into his little Karmann Ghia heading speedily towards their destination.

Their lovemaking sessions were epic. They'd begin at the station, spill out into the car and barely could they contain themselves long enough to make it up the long stairway into the bedroom. The years of living experience that Mike had were clearly demonstrated through his sexual maneuvers and appetite. He matched Piper in his tastes for the exotic and exploration of the unknown. He was a master in the bedroom infusing his tantric liberties and yogi postures to take Piper to sexual heights she'd never experienced and she felt in no position, literally, to deny herself of these pleasures. All of her senses were enlightened and stimulated as he guided her around his body to reciprocate the sensations, an ever-eager student to this highly accomplished sexual guru.

"You must thank your sister for allowing us to use her pad," Piper reiterated after they made several visits to the house noticing that she always got the same vague response.

"For sure." Mike diverted. "I've gotta take a shower; wanna join me?" Their sudsy vertical skills were second to none.

However inviting as it was, Piper declined. She dressed, ripped the bed sheets off and expertly remade it with the fresh sheets Mike had retrieved from the linen closet. She went over to the dresser to upright the bottles and pictures that had fallen during their sexual gymnastics. She tried not to be like her more curious self when she was with Mike because she wasn't really sure she wanted to know about all his dirty laundry. After all, she wasn't exactly a saint herself. But she couldn't help but notice a wedding picture in one of the frames that had toppled over. She looked closely and could see that the groom was definitely Mike and with one more, quick glance, because she could hear his footsteps approaching from behind her, she noticed a very pretty, young bride.

"Yes. I'm married, but separated." Mike admitted from close behind her.

"Why did you not mention it to me before?" Piper said shyly worried that her investigating was getting her into trouble.

"Long, boring story. Didn't think you'd need to know." Mike briefly concluded. Piper realized that Mike wasn't going to confess anything else at the moment and that was more than enough for her to swallow.

Mike never actually again mentioned his status at home and Piper never raised the issue. She had struggled enough until the end of her own marriage while things at work were pretty crazy as well with her newfound stardom. Her on-air partnership with Mike was elevating her to radio goddess and she was reveling in the glory of it. So there was no need to stir the pot. It was bubbling quite sufficiently on its own.

The months passed relatively uneventfully. It seemed as though *'the world was unfolding as it should'*, when one day Piper woke up with a tenderness in her breasts and shooting pain through her nipples. *"Well that's reasonable,"* she thought. *"I'm due for my period and sometimes sore breasts are part of the deal."* She went to the calendar and noticed that she should've had her period the week before. "Oh no!" she gasped out loud. "Breathe, stay calm," she tried to convince herself. *"There's probably a good explanation for this. I haven't been eating very much lately; my weight's really low. I'll give it another week and then take a test. No point in alarming Mike,"* she continued rationalizing in thought to herself.

Much to her dismay, the week came and went with still no sign of bleeding. She bought a drugstore pregnancy test kit and held her breath while she looked at the results. *'If a red line appears in the second window then the results are positive and you are pregnant.'* She read the instructions over and over again, each time looking back into the window to see the little, bright red line.

Mike had been away at a music conference when Piper discovered her predicament. And when he got back she'd already made up her mind that there was no way she could carry on with the pregnancy. She and Mike just had not talked about this kind of a future together yet. She knew they weren't ready for the responsibilities of raising a child. It would destroy them; which would mean that she'd ultimately be left with a baby on her own. There was no other recourse. She'd let Mike know as soon as he returned.

He was very quiet when she told him; he gave her space to come to terms with it all without condescension or disagreement. He did manage to say that he believed as she did that it was a woman's right to make the decision, as it was the woman who had to bear the burdens. He also didn't give her the feeling that he would drop everything and marry her to help raise the child either, which just added to her fears about being alone through the process, thus giving her more reason to believe that abortion was the right choice. Mike remained very affectionate and tender towards Piper for the next few weeks while they awaited her appointment at the Morgentaler Clinic downtown. He wanted her to go to the most reputable abortion clinic because he figured she'd get treated with the greatest respect and be given the best in care and treatment. He offered to pay the $400 bill; at the time, the cost was not covered by OHIP and he'd drive her to and from the clinic. He claimed it was the least he could do.

One early December morning, Piper and Mike entered the back door of the small, unassuming old row house on Harbord Street. The sign out the front was withered and worn but somehow procured a feeling of great consolation. The clinic nurses had advised them to take the alleyway emergency door rather than the main entrance as there may have been some picketing going on and they didn't want their patients to have to be subjected to the sometimes angry mob and placards on their way in. Mike told Piper he'd take charge and showed her to a seat in the waiting room. He paid the cashier and was handed a clipboard to fill out all of Piper's personal and medical information. He filled in what he could then returned to the waiting room and took a seat beside her. He passed her the clipboard and whispered, "Pipes, I don't even know your middle name." They looked at each other with tears in their eyes. This last acknowledgement solidified their decision to go through with the abortion. They just weren't ready for parental responsibilities.

Piper said, "It's Jane. Like Jane Doe." Piper finished the questionnaire on her own in silence. The nurse came out fairly soon after with a big smile on her face and a warm sparkle in her eyes.

She said rather boastfully, "We've got Henry in today. Doctor Morgentaler will be performing your surgery. You're very lucky!" Piper turned to look at Mike, who nodded affirmatively and squeezed her hand.

"You'll be in the best of care, Piper."

She was ushered into the prepping room by the nurse who told her to undress and put on the surgical gown.

Although the room was temperate enough, a chill ran down her vulnerable spine. She used her free hand to hold together the enclosure in the back. She was then led to the bed where she'd undergo the surgery. Another nurse came around to discuss her options. Was she still really thinking she needed to terminate her pregnancy; was she aware of other options; did she understand the mechanics of birth control and had she been informed of the risks involved. There was one final question asked by the nurse and again by Morgentaler when he arrived and that was, "Are you making this decision entirely on your own, free of duress, threats and physical and mental coercion?" When the answer to this was a resounding 'Yes' both times it was asked, it was marked with a check on her file.

The anesthetic needle drip was attached to the back of Piper's hand and within minutes she was out. And back. Although much of the recovery, hours and days afterwards were hazy for her, she remembered vividly the kind, sparkling eyes of Dr. Morgentaler as she awakened groggily from the procedure. She remembered his soft, squeaky voice and his gentle hand as he patted her comfortingly on her shoulder saying, "You'll be okay, Piper. You've got a long, healthy life ahead of you."

Piper's aunt, her dad's sister, had offered the Browns' use of their condo in Florida over Christmas while they were in Europe. Emily and Patrick had other things going on; Finn was going to be in Ottawa with her boyfriend and the others pretty much had their own families to organize so Piper took her up on the offer. She figured it would be a good, peaceful time for her to recover. She and Mike weren't really connecting. Mike was probably trying to give Piper some space while Piper was vacillating between moments of sadness and loss to anger and blame. They did both vow that with the coming new year, would come new dreams and a fresh start.

It was a fresh start all right. On Tuesday, January third, 1989, at 3 am, Piper heard her phone ringing in the next room of her tiny apartment. As she was in a dead sleep, her body felt like it was moving in slow motion to get to the receiver before the caller would hang up. After what seemed like hours, she put the phone to her ear and heard a soft female voice on the other end say, "How long have you been sleeping with my husband?"

Chapter Six

Stunned and feeling like she was in the middle of a strange nightmare, Piper took a few minutes to become cognizant. "Um, since the summer. I guess about six months?" Piper felt no reason to lie.

"He said he only slept with you once. Is that true?" At this point Piper could hear the clicking sound of someone on another extension.

"Over a six month period, you think we'd have sex just one time?" Piper became snarky.

"You don't have to answer her questions, Patricia." Mike interrupted from the other line. *'Patricia,'* she thought. No one ever called her *'Patricia'* except for her father when he was angry, and that was many years ago.

"Well, Michael..." Piper reciprocated the patronizing tone. "She has a right to know the truth. A right you denied me as well."

"Thank you," she uttered maintaining her demure composure, "but I need to hang up now and speak with my husband. Can I call you later if I have any further questions?"

"Just lovely!" Piper thought to herself, but composed a more civilized response. "I guess so. I realize you're hurt and I'm sorry for that. If this helps you, then I'd like to do that for you but just so you know, I'm hurting too. He lied to both of us." Piper confided.

"Do you love him?" She continued.

"I thought I did," Piper replied with the familiar feeling of that fireball knot getting tied tighter and tighter in her stomach. "But I'll back off. I didn't know. I'm sorry."

"Thank you!" she said again. Her receiver clicked and I waited to hear if Mike was still on the line.

"You really shouldn't talk to her. It's not helping," Mike pleaded, answering my curiosity.

"Helping you?" Piper stammered. "She has a right to know, Mike."

"Yes she does, but you don't need to go into all the bloody details. Let me handle it, will you please?" Mike urged.

"Just like the way you've handled it so far?" Piper was starting to rage.

"I'll talk to you later, Piper." The phone clicked off.

Piper sat there in the middle of her tiny living room staring at the clock on the wall, watching it click away each vital second. She sat there until the clicking and the beating of her heart were working in unison. She sat there staring, as the flood gates opened wide and big, juicy tear drops rolled like fountains down her cheekbones. At some point, hours later she must have fallen asleep with the monotony of the beat synchronicity. She awoke to a bright winter mid-day sun streaming down on her through her curtainless window. She didn't know where she was at first then moments later gasped for a breath in realization at what had occurred earlier that morning. She began to panic. Anxiety was setting in. *"I've just gotta go see him, talk to him, hold him."* She uttered as she ran into the bathroom to fix herself up for work.

If there are seven stages of grief, then Piper felt them all and perhaps found a few more along the way. She certainly had her share of loss lately with the abortion just weeks earlier so this was enough to almost put her over the edge. She vacillated between shock and disbelief to desperation and denial. She was a dichotomy of emotions; while she was overwrought with guilt and shame, she bargained with Mike for days afterwards, begging for him to give her another chance.

"Piper, I'm trying to get things back on track with Allison. And why would you want me after what I've done to you?" Piper's answer should've been, *'you're right. I shouldn't want you. You're no good for me.'*

But instead she blurted out. "Because I love you, Mike."

Despite her inability to control her emotional bargaining, her tug-of-war in anger and acceptance, she maintained her distance from him for the next few weeks because she had a desperate plan in place.

Back in November, the station had arranged to send Mike to the MIDEM Festival – Marche International du Disque et de l'Edition Musicale - in Cannes, France at the end of January. He was going to cover the trade show's latest developments and be there for 5 days. As the station had only promised enough financial coverage for one of them to go, Piper had contemplated buying her own plane ticket and meeting up with him. She'd piggyback the work trip to Cannes with a visit to her sister in nearby Verona, Italy, who was living there with her medical school interning husband and their young family. But since the trauma with her pregnancy, abortion then the Christmas holidays, she hadn't really made any concrete plans to go. Until of course discovering that this would be a great time to get Mike alone, so that she could at least talk it through with him. *'And besides,' she thought. 'How could he resist me in such a romantic city half way around the world?'* She booked her ticket to arrive a day after Mike was going to, so that he'd be settled in, and then meet him there at his hotel. She'd keep it a secret. There was no point in revealing her plans to him ahead of time. It would just make him anxious and this way, it would seem more magical and like the whole thing, from start to finish, was all just a dream.

Piper was unusually cheery those last few weeks in January, Mike thought, and chalked up her change in attitude to her Irish resiliency. They continued to work together, uneventfully. She wished him well for his trip and off he went.

~~

"Oh my God!" Piper sighed in disbelief and stared at herself in the vanity. *"What the hell have I done?"* She'd picked up a handmade farewell card that was sitting on a tiny dusty TV set in the rundown room of an old 3-star Inn in Cannes and as she read and reread the message inside, she stood face to face with her own reality. The card was from his ' *eternally loving wife, Allison'*.

"Room 11, Mademoiselle." The front desk clerk had offered when she asked him what room Monsieur Gryphon was in. "Le chamber d'amour," he continued teasingly. "I'll let you in. He's at the festival maintenant," as Piper translated and nodded in appreciation.

"Merci monsieur." It was such an eclectic and quaint little inn, so very much in keeping with Mike's sensibilities. Her heart heaved a heavy sigh.

Piper wasn't waiting alone for very long in his room. Mike had finished up the day of conferences and came back to change clothes for the evening. He was shocked but seemed pleased enough to see her. There was some hesitation on both their parts but within a few moments they were in each other's arms again. They made love throughout the evening and into the night, stopping briefly to sip on wine they shared from the bottle. The morning light seemed to come up so quickly. They'd barely slept. Piper didn't want to lose a moment with him because she knew this was really the end. They both knew. Mike went back to the festival the following morning to get an interview that he'd booked previously while Piper put on her running shoes and set out to get her bearings. For her, there was nothing more reassuring than running: the wind in her hair, the feel of her muscles taut against her skin, and the ease at which her breath and blood pumped life into her veins. She ran long and far. At that time, as familiar as this directional exercise was to Piper, she felt lost; she wasn't sure whether she was running to or away from herself.

They planned to 'do the town' together that evening. Mike was interested in showing Piper around a bit and

seeing a MIDEM show booked for midnight in the main
ballroom of the *Palais.* He also wanted to try a hash café.
They were pretty popular in France at the time. You
could go into the shoppe, which was really more like a
restaurant, and order hash, of any flavor or variety, to
smoke at your table. Not being a smoker, Piper didn't
care for it much, but the notion of it was interesting
enough.

Another eclectic experience with Mike, Piper thought,
but began to feel that this was wearing thin. She had to
face her life, meet her maker and bare the
consequences. During their second night of intense
lovemaking, Piper broke down and said she had to
leave. Mike complied and went with her to the train
station. It was still dark when the passenger commuter
train pulled out of Cannes station headed towards
Piper's unknown destiny.

Piper tucked her feet under her on a passenger seat in
the economy section. She grasped and crossed her legs
and bowed her head onto her thighs hiding her face
between her knees. She cried and cried and cried. She
told me some years later that she'd cried so much that
when other passengers came on board to take a seat in
her car, some would ask if she was okay, but most
others would turn away not knowing what to do or say
in her despair. She cried until there were no tears left to
cry. When she started to come out of her misery, she
began to notice just how beautiful the Mediterranean
view was: from the cliffs sculpted by the thrashing of
the seas as they pounded the shoreline, and the villages
checkered with old and new pastel-colored buildings,
the way she'd see from the tourist brochures. She hoped
to come back to this place when she could see it for how

breathtaking it was supposed to be, see it with greater clarity, without the hazy film upon which her heartbreak bestowed. Some day she felt certain that she'd be in a better frame of mind to see its reality and enjoy its entire splendor.

Some 10 hours later, when darkness had again set in, the train stopped at its final destination, the land of Romeo and Juliet, in Verona, Italy. Piper's sister was set to pick her up at the train station. "Just call me when you get in sis! We only live about a half hour away and I can put the little ones in their car seats and be there when you need me." Angela Brown had married her high school sweetheart, Toni Vitucci, an Italian Canadian, years earlier. He was doing his year residency in medical school and had selected his ancestor's hometown of Verona, for his practice. He, Angela and their two little kids, had been there since the fall.

"What do you mean, you can't come to get me?" Piper pleaded over the phone.

"The fog has moved in again, Piper. It's as thick as pea soup. It's been like this on and off for weeks now. I can't set out in the dark with the kids. It's not safe. But get in a taxi. I'll pay him when you get here."

"I don't even know where you live, Angie. And I don't speak any Italian. I've just come from France remember? I don't know how to communicate with the cabbie." Piper cried.

"When you've hired one, put him on the phone and I'll explain it to him," Angela replied.

The fog was so thick that even the cab driver had a difficult time finding their address. What was supposed to be a forty-minute fare, turned into close to a two-hour ride, a pathetic fallacy to synchronize her despair.

Angie was very generous with her payment when Piper finally arrived by taxi and kept saying, "Gracia, gracia!" to the driver making use of her new language skills.

"You must be hungry, PJ." Angie consoled. "How about some chicken soup? That'll cure whatever ails you," choosing a line that their father would often say.

"Gracia," said Piper wearily.

~~

The next thing Piper remembered was waking up to the sound of children giggling. She rolled over to see where she was and who it was. Angie was sitting on the edge of her bed tickling the younger one while coloring in a book with the older.

"What time is it?" Piper asked.

"About 5 o'clock." Angela replied.

"In the afternoon? I've been sleeping for almost 24 hours?" Piper blinked away the dreams she had clearly experienced.

"It was a while. We were getting worried about you. Mum called and said you would be arriving later at the airport than expected because your flight had been delayed out of Toronto. There was a big winter storm when she dropped you off at Pearson and she figured it would've affected your arrival time".

Piper replied confused and shaking the dreams out of her head. "You picked me up at the airport? What about the fog?"

"The only thing that's foggy around here is you; are you okay? What's going on?"

"No I'm not okay, but I will be, and I'm just not ready to talk about it right now."

Chapter Seven

Piper came back to Canada completely annihilated. She felt defeated, lost and lonely. As was seemingly becoming her nature, if it hadn't been already, she moved very quickly and perhaps quicker than her psyche could handle. She hadn't even worked a full year in the media world before major market took her under its wing, and elevated her to star status; meanwhile, attached to the pressures of this fast-paced career and success, were the troubles of the ego. Piper's barely 25-year-old heart, had taken a beating. What had seemed like rewards for doing such a superb job within the industry: her relationship with Mike, growing popularity as a broadcaster and thoughts of a clandestine romance in Europe, quickly became her punishments; however high to which it had once very recently raised her, soon dropped her into a pit of despair.

She refrained from any social activity, came home late from work and would barely flip a light switch on. She wandered or just even sat for hours in the dimness of her studio apartment as she repeatedly played Sinead O'Connor's "Troy" on her stereo, screeching and crying out in angst, imitating her favourite Irish artist or favourite artist of any culture at that time, for that matter. Although the song had been written about the tragic death of Sinead's mother, Piper found the lyrics to be fitting to her own situation and in keeping with her sorrowful grief.

> "I'll remember it
> And Dublin in a rainstorm...
> Does she love you?
> What do you want to do?

Do you love her?
Is she good for you?
Does she hold you like I do?
Do you want me?"

I would've given anything to shield her from this suffering but knowing what I came to know about her, she was being molded and shaped by these experiences and she would never have allowed me to enter this shrouded tomb at the time anyway. She had said it was a moment for her to share with her Irish sister who seemed to know as much or more so than she did, about an angry world.

Piper buried herself in her work. She asked if her shift could be moved to one earlier in the day and back to doing mostly news reports and casting. She just did not want to have to run into Mike at all. Their relationship and termination of it was by no means a secret. The news director saw the pained expression in her face, every time that Piper got near Mike, let alone getting confined in the tiny broadcast booth with him, and realized it was in everyone's best interest to separate the two of them. He knew that she was worth hanging onto and if she became so distraught over having to continue co-hosting with Mike, then she may reach out and be picked up by some other, 'keen to notice her particular talents', radio station. And besides, the news business had bigger issues to deal with and they could certainly use Piper's skills as a news anchor for the drive shift in the time slot for which she had been asking.

As art often imitates life, it was midway through 1990 when the Persian Gulf War heated up; it was a becoming an angry world for everyone. Though the long-running battle between Iran and Iraq had ended in a United Nations-brokered ceasefire in August 1988, by mid-1990 the two states had yet to begin negotiating a permanent peace treaty. When their foreign ministers met in Geneva that July, prospects for peace suddenly seemed bright, as it appeared that Iraqi leader Saddam Hussein was prepared to dissolve that conflict and return territory that his forces had long occupied. Two weeks later, however, Hussein delivered a speech in which he accused neighboring nation Kuwait of siphoning crude oil from the oil fields located along their common border. He insisted that Kuwait and Saudi Arabia cancel out $30 billion of Iraq's foreign debt, and accused them of conspiring to keep oil prices low in an effort to pander to Western oil-buying nations. Piper was on top of it all.

In addition to Hussein's incendiary speech, Piper reported that Iraq had begun amassing troops on Kuwait's border. Alarmed by these actions, President Hosni Mubarak of Egypt initiated negotiations between Iraq and Kuwait in an effort to avoid intervention by the United States or other powers from outside the Gulf region. Hussein broke off the negotiations after only two hours, and on August 2, 1990 ordered the invasion of Kuwait. Hussein's assumption that his fellow Arab states would stand by in the face of his invasion of Kuwait, and not call in outside help to stop it, proved to be a miscalculation. Two-thirds of the 21 members of the Arab League condemned Iraq's act of aggression, and Saudi Arabia's King Fahd, along with Kuwait's government-in-exile, turned to the United States and other members of the North Atlantic Treaty Organization (NATO) for support. That brought forth the pertinence of the western world; its attention and significance on the universal scale relied on the power of the western media, which further intensified Piper's addiction to it all.

Piper broadcast that, "U.S. President George H.W. Bush immediately condemned the invasion, as did the governments of Britain and the Soviet Union". Canada was to remain neutral but was on watch for change in status. On August 3, the United Nations Security Council called for Iraq to withdraw from Kuwait; three days later, King Fahd met with U.S. Secretary of Defense Richard Cheney to request U.S. military assistance. On August 8, the day on which the Iraqi government formally annexed Kuwait–Hussein called it Iraq's "19th province"–the first U.S. Air Force fighter planes began arriving in Saudi Arabia as part of a military buildup dubbed Operation Desert Shield. The planes were accompanied by troops sent by NATO allies as well as Egypt and several other Arab nations, designed to guard against a possible Iraqi attack on Saudi Arabia. The world was officially at war. And so too, was Piper.

She was both fascinated and fearful of what it all meant. Having been born in the 60s and in Canada, she felt very far removed from the impact of a war and she believed she shared that sentiment with her fellow Canadians. This was the closest she'd ever come to the real deal, and with her growing credibility in the news world, she covered the day-to-day atrocities with immense passion. She became addicted to the frenzy, the intensity and the sensationalism of all the events as they unfolded. She got swallowed up by the reality of what she was broadcasting while she spat out the illusion of the conflicted possibilities. This was the first true sign of her imbalanced psyche, the obsessive-compulsivity of her passionate ego.

People long remembered her announcement on November 29, 1990, that "the U.N. Security Council authorized and threatened the use of 'all necessary means' of force against Iraq if it did not withdraw from Kuwait by the following January 15." By January, the coalition forces prepared to face off against Iraq numbered some 750,000, including 540,000 U.S. personnel and smaller forces from Britain, France, Germany, Canada, the Soviet Union, Japan, Egypt and Saudi Arabia, among other nations. And again on January 17, 1991, she broadcast "that a massive U.S-led air offensive hit Iraq's air defenses, moved swiftly on to its communications networks, weapons plants, oil refineries and more. The coalition effort, known as Operation Desert Storm, benefited from the latest military technology, including Stealth bombers, Cruise missiles, so-called 'Smart' bombs with laser-guidance systems and infrared night-bombing equipment."

With Iraqi resistance nearing collapse, Bush declared a ceasefire on February 28, ending the Persian Gulf War on which Piper also proudly reported. According to the peace terms that Hussein subsequently accepted, Iraq would recognize Kuwait's sovereignty and get rid of all its weapons of mass destruction (including nuclear, biological and chemical weapons). In all, an estimated 8,000 to 10,000 Iraqi forces were killed, in comparison with only 300 coalition troops as Piper summarized in one of her final broadcasts of the events. It was a significant time in history and a time to show her true colours as a journalist. And that she very well did. But it seemed as though now, she had her own inner battles to face and had become a victim of confliction through contagion and osmosis. She ate, drank and slept war.

Getting too intently caught up in the news grind was something that Piper was warned about. It was common among young broadcasters with such a passion as hers. She'd spend hour upon hour checking the latest advancements in the war and write and rewrite her copy to appreciate the changes. Sleep at the best of times for her was perhaps 6 hours a night, but during these stressful months, Piper stayed awake well into the night watching live CNN reports and rising early or awakening with clenched teeth, just a few hours after falling asleep. Her therapist recommended that she see a dentist to order a mouth piece for her grinding teeth issue and advised her that she'd maintain a longer broadcasting career if she became more detached from the reality of it all.

Seeing a therapist was one of the best things she ever did for herself. Dr. O'Reilly, having come by it naturally, was an elderly Irish psychiatrist who knew very well the nature of Piper's cultural eccentricities. He was instrumental in helping Piper maintain her often-questionable sanity.

It was ironically during this time of great significance in Piper's life as a broadcaster that she met her second husband. As the saying goes, "If you truly want to find something or someone, then stop looking," and that seemed to be true for Piper. She was caught in the whirlwind at work, ran further and faster than she ever did to maintain her health and abundant energy, and thus she was oblivious to her own magnetism and the attraction that others had for her. She'd just started teaching fitness classes at a new, local gym when her boss approached her with a request for a 'run date'.

"Sure," she promised. "Would love to. I love running and it's always nicer to run with someone else," she affirmed.

Richard Sirko was a tall, confident yet unassuming man with obvious years of athleticism in his strong, healthy build. "Built like a horse and strong as an ox, as my Baba always says about us Ukies." Piper would go on to learn that Richie, as 'all-star American' as he appeared and seemed, had an equally strong family heritage with intelligent, and artistic roots. *'Good baby-making material,'* I remember teasing her in trying to hide that jealous flutter in my heart. She'd just curl up her nose at me and frown.

And Richie as it turned out, was a big fan of Piper's radio talents. This guy was just not your average Joe Quarterback. He was as much a sensitive *artiste* as Piper was. They had a great deal in common in fact. He was an accomplished classical guitar player, a budding songwriter and knew his way around a camera. While he may have managed the fitness programs at the gym for a living, and which was Piper's side job, his main hobbies were those of Piper's career. It sounded all so balanced and yin-yang on paper.

With the war down to a dull roar and still sensitive over her losses, Piper realized that spending some time with Richie might be therapeutic. He had just come back from a three-month trek through the Cappadocia mountains in Central Turkey – *'Wow! Another adventurer?' I teased* – He had a ton of pictures he'd taken and was dying to share them. He thought they were particularly timely considering the state of Persia and its ongoing conflicts. Although Turkey was such a peaceful nation at the time and certainly more of a safe place to travel, appreciating its history could help Piper in her perspective on its global presentation and it certainly would help to appease her wanderlust since she felt she couldn't get away at the time.

"Cappadocia, comes from the combination of the Turkish and Greek in what is known today as Old Persia," Richie began during the first of what would be many dates of photo sharing with Piper. "The name was traditionally used in Christian sources throughout history and is still widely used as an international tourism concept to define a region of exceptional natural wonders, in particular characterized by fairy chimneys and a unique historical and cultural heritage."

Piper suddenly perked up with the idea of 'fairies'. She was enthralled by the spiritual world, beginning to believe more and more that the greater faith one had in the notion that the soul was eternal, one could actually tap into hearing, touching and perhaps even seeing that which was only imagined before. "What do you mean by *fairy* chimneys?" Piper asked.

"A fairy chimney is a tall, thin spire of rock that protrudes from the bottom of a drainage basin. They could be 5 to 150 feet tall. There are a lot of them in the Grand Canyon and also in the Cappadocia's. The Turkish people have even carved houses from these formations. Their shapes are affected by the erosional patterns of alternating hard and softer rock layers." Never had geology been so intriguing to Piper.

"I'm not so concerned with the geological history," she continued. "What do they say about the spirituality of these formations?"

"Well, due to the changing weather patterns and the layers of harder and softer sediments, the area could lend itself to the belief that it was easier for spirits to get trapped within the layers. The Turkish are highly spiritual and throughout ancient history they'd lay their dead in open caskets among the rocks so that their spirits could be free to dance around while their physical bodies were being swallowed up by the ongoing erosional process. It would get very cold in the winter in the mountains and this was often disconcerting to those who had loved ones laying there, so they'd imagine that these formations were 'chimneys' keeping their spirits warm; they believed that they could even see these fairies dancing sometimes. Perhaps it is also where we get some of our more modern notions about cremation. They're beautiful people really. Everyone talks about how amazing Greece is and it certainly is, but Turkey is always so highly overshadowed."

Piper was in awe. "I've just to go there some day. That sounds fascinating!"

Life was pretty good for the young couple. They shared many similarities that would, essentially, lead them into many adventures.

Chapter Eight

I missed her smell, her touch and her taste. I missed the way she smiled when she greeted me, her laugh that so easily spilled out of her in bouts of joy and her voice as it soothed my aching soul. I wanted to wrap my arms around her and protect her from any possible harm that could come to her. I wanted to rescue her in her times of poor choices and indecision. I wanted her to want me as reciprocally as I wanted her so it was no wonder that I'd wait endlessly by the phone to hear her plans of our next clandestine meeting.

"Guess where I'm going?" Piper's exuberance was overwhelming even over the phone.

"Uh oh! She's got the bug again!" I reply to her in the third person, trying very hard not to reveal my true feelings; the only place I want her to be going is with me. "I really can't play this game, Piper. I have NO idea."

"Well. You know that my parents finally separated when my dad moved to Africa last year, right?"

"So you're going to Africa to visit your father?" I shrieked very worried about her safety and her sanity. It was no secret just how she felt about Patrick, her fears and insecurities, and I always thought, with very good reason.

"Whoa, back up a bit!" She interrupted. "Yes and I get where you're coming from, but here's the deal. My dad's working in Malawi; it's a tiny country south of Kenya and north of South Africa. Well, there are a few countries in between but it bodes well for an Eastern

African excursion, something I've always wanted to do. AND..." she emphasized, "It just so happens that there's a big Apartheid aid concert scheduled in Johannesburg that the station is willing to pay for me to cover for them; with the increased tensions with the ANC in Pretoria, and Mandela's newfound freedom, it makes for a triple threat journalist!"

"So you're going to mix business with pleasure?" I queried. "Not at all like you Piper." I teased.

"Doesn't that sound thrilling?" she diverted.

"Frightening, actually." I admitted.

"Because I'm there as a journalist I'll be protected by security at the Canadian Embassy in Jo-Berg," Piper justified.

"No, I meant your father." I was no stranger to her stories of his rage.

"Well, I won't actually be staying with him for very much of the trip. I'm sure he's on his best behavior, anyway, now that he's shacked up with his new squeeze in Lilongwe and Richie's going with me." She offered, while trying to sneak by me, this latter part of her plans.

"Again, the triple threat. Wow!" I managed to eek out. Sarcasm was my way of avoiding my true feelings. I was desperate; I felt like I was losing her with each passing year that we were apart. "Are you sure that you want to get serious with this guy?" I questioned, taking a stab at my dormant courage.

"My father?" She laughed; sarcasm was her way out as well. Our similarities were overwhelming. "Don't worry, baby; you'll always be (she paused and placed her hand on her heart)...right here."

"And where is that?" I asked, as I naturally couldn't see any of her hand gestures over the phone.

She made a kissing sound by pursing her lips. "Smack at ya, Steve!"

"And are you sure that you're well enough to immerse yourself in another heavy journalism story? What does your therapist say about this?" I made one last attempt to detain her from moving forward in her new life.

"What gives, Steve, geez?" She sounded frustrated.

I needed to see her and fast and I needed her to tell me that she saw me as someone other than her friend or a former boss. "Can you meet me at the airport then?" I said breathlessly; I didn't breathe because I didn't dare. "I'm coming to town to meet with my new station manager. If you could come meet me then it would save some time for me. I'd really like to see you before you travel. It may be awhile before we can get together again."

"You know I would move 'Heaven and Earth' to get there when I can," she paused and then continued, "Look bud..." *There's that bud again*, I thought. "I need you. Who else can I share my heart to? You're an important chapter in my book of life."

"How could I tell her that I didn't want to be just a chapter? I wanted to be thee book," I thought. Maybe I would find the courage this time.

How could I speak my mind and be true to myself without it having some permanent altercation? I didn't yet know whether I was prepared for its consequences. I always considered myself to be a person of high moral character, one full of great integrity and adhered to the humble words of *The Desiderata.* But to, "Speak my truth clearly", at this point to Piper, ultimately entrapped me between two philosophies: the teleological and the deontological. I was faced with an ethical dilemma. Was I right to merely standby, in my dishonesty, and wait for her or should I move forward and express my true self? The deontological realist in me would believe that I needed to speak my truth at whatever the cost. The teleological thinker would say that I had to weigh out the responsibilities of my words. There was a real possibility that my honesty might hurt her and send her away.

Piper, it seemed to me at the time, needed more freedom to grow and realize her potential for love. I would be taking a great chance in sharing my honesty and thus could be inflicting more pain for both of us. I decided that having her in my life in any capacity was more important than losing her altogether. I didn't want my desperation to destroy what clearly, we already had. I decided to wait.

BOOK TWO

Avoid the loud and aggressive,
They are vexatious to the spirit;
If you compare yourself with others
You may become vain or bitter
For always there will be
  -greater and lesser than yourself.
Enjoy your achievements as well as your plans,
Keep interested in your career
It is a possession in the changing fortunes of time;
Exercise caution in your affairs
  -for the world is full of trickery
But let this not blind you to what virtue there is,
Strive for high ideals.
Everywhere there is heroism,
Be yourself
Do not feign affection; be not cynical about love
  -as it is as perennial as the grass.

Chapter Nine

The months following were filled with eager plans and preparations, I learned later. I didn't again connect with Piper for a long time. She let me know in no uncertain terms that she wanted to make a good go of this relationship and didn't think any outside 'interference' would help her initiative, despite the fact that I don't think she even entertained the idea of me being an actual 'interference' in any way, shape or form. Since Piper seemed to know what she wanted, which wasn't me, I decided to work on my own relationship.

All hands were on deck for this project. CNDY's corporate sponsors had arranged to cover the advertising costs and were busily scheduling TV and print ads for the Apartheid concert. The creative department was working on the ad campaign, developing spots, industrial video, and promotional radio flyers. The news team was providing Piper with the background. They'd researched the current state of Pretoria following the release of Mandela considering the recent ANC (African National Congress) developments.

Piper had her own personal life to attend to. She wired Patrick to let him know her itinerary. They'd be flying into Kenya, where they were going to stay for a week or two, depending on the need, at one of the International Youth Traveller (IYT) hostels, which Richie was a member. The station had been in touch with the Canadian Embassy in Nairobi to arrange their stay. In exchange, Piper was to do a story on the newly founded *Kenya Television Network.* Her plans were then to fly from Nairobi, Kenya, into Tanzania, and then move onto Lilongwe, Malawi, where Patrick was the chief and attending surgeon at one of two of the country's medical emergency clinics. Due to the fact that communication was difficult and she didn't really want to go into details about her 'partner' with her father over the wire, she just mentioned that she'd need a place to stay and that she'd be accompanied by a 'male companion'. *'There was no point in giving the man a heart attack,'* she rationalized to me later. But she kept the message rather cryptic regardless. *'And besides, sleeping arrangements could certainly be dealt with at a later date.'* If it mattered to Patrick that Piper was bringing a man, it didn't seem to affect him. In fact, he mentioned that it was probably a good idea and much safer for her to travel with a male counterpart in these volatile areas of the world. *'Counterpart'; Yes that's what I'll call him!* Piper chuckled in agreement. From there, she was going to go on down to South Africa but the concert was over a month away and she wanted to make good use of her travel time to cash in on some of her own adventures. Seeing Victoria Falls and a safari trek through a national park or reserve were high on her list of attractions but she didn't let Patrick know of all these details, just that her schedule only permitted her a few days with him in Malawi.

The months leading up to their journey were filled with medical appointments and blood tests. Both Piper and Richie were screened by the physician for infectious diseases and received the recommended immunizations: measles, small pox and proof of the yellow fever vaccine were requirements from the African government at the time for visitors intending to travel through Kenya and Malawi. The various rounds of needles and medications were making Piper sick and she often thought about whether 'this whole thing was worth it.' By the time the pair boarded the plane to the U.K, they both felt they understood what it was like to be a pincushion.

"Geesh," Piper complained. "My arms are so lumpy. I haven't been able to lift any thing in days from the stiffness."

"Well don't you worry about a thing, Pipes. I've got the bags covered," offered Richie.

"Yea right! You've got more baggage than I've ever seen. Add to that a guitar case and a camera. Ever heard of traveling light?"

"One just never knows when they'll be breaking out into song!" he teased in his effort to be funny.

"I think I feel more like I'm breaking out into an allergic rash. My skin is so itchy!"

"That was the measles shot. Piper, that doesn't look too good. You should've had that checked out before we left. Maybe we should drop into a clinic in London when we land," he said.

"We'll see. If it gets worse, maybe, but it can probably wait until we get to Africa. Don't forget that my dad is a doctor and works at a clinic," she said.

"Yes I know. Dr. Brown. I didn't forget. Just trying to be proactive. Besides, I really think I'd make a bad first impression bringing him his daughter with sumo wrestling arms." He argued.

"I hate to tell you this but he's my dad. He's not going to like you anyway."

The flight was an overnighter so they tried to get in as much sleep as they could. They knew they'd have a day of traipsing around London when they arrived in the morning, as their flight into Nairobi was another red-eye so if they hadn't slept, then it would make the adventure a lot less enjoyable. But neither slept too well. Piper was excited and anxious about all the responsibilities she had in front of her and again being reunited with her father. Richie was just a big guy and those plane seats must *be made for midgets. Okay vertically challenged then,'* he corrected himself when he saw Piper's look of distain.

The day in London was all a fog, not just in typical U.K weather but because the pair had done nothing but argue and usually over the smallest of things. They were really both too tired and too bogged down with their luggage to call it an adventure; it felt more like a punishment Piper recalled. Richie had snapped some pictures of her throughout the earlier parts of the day but got fed up with her sneers and covering her face with her hand to hide her less-than-perfect travel appearance. By the time the two of them passed through the security gates, the immigration cues and the infectious disease line-up at Jomo Kenyatta International Airport in Nairobi, the following day, they were about ready to kill each other. *We must've been quite the sight for the embassy guide who was sent there to greet us. Picking away at each other like we were an old married couple,* she recanted to me. Rich used every last bit of his strength to help load up Piper's recording gear and all their luggage into the tiny van rented to them for the duration of their stay in Kenya. He was supposed to then follow the guide who had pulled out in front of them several minutes earlier.

"Hurry up, Rich! We're losing him. I really don't feel like getting lost out here in no man's land." She warned.

"And you think I do?" He argued back.

"Then put a little lead into it. "

"I'm trying but I'm really not used to driving a standard transmission."

"I could hardly notice," she said sarcastically.

"Just stop!!" Richie used all his force to slam down hard onto the brakes, a force which threw all the gear forward with one of the duffle bags managing to hit Piper in the back of the head.

"Look what you've done now, you idiot! And that car is nowhere in sight." He got out of the driver side and went around to open Piper's door. "What are you doing?" she said.

"You think it's so easy? You drive." Piper begrudgingly made her way over to the driver's seat and put the car into first gear. With no less than 3 stutters the car lurched forward and they were back in action. Thankfully the driver of the car they were following had noticed that the pair weren't behind him so he pulled off to the side of the road to wait. Within another 30 minutes they were settled into their tiny private room in the student hostel. They had a full 24 hours to get accustomed to the time change and jet lag before Piper was to report to the television station. They forewent eating the fresh fruit that was left in a welcome basket at their bedside and hit the pillows like there was no tomorrow.

They were up fairly early the following day. Piper eagerly got her gear and notes together for her first assignment while in Africa. She mentioned to Rich that he'd probably be bored while she worked so suggested that he just drop her off and then go get food supplies and essentials for their room. He figured he'd want some time to get adjusted maybe take some pictures too, so for once they weren't at each other's throats.

The station was in a fairly new building and looked rather modern for the time period. KTN had been founded only a year or so before and had quickly become one of the leading television stations in Kenya with its headquarters located along Mombasa Road, one of the main thoroughfares in Nairobi. Piper learned, upon interviewing its founder, Jared Kangwana, that "it was the first non-pay privately owned TV station in Africa." It became famous for activism journalism, "developing a sophisticated, aggressive and unique style news coverage." KTN had just won their bid to carry the 1992 Albertville Winter Olympics and Barcelona Summer Olympic games; so all energies were afforded in that direction, Piper noted. She also reported that this was an opportune time for media and for the country's political parties. Kenya was in the middle of a multi-party democracy movement and KTN was becoming known "to give voices to the subversives, dissidents and opposition politicians." They were entering in a new age of electronic media and Piper was proud to be part of the 'civilized rebellion.' The day's work went expediently without a hitch. She went home to the couple's hostel room exhausted and exhilarated. She only had the energy to gobble down a few bites of bread before she hit the pillow for another full night's sleep.

When she awoke, Richie had already left with the van. She showered and went into her work pack to listen to the recorded interviews she had done the day before. She rewound the tape to the beginning then fast-forwarded over each of the questions. It wasn't until she got to the final few minutes that she heard a *blip* in the tape. She reversed it to go over it a second time. She played through the disruption and noticed that she could hear her muffled voice but it seemed rather distant. Someone had clearly recorded over it. She let it run for another few seconds when she heard a man's voice unfamiliar to her, speaking harshly in what appeared to be his native tongue and considering they were in Kenya, it was more than likely in Swahili. Her puzzled expression was the first thing that Richard noticed as he entered the room. "What's wrong?" he asked.

"I'm not sure. Listen and tell me what you think happened."

They agreed that it was best if they inform the station right away. Kangwana, without trying to alarm them, told them they should return to the station immediately. He'd have his security meet them at the gate. When the pair arrived back into his office, he had 2 armed security men with him and what appeared at first to be a note-taker. This man was introduced to Piper as Robert Ngali, a translator.

"Play the recording for Mr. Ngali, Ms. Brown, will you please?" urges Kangwana.

"Oh yes sir. It's right here." Said Piper. Kangwana and Ngali listened repeatedly and conversed in an African tongue. Kangwana was the first to address the duo.

"Mr. Ngali is in agreement with me that this is a very dangerous warning in Swahili. The speaker is basically telling you to stop and to not get involved or there would be dire consequences. He doesn't go into details as to what is his cause or reason for his threats but our belief is that he's part of the movement to defend the single political party system in favor of democracy.

Some of our reporters have been tear gassed alongside the opposition luminaries during this time of great upheaval for Kenya. We're paving new grounds for African journalists and becoming more universal isn't sitting well among the staunch traditionalists."

Piper and Richard nod accordingly and then he went on to say, "You mustn't worry but it would be in your best interest to move along now on your journey. Perhaps you should file your story here first so that you're not carrying it with you. That would put you in greater danger. And I'll see that you get an escort back to your residence."

Once back to the room, Piper started to panic. "Oh my God, Richie. I just wanna go home."

Richie picked up his guitar and strummed the first line of a John Hiatt classic, *Have a Little Faith in Me*. "It'll be okay, kiddo. And you thought it was going to be your dad who was going to terrorize us?" Richie teased trying to ease the tension. He held her while she quivered in his embrace. "Want to hear what I've been up to?" He added.

"Okay," Piper replied.

Richie put down the guitar and began his prologue into the research he was doing and the photographs he was taking on the poaching issues in Africa and the recent ban on the ivory trade. He told her that he got some remarkable footage over the past day or so and that it would only increase the closer they got to the Cape (Cape of Good Hope).

"Gee, and I thought we were just going surfing once we got to the south coast; I didn't realize we'd be on a hunt to protect the elephants. Good on ya!" Piper declared.

"Good on us!" Rich added.

Chapter Ten

Later that day the duo found themselves back at the Embassy. They mapped out their route to their next destination. They bought cheap charter flights from Nairobi to get into Mombasa and from there they'd do the overnight commuter train into Dar es Salaam. Their flight was going to be leaving in less than 90 minutes so they had to 'get a move on' as Piper claims Patrick would always say. They arrived to Tanzania's most luxurious city by mid morning, hungry, tired and with very sore feet.

"Man, oh man," Piper howled. "Got to give these puppies a rest. I was really hoping to get in a nice long run, Rich. Haven't had one in a week but my feet are so swollen."

"Mine aren't much better. Let's just take a beach day and enjoy what the city has to offer."

In fact, they took 2 days off to get rested and organized for the second week of their journey. Rich was itching to get started on his shoot with the elephants. Piper had already wired *The Toronto Star* to see what angle she was to take on her story about the ivory ban. They awoke wide-eyed and bushy-tailed on their third day in Tanzania. The safari jeep with a guide was arranged to pick them up for a two-day adventure of 'elephant tracking'.

"How does this sound so far?" Piper began. "The ivory ban was a significant victory, but the cause for the elephant has not yet been won. Human encroachment on elephant habitat continues to threaten its survival. As a result of the ban, the price of ivory has plummeted, and poaching brought under control but the elephant is still in danger."

"Great and I've got some footage to add to your story." Richie said proudly.

"I don't imagine you got a shot of yourself getting chased by the bull today?" Piper giggled. "You should've seen your face. I've never seen you move quicker."

"Very funny!" Rich sneered. They were back in the jeep early the following morning for their final day of their trek.

~~

"Are you getting anxious about seeing your father?" Rich queried as they packed up their things to go to Malawi.

"Yes and no. Trying not to make it a big deal 'cause that's exactly what he wants...a reception fit for a 'king'. You know he's here in Africa so he can maintain his 'king' status. White manliness in these parts of the world is next to godliness. I'm sure he's got servants and slaves to do all his work for him. And that's just his wife." Piper exaggerated.

"I'm sure he's here for more reasons than that, Piper." Rich defended. Piper just shrugged. "Yea sure; just take his side."

Piper was pretty quiet during the boarding process and flight itself, except for her usual request to hold her flying partner's hand every time the plane took off and landed; she didn't speak very much. Rich could tell that she was nervous about the reunion. She made it even more evident when she leaned over to him while they were undoing their seatbelts to ask if she looked all right. Piper was never known to care too much about her personal appearance. She had natural beauty and innate fashion sense. "You look great, Piper, beautiful, in fact. Don't worry." She didn't respond to him but just stared blankly out the window onto the tarmac below.

"Welcome to Lilongwe!" the couple heard as they were greeted by the airline crew and escorted into the single gated airport. Piper scanned the small crowd, watched as others were hugged and hands were held, giving her back that old familiar feeling that she craved and knew so well...but no sign of her father.

Patrick was renowned for being late due to not paying attention to detail or *'not giving a fuck'* as Piper believed so as disappointed as she was, she certainly wasn't surprised. *"Okay now what do we do?"* Piper thought.

Just as she was beginning a new plan, she heard her name being paged over the airport's P.A system. "Attention all visitors: Would Patricia Jane Brown please come to the guest services desk? Patricia Brown to the guest services desk, please." She motioned to Rich where she was going as he was gathering the last of the bags from the baggage carousel. The look on her face said everything.

"He's had a heart attack." She whispered upon his arrival to her side. "He's at the south clinic in Blantyre about a day's drive, which they don't recommend, or another flight away."

"What did they say about his condition?"

"It's pretty bad. When he didn't show up to work on Monday morning they called his house and didn't get any response. They got his neighbor to come over to check on him because she'd said his car was in the driveway. She found him on the kitchen floor. She revived him briefly but it's been touch and go ever since. There's no flight outta here until tomorrow, so that means it'll be Wednesday or possibly Thursday before we can get there. I guess we just have to do our best and get there as quickly as we can".

Richie thought Piper was pretty composed despite the news and in fact noted that she was a fairly calm person under pressure on most occasions. It's not until some time afterwards that she would break down.

The next 24 hours were excruciatingly painful. Piper was jumping down Richie's throat every time he made any kind of a suggestion to help ease the tension and to provide her with some hope. He decided it was best to just leave her be, stay within proximity but remain out of her personal space. By the time they arrived to the tiny southern town, Rich squeezed her hand, in what became his traditional method of support, and waved her off at the front steps of the five-story clinic. "I'll wait here. Take whatever time you need." He assured her.

Piper had her car door open even before the car had come to a full stop. She raced into the front lobby, noticed an obstruction at the elevator so veered off quickly to the stairwell, taking 2 and 3 steps up at a time. Her heart was pounding by the time she arrived to the fifth floor. She brushed past some nurses and burst through the first open door to see her father's eyes open. With a gravelly voice she heard him whisper, "Look who's here!"

"And look who's alive! They told me to hurry 'cause it looked grim." Piper replied.

"Apparently the guy in the sky is not ready for me yet," he grinned. Piper kind of squirmed and thought that perhaps it was more like *the liar in the fire* who was going to select Patrick's fate but then she felt awkward thinking such thoughts under the circumstances.

She hugged him and started filling him in on her adventures. Not even a few minutes into her story Piper realized that Patrick seemed disinterested in what she was offering and turned the conversation towards himself. *Yes! He still thinks he's a king*, she thought to herself. But then again readjusted the thoughts in her mind and figured he was really just worn out; after all, he'd just had a massive heart attack.

"How's your mother?" he finally asked.

"She's fine," she replied. Piper could not, as was the case for the rest of the Brown clan, forgive her father for his treatment of their mother: the lying, the cheating, and the violent threats. "But do you really care? You're here in Africa where the world seemingly adores you; you're remarried and I'm sure, have your share of a harem here at the hospital, the way you did back home." Piper became enraged.

"Is that anyway to talk to your dying father?" Patrick managed to say beneath what sounded like an excruciating inhalation. Piper was adamant.

"And is that how one is supposed to treat the living?" Piper lit into him long and hard for quite some time. It's like she finally had the opportunity to say what she'd been feeling for a long while, perhaps even her lifetime. She'd always been so afraid of him; his physical strength combined with his quick temper and drunken binges made for very treacherous communication. But as he lay there before her, he looked so less threatening, almost meek. It never occurred to her just how much he'd aged since the last time she saw him.

"I'm not going to defend my actions, Piper, nor excuse my behavior. I am who I am and I'm very proud of the accomplishments that I've made. I was really hoping that we could just get a fresh start but it seems as though you can't let go of the past. Just why did you come here, Piper?" Patrick questioned with his eyes closing narrowly.

"I don't know. I guess I thought you'd be different somehow." And with that Piper turned and ran out of his room. She hopped into the elevator in tears. It was a few moments later where she noticed that she wasn't alone in the tiny space.

She felt too emotional to make eye contact but nodded when the stranger said, "Are you okay? Death is very difficult for the living. Whatever you need to say to your loved ones needs to be said. *Be yourself; do not feign affection.* It is important that we make amends not for those leaving this life, but for those of us left behind. We can become so narrow in our visions that we fail to see the bigger picture. There's a lot more to people than meets the eye. It is true that *the world is full of trickery but let not this blind you to what virtue there is. Keep peace with your soul*, Piper. Follow your spirit and you will come home." With that, the elevator door opened and Piper stepped out. She wondered how the stranger behind her knew her name. She looked down at her chest to see if she had been issued a nametag then looked back at the elevator to notice it was empty. Although she knew she'd never seen the woman before, there was something so oddly familiar about her and what she had said.

"The Desiderata," she thought out loud. *"The Desiderata"* was a prose poem found in the old Church of England and copyrighted many centuries later by American writer Max Ehrmann. It had been framed and hung on the walls of the Brown estate for most of Piper's life. She was often found standing in front of it, staring. "I just like the way it sings to me," she would say when one of her teasing siblings noticed her trance.

"You're just plain weird, PJ," was the usual response. Her mother understood the magnitude of the poem's significance or it wouldn't have hung in the hallway in the first place and appreciated Piper's devotion to it by giving her, her own copy of it one year as a Christmas gift. She'd memorized its eloquence some ten times over.

Just as she thought she had pieced it all together, an attendant walked by her in the hospital hallway and asked, "You seem lost. Are you looking for someone?"

"Yes, my father. Am I on the right floor? I just got off the elevator." Piper admitted.

"You're on the fifth floor but you couldn't have taken the elevator; it hasn't worked in months." Piper was more confused than ever but continued. "I'm looking for Patrick Brown. I'm his daughter."

"Ah yes, Dr. Brown's daughter. He spoke highly of you. He said you were coming to Africa to visit him. Come this way."

She was taken back to the room where she thought she had been just a few moments earlier. This time, it was empty. A lovely doe-eyed nurse entered the room looking mournful and compassionate towards her. "I'm sorry Piper. We tried to keep him alive long enough for you to make one last visit to him, particularly since you've come all the way from Canada. He had a massive heart attack on Monday and didn't recover. Just know that he was a good man, a wonderful doctor and that he loved you and his family very much. He did a lot of good work at this hospital in the time he was here. We're arranging for the new wing to be named after him. It would be wonderful if you could be part of the ceremony in his honour."

Piper bit her lip to prevent it from quivering and nodded. Big juicy tears rolled down her cheekbones. She tried to keep the wise words from the stranger in the elevator foremost in her mind and she felt solace that perhaps Patrick had found his *home.*

Chapter Eleven

The few days following were sketchy from Piper's recollection. She told me that she had called her mother to find out whether it was important for her to have Patrick's body shipped back to Canada or not. Emily said that Patrick had always wanted to be cremated and his remains to be spread around the grounds of the Brown country estate. If his new wife and family could accommodate his request then it would certainly be appreciated. Piper met with Evelyn Jacobs to go over the options available to them.

"I'm sure it would be absolutely fine for you to hold a wake and service for dad here. He chose to be here and obviously very much wanted to be with you and your family in Malawi at this time. It makes sense. It also makes sense to me that his previous wishes are honoured, that he is cremated with his ashes spread across the Canadian countryside. He left Ireland over 60 years ago for the wonder and wealth of Canada and he was a Canadian through and through." No one could argue with Piper's logic so her compromise was put into place. The Jacobs family would arrange and pay for the cremation and funeral in Lilongwe and then they'd send his urn back to Canada where the Browns would pay for its arrival and take over from there.

Piper and Rich spent the next few evenings over dinner with the Jacobs, going over plans and details of the ceremonies, his funeral service and the naming ceremony of the new hospital wing in his honour. Piper learned that the Jacobs' family had pretty much taken Patrick in and claimed him as one of their own. They worshipped the ground he walked on because of the work that he had been doing in the clinics. Malawi had no medical school and no way to train local students who had any scientific background. Any young person who wanted to become a doctor had to train elsewhere, even as far away as London. They found that the medical school students wouldn't return, choosing to stay in a more affluent environment and this really wasn't doing Malawi any good. In fact, it almost bled the country dry of qualified emergency personnel. Patrick saw at least a temporary fix to the problem. He'd been organizing grants issued by the Canadian government to award to local Africans to study and graduate from a local medical school, under Patrick's auspices. He'd taken the best of the best emergency clinicians and provided them with 4 years of more specific medical training. Malawi still lost so much of their population annually to polio and he thought this might ease some of this epidemic. The degree he was sanctioning to issue was only recognized within the continent, in hopes that the country could hang onto some of their young doctors. Patrick had been only into his 2nd year of training the first group of students when he died, so it was too early to prove whether this was actually going to work; however, on paper it sure looked altruistic.

Her father's ceremonies were small and intimate and went on without a hitch. She remained ambivalent in her feelings toward him but felt sad when she saw how it affected the Jacobs' family. She also felt badly that her siblings didn't get a chance to see the more benevolent side of their dad. She would make it a point to communicate the compassionate component of his life once she got back home.

It was a very busy few days. Piper, as worn-out as she was physically from her cross continent trek, and emotionally from her father dying, had to keep moving. The main reason she went to Africa in the first place was to cover the anti-Apartheid concert for the station and that was only 8 days away now and in another country no less. She felt achy and sore. It wasn't until she was undressing to get into bed the night after the hospital inauguration that Richie noticed a big red, oozing rash across her back.

"Oh my God, Piper. What is that?"

"What is what?" she cranked her neck to see what he was pointing at.

"You've got a massive rash along your upper back from shoulder to shoulder. Is that from your vaccination a couple of weeks ago?"

"It must be," Piper decided.

"Isn't it bothering you?" he said.

"Yes I guess it is! I've been feeling like crap the whole time I've been here but I've just chalked that up to the travel bug. As much as I love being somewhere else, I hate getting there. I better mention it to Evelyn and see what she says."

The Jacobs were having a big family dinner that night. Evelyn's daughter and son-in-law were invited. Julian had just come back from a 3-month gaming hunt and had many adventures to tell. Julian was a professional big game hunter and although it was an insanely dangerous career, he never seemed to let the risks scare him away so he naturally had many exotic and thrilling stories to share.

"I'll be going into Harare tomorrow guys. You're welcome to come with me," Julian offered. "I've got to set up another crew for a hunt into Hwange National Park. There is a pesky lion pride disturbing the campers that we've got to look after. I've been told as well that you were interested in seeing the falls (Victoria) and that's really the best vantage point."

Richie continued. "That sounds great! Um, has Piper mentioned anything to you about her rash and high fever?"

"I'm right here, Rich." Piper retorted indignantly. "I've just finished showing Evelyn and she mentioned a special salve that I could try. You use that in conjunction with an African herbal liquid only available in Zimbabwe, so I guess it's 'Hi ho, hi ho, off to Zim we go."

"You might actually want to try one of the native herbalists while you're there." Julian said with a bit of a grin.

"What's the face for?" Piper asked.

"Pardon my sarcasm but if your father hadn't have been cremated, he'd be rolling around in his grave with that suggestion."

Piper took no time to decide. "In that case, that's exactly what I'll do."

It was a long bumpy ride into Zimbabwe through Mozambique. Piper felt more feverish than ever but she was alert enough to notice just how poor and desolate this war-stricken country was. The foursome had to stop twice for gas and every time the 4 x 4 pulled off to the side of the road headed toward the open pumps, a horde of children surrounded them. They tugged at Piper's arms and pulled at her skirt.

"I've got to give them something," she shouted out to Julian above the noise from the crowd.

"No don't do it. You give something to one kid, and then they will all want it and will rape, rob and pillage the one you give it to. It's just not worth it, for anybody."

Piper just couldn't take it. She saw deep into the dark eyes of the barely clothed little ones; their protruding bellies and cracked swollen lips only told part of the story of how desperate and hungry they were. It was at that time she vowed to do some fundraising once she got back to the station in Canada and to make sure that the money would be sent to the children in the villages of war-torn Mozambique. When she told me this story some time later, it made me further realize just what a wonderful mother she would make some day.

"We're here and not a moment too soon," uttered Julian. "Can you pick her up and follow me?" he said to Rich, referring to Piper. Her fever had spiked in the last hour of the trip and she had been in and out of delusional sleep. Julian thought it best to go directly to the herbalist in town. He could attend to his crew after he got Piper and Richie settled.

From Piper's recantation of the experience, it sounded more like she had been treated by a Haitian witch doctor but it could've been the fever talking. They weren't inside the tiny cobblestoned house for very long before Piper opened her eyes. In front of her, propped up with a cane, stood a short, native black man with very long graying braids. Because African skin isn't prone to visible, rapid aging, the way white skin is, Piper had ascertained that he was much older than he appeared. He didn't speak any English and mumbled something to Julian who nodded. He stumbled his way across the room to a shelf filled with ceramic bottles and bins. He measured some various substances out and poured them into a flask. He brought the flask up to his eye level and then nodded. He beckoned for Julian to come and help him return with the potion as he couldn't manage the cane and the medicine at the same time. From another shelf he reached his hand into a tub and brought out a scoop of a white ointment. He motioned for Piper to roll up her sleeves and lift up the back of her shirt, so that he could access the tops of her shoulders. The salve had a cooling and de-itching affect and almost instantly made her feel better. She sipped the liquid at first gingerly, not sure exactly what she was in for and then gulped it after she was assured of its sweetness. Richie sat on the hard-mud floor beside her seemingly worried but began to feel some relief as Piper did.

"This is amazing!" Piper said 15 minutes after the procedure. They could still hear the old pharmacist chanting and murmuring off in the distance. "What did he give me?"

Julian laughed. "Sorry to tease. It's our way here in Zimbabwe. That was liquid acetaminophen, kind of like

Tylenol. Ever heard of that? And the salve is a combination of aloe, antibiotic ointment and petroleum jelly."

"Vaseline and Polysporin?" Piper squealed.

"'Fraid so," Julian chuckled. "Nothing fancier than that. And that's Mr. Huulu our resident medic. Harare is becoming very touristy and so we like to give the crowd what they want, or so it appears."

"I didn't care what he was going to do," Piper exclaimed. "As long as I was going to feel better. And I do. Thanks very much." She smiled as she figured out that Evelyn was probably in on the joke too.

"Well, he hasn't cured you but it has relieved your itch and getting a solid night sleep tonight will get you back on the road to recovery. I've booked you two into the Victoria Falls Hotel, a gorgeous 5-star resort, where you can eat, rest and enjoy for the next while." Julian looked very pleased at his tomfoolery.

"Thanks guy," said Richie. Piper nodded.

~~

Their view from the old Victorian-style hotel was gorgeous, lush gardens, live monkeys high atop the eucalyptus trees and landscaped walkways along a winding tributary. About a ten minute walk along the pathway behind the hotel was a popular entrance to the Zambesi River. That's where the couple was to meet their guide for their half-day kayak and half-day savannah trail hike.

Rich was in his glory. He'd been a bit of a competitive kayaker back in Canada and was aching to show off his skills. He had, had quite enough of Piper leading the parade lately and this was his turn to shine. "We must be at the bottom of the falls then, right?" Piper asked.

"Oh no, missus," said the guide with a seemingly British accent. "We're at the top of the falls. Don't paddle too far or you'll go over," with not even a hint of sarcasm in his voice.

"These Zimfolk are killing me!" Piper shrugged.

"Certainly entertaining," added Rich as he grabbed a paddle and threw it across to Piper. "Get in front, kid. It's time to go."

There were 6 kayak doubles and 2 kayak singles, one each for the guides. Everyone set out and paddled rather merrily and easily for the first few minutes, getting familiar with the ebb and flow of the streaming river. It was about 20 minutes later that one of the guides mentioned that they saw a crocodile in the reeds along the inner bank. They warned the kayakers to steer clear of that particular area. They said the crocs wouldn't likely bother with them but if this were mating season, they would certainly be on the defensive.

"Gawwwd," Piper groaned. "I've had enough adventures to last a life time already."

"Let's just paddle our way across this narrow passageway and touch down on the other side. Zambia is on that side. If we touch ground with our paddles over there, we can say we've traveled to yet another country in Africa."

The guides corralled the kayakers off to a sandy beach area. Everyone got out and hiked up a little hill. When they got to the other side, there were lovely table-clothed tables set up with buckets of sparkling wine. Piper hadn't realized how hungry she was until she saw the feast.

"Wonderful! Just what the doctor ordered."

It was the afternoon trek across the Hwange Reserve, however, that was the highlight of her entire month's adventures. A short walk up the river she began to hear the rushing of water. She knew full well what to expect having grown up near Niagara Falls but despite all, her heart raced in anticipation of the magnitude of its glory. Another few quick steps toward the viewing platform got her in a good position to peer over the edge. She gasped as if the power of the falls had actually hit her in the chest. "Ah, this is truly magnificent! I am so blessed," Piper realized.

The remainder of the afternoon she was entirely in her element, in harmony with nature's peace and tranquility. She had shimmied her way up the side of a rock and sat out on a tiny ledge that jutted out from the side of the cliff. She sat cross-legged and clasped her hands to heart center, as a budding yogi, breathing in solitude to find oneness with the world. It was here where Piper first began to appreciate the many sounds of silence, amid the noise and haste.

Chapter Twelve

By the number of adventures the pair had already had, it was easy to negotiate just how quickly the month away from home got soaked up. They arrived into South Africa with only 2 days left before the big concert. Piper felt relieved to see that the tech crew she'd organized and sent for from CNDY had arrived and they had already met with the locals to begin set up for the big event. She also felt excited to see some of her buddies from back home. It suddenly made her feel like she'd been away for a very long time and that perhaps it was time to go home. So much had happened while she was away this time that she almost felt she had become a different person.

"That may account for the voices in my head," Piper managed to say out loud.

"What was that?" said Joe, the good-looking roadshow kid.

"What was what?" she pretended not to hear him.

"You talking to yourself again, Piper?" he continued. "They say it's fine to ask yourself questions but if you're answering them out loud, then there's a problem." He chuckled.

Piper sighed and managed to say under her breath this time, "Well then, there's no hope for me and the bucket load of people I hear talking inside of my head."

As usual, Piper got right down to business, arranging for the interviews with the artists flying in or already in town for the show. Hugh Masekela was on his own tour and had been in Johannesburg for a few days, so his agent said it would be easy for her to speak with him right away. Both Johnny Clegg and Ladysmith Black Mambazo, a 20-piece male choral band, were native to Joberg, and were in town doing promos and station stingers for the concert, so they wouldn't create any snags either but it was the new up-and-comer Angelique Kidjo, coming in from Senegal, who might have created a scheduling headache, if her flights were delayed. Since time was limited, Piper thought it best to go and greet Kidjo at the airport and did the interview on the fly.

"What an absolutely lovely woman?" Piper told Richie later that day. "She's special and going somewhere. I can't wait to see her perform and share in her energy. She's got fire breathers and Zulu warrior dancers up on stage with her and she wears these witch doctor types of masks and skirts. She calls them her 'roosters'. Remind me that I've really got to add more of these moves and promote this stuff in my fitness classes at home. It's all the rage and it's a great workout. I actually got her New York City agent info so we can maybe connect later."

"How was the choir?" Richie asked, in reference to Ladysmith Black Mambazo.

"Well, they didn't actually perform for me but I've been listening to their promos and I just love them on Paul Simon's *Graceland* album. He really scored with that one," Piper replied. "I interviewed the headmaster today, Joseph Shabalala; don't you love his name, shaba-la-la-la-la (she said singingly); even that's musical.

They've got such a great concept. When I asked him how all that came together he said 'it all began with a series of dreams he had back in 1964, over a six month period in which featured a choir singing in perfect harmony'. He gathered the finest Zulu male singers in the area at the time, from here through Durban Township, and they began to perform at weddings and then in local competitions. He actually taught these choirboys the harmonies from what he'd heard in his dreams. I find that so fascinating! Was it really dreaming or something more like having voices in his head?" Piper asked this out loud on purpose. She certainly felt a kinship with this ability and wanted to know if there were other people who could relate or at least, believe in it. She had always questioned from where some of this musical genius came. She felt it had to be linked more to one's immaculate spirit rather than just a superlative physiological wiring of nerve synapses.

"Hmm..." was all the response that Piper received in return.

"It'll be Masekela and Clegg tomorrow. These guys will be the center of my focus on apartheid."

"I actually heard Masekela at the Rivoli in Toronto," offered Richie.

"Really? I'd never heard of him until the station booked him for this show and clearly he's well loved around here. Our posters feature him front and centre."

"Yes you have, Piper. He was musical director on the CD for *Sarafina*, which you actually gave me." Rich admitted.

"Was that he? That CD is one of my favourites!" replied Piper. "He's getting on too, he's not much younger than my Mum."

Rich agreed. "Something to add to your knowledge bank for when you interview him tomorrow. Say 'thank you, Richie'," Rich teased and strummed and sang his usual, *Have a Little Faith in Me.*

"Ay-yay-yay! I hate it when you do that. Seriously, you make me sound so ungrateful."

Piper laced up her running shoes and set out for a nice long, flat run. It felt so good to be able to run without having to be covered from head to toe. The last time she ran she was in Malawi and that country had an archaic dress code for women. According to the statute legislated by the thirty year reigning President Banda, *'women were to be covered at all times while in public and were never to show any nudity in the lower regions of their bodies.'* Actually Piper rephrased that and told me that women were allowed to be topless but had to have everything else covered from the waist on down. That applied to female runners as well, not that any woman could run without at least a sports bra, but the running in a skirt made it pretty awkward. Piper said that she didn't want to get her skirts sweaty so she'd wrap herself up in a shower curtain before she'd head out. I laughed every time I pictured it.

~~

The show was quite a spectacle from start to finish. Piper's hosting skills were brilliant as usual and her pre-concert interviews, although weren't used during the show, would be dubbed in for the recorded version and sent back with her for use at the station for its biographical library. She did a piece on the status of Apartheid at that point in 1992 that included the more recent talks and installation of reforms. The latest move to end it had been in 1990, two years earlier, when South African President Frederik Willem de Klerk began negotiations. But it wouldn't be until 1994 with the success of the multi-racial democratic elections, won by the African National Congress under Nelson Mandela, where Apartheid would be defeated altogether. Piper felt so accomplished in being part of this fundraising initiative to raise not only money, but also further awareness to the western world.

She'd also had a great deal of fun doing the 'live' hosting of the show itself, an opportunity of which she wanted to do more. Most of the full-time announcers, like Mike Gryphon, her ex beau, and Todd Sullivan, fast becoming her best friend in the business, got asked to do those kinds of gigs; as she was considered a 'newsie', she didn't really get invited to host as much as she'd liked; not only was it fun to do but it put her on a higher pay scale at the radio station and added to that, often times, the host would get paid cash, which increased the windfall exponentially.

Kidjo had kept her on stage after Piper's introduction of her and added her to her flame-throwing act. It meant that Piper could show-off her tribal dance moves that were becoming such a popular trend in the Toronto fitness scene. It seemed every year there was another vogue form of workout that Piper kept right on top of for her clients, in order to keep boredom at bay. In some studios they actually had live African drummers set-up in the corner of the studio to entertain the fitness enthusiasts while they sweated to the beat.

Both her interviews with Masekela and Clegg were a vital part of the cause. Masekela, she learned, played and recorded music that closely reflected his life experiences. 'The agony, conflict and exploitation South Africa faced during the 50s and 60s inspired him to make music thematic of political change." Clegg on the other hand, seemed to embody anti-apartheid philosophies just by his heritage and culture alone. Although British-born he moved to South Africa early on in his life and recorded and performed with his first band called, *Le Zoulou Blanc*, meaning 'The White Zulu'. He was renowned for his mixture of Zulu with English lyrics combining a blend of African rhythms. He was the first prominent racially mixed South African musician and due to the fact that he was ahead of his time period, he was restrained from performing in his hometown areas and received no airplay on state-owned radio for his first album appropriately named, *Universal Men*. The moderate success he received at that point in time came all by word-of-mouth. He took risks to maintain his mixed racial band members but suffered the consequences; he had been arrested several times and had concerts broken up on account of his more progressive ideals.

"It just doesn't seem fair to me that a plain and simple musician can be put in jail for creating something so beautiful. What happened to freedom of speech, not to mention freedom to create?" Piper exclaimed to me, in wrapping up her African adventure. "Isn't it the point of art to envelop the ideals of the community at the time or conversely, to challenge the postures put forward by the society in which it resides?"

I had to remind her that her views were highly civilized and what she was arguing was a moot point in the third world countries in which she traveled.

"Steve, seriously, South Africa is definitely not third world and I bet you that we wouldn't have to search too far to find such similar atrocities with musicians in our part of the world as well." She was right as usual. Shock rockers were already in abundance in North America with artists like Marilyn Manson and Eminem were in the early throes of their careers at the time. Despite the fact that these were some of the more controversial artists, they didn't ever have to spend any time behind bars for their highly suggestive and even explicit lyrics and ideals.

~~

"Impactful stuff, Piper!" her boss praised over the phone the day after the concert. "When are we going to get you back here in the driver's seat?"

"Our flights leave tomorrow. It'll be another day or so to come back down to earth. We'll see you soon."

"Tomorrow's Sunday and there's one last thing I've wanted to do here which we could do tomorrow morning," Richie suggested.

"What's that?" Piper asked.

"I'd just love to hear a gospel service at a church somewhere, possibly Soweto?"

"We can do that. I'm sure the Embassy folks here know of a safe zone for us."

The duo was all packed and ready for their flight later that day when they headed out for the morning service. And it was absolutely everything they'd imagined it to be. The taxi ride through Soweto was dark and dreary juxtaposed to their warm welcome into the open-air church. They certainly couldn't hide their tourist stature as their whiteness made them feel naked encompassed by the depths of the darkness of the locals.

"Praise the Lord, have mercy on our souls," bellowed the preacher from his pulpit high above the congregation.

The choir echoed, "Praise be to the savior, our Lord."

"Stand up, raise your hands and repeat after me, 'Oh Lord take us into your house and keep us safe from all the sinners.'"

The congregation stood and repeated as he requested. Piper leaned in towards Rich and whispered, "And all this is done in 4-part harmony! Incredible!"

As Piper recapitulated her Soweto stories to me afterwards, she couldn't speak highly enough of her experiences about South African culture and music, touting it as being 'next to godliness' and 'simply heavenly'.

Chapter Thirteen

Things settled down nicely for Piper back at the station. Much to my chagrin, she seemed very happy with Richie and her anchor position at the radio station. She seemed to have let go of the past and moved on.

Her family had held a small wake for Patrick; only Finola had shed any tears. Emily had been particularly moved by the service; not only did she have her children back in the same place at the same time, which seemed to happen rather infrequently as the years went on, but also because it had always been a particular dream of hers to have her children perform at her own funeral; it seemed though, that every time she'd raise the notion with the kids, they seemed to ignore the idea, not because they didn't want to do it exactly; they just didn't want to have to think about preparations for the death of their parents. They performed a family rendition of *Amazing Grace,* while Emily tossed his ashes along their garden walk. Piper sang lead vocals with Angela on harmonies and the pennywhistle when it was required; Finn played keyboards while Jonny was on drums and was the musician responsible for the arrangement; the Browns always amazed me with their talents.

Although Piper certainly got a good taste for what Richie was all about as a traveler and trip mate, they'd never really spent a great deal of time together with the day-to-day humdrum of life, so the months following the big African adventure were intended to be the ground-breaker for that part of their relationship. She had told me that she needed to see if she could live with him when everything was just 'ordinary' and I thought to myself *just how ordinary can anything be with Piper who is so extraordinary.* She mentioned that they tended towards arguing too much. They were both pretty headstrong. Well, Piper was, that much I knew to be true.

As Richie was a personal trainer he encouraged Piper's running hobby. He set up a training schedule for her and thought that she was ready, if interested, to tackle a marathon. She'd already done a few 10 k races and fared well, even picking up some placement medals, so he figured she had it in her.

"What do you think, Piper? The Forest City marathon is about 6 months away. That'll give you time to run a few 10 or 12 milers first before we even begin the marathon training and with that kind of base, you're already well on your way."

"Sure, whatever." Piper believed that after traipsing through Africa for a solid month with recording gear strapped to her back, that she could probably just about tackle anything now. "Are you going to run with me at all? I could use the company."

"Yea I guess I could. Perhaps one or two days a week and maybe sign up with you for a 5 or 10 k race beforehand. Is that good?" Richie offered.

"Perfect! What about tonight? What have you got me doing?"

"We'll be doing timed runs at the track."

"Arrrrrgh!" Piper groaned. "Seriously, long distance runners hate speed work that's why we run further to avoid the sprint and that crappy feeling you get when you're killing it."

"Nah, I've got a system worked out for you. It'll be fine." Richie assured her.

"That's what they all say," Piper grumbled.

By the 3rd week of training and a regimen in place, Piper started to feel much better about her goals. Mondays and Wednesdays were track days for speed work, Tuesdays and Thursdays were anything from 8 to 12 km runs depending on the hills involved and Saturdays were dedicated to the 'long' run. Each Saturday, beginning with a 2-hour run, she was to increase her distance by 15 minutes or 1.5 miles more each week; that would put her at just under the 4-hour marathon mark, not too shabby for a first timer. Sundays were left for rest and recovery.

The training went well and the two seemed to be getting along famously. On the shorter run days, Richie would often head out with her but on the longer runs she was left to her own devices; she mentioned to me that sometimes she'd meet up with some old running friends of hers, so I always felt she was in good hands.

"Whom were you talking to on your run today, Piper?" Richie asked.

"Um, well the usual. I cover a lot of distance and that tends to make me run into a lot of people," Piper defended. "What did they look like?"

"You were actually alone at the point I drove by you," said Rich.

"I guess I wasn't talking to anyone then," Piper admitted. "You answered your own question. That's a sign of insanity don't you know?"

Richie just shook his head. "You're a strange one, Pipes."

"And that's why you love me, right?" Piper continued, "And since when have you called me Pipes?" as she reaches out for a big hug and smooch.

"I heard the guys at the station calling you that and so I thought I'd try it. It's a good name for you. A strong voice and strong arms."

As was required in the training program, Piper had spent the last 2 weeks before race day, tapering down and spending more time with stretching. She'd trained hard and well. Richard made her a nice plate of pasta the night before that they shared and she was already getting butterflies as she hit the pillow.

"I'm not able to fall asleep," she whined.

"Well that's because you're talking and too loudly. Your body surely can't sleep through all the noise."

"Wow! What a help you are and stop calling me Shirley!"

"Funny girl," he said. "You've been sleeping well for you lately," referring to just how troubled of a sleeper she normally was. "Don't worry about it so much. Often the night before a big race, the competitors don't get into their REM sleep; just relax and close your eyes and your body will get the rest it needs."

"If you say so, boss," she consigned. Within moments her body started to relax and she felt herself drift off into a gentle slumber. Suddenly she heard a noise that startled her. She sat up in bed and had a very odd sensation that there was someone watching her, someone hovering over her side of the bed. "Rich, Rich, wake up," she stressed urgently and dove for cover underneath him. "Ah, it's coming closer, Rich. Wake up. Help me." When that didn't seem to stir him she jumped up and over him and landed with a thud on the opposite side of the bed. That was finally enough to awaken Richie who flicked on his night lamp. He found Piper sound asleep curled up on the floor on his side of the bed.

Wow, she's intense! He thought and swept her up and put her back into bed. Rich off-handedly mentioned the following morning, whether she'd been dreaming or not the previous night, and she seemed to have no recollection of it. He just let it go because he didn't want to disturb her any further before the big race.

They were up early. He drew her a bath that she felt was a huge luxury and couldn't stop thanking him for it. She tended not to pamper herself very much. "It's really not luxurious, Pipes. It's part of the muscle stimulating process. A cold muscle is a slow muscle therefore a warm muscle is a fast one."

"It sure feels good regardless. Okay now I'm ready." And off they went.

Piper positioned herself at the back of the fast pack for the first 7 k or so then got a bit of a burst of energy to move her closer to the lead. Richie was going to meet her at the 10 k mark where he would ride his bike with her for a while so he was rather surprised to see her appear at the water station with such a commanding lead and a record-setting pace.

"You look awesome, Pipes, but you can slow down; it's still early, you're not even a quarter of the way through. You're 10 k split was 48 minutes. Remember that it's always better to be passing people than have them passing you. It can hurt your confidence when you need it the most."

"Who died and made you boss?" was her retort.

"C'mon, do you want me to ride with you or not?"

"Yes please. I promise I won't be mean. No I can't promise," she said, "but I'll try not to be mean." Richie just shook his head.

"I just really feel good at certain times and want to make the best of it while I have the energy. I just never know when I'm going to crash."

At the 10-mile mark she clocked in at 84 minutes and then 1:45 at the halfway point.

"Still looking strong, Piper. You haven't had to slow down at all yet, eh?" Richie said as she caught back up to him at the 12.5 mile water station. He'd gone ahead when she said she was okay and wanted to be alone in her thoughts.

"Feeling good so far." She chimed back.

At the three quarter mark she was starting to feel the burn in her legs and her vision began to blur. She thought to herself that she would ask Rich to stay back with her the next time he passed. Just up ahead another kilometer was the next water station. She decided she was going to take her time through that one as that was what seemed to be appropriate marathon protocol anyway, at least according to Richie.

She slowed her pace and reached for one of the many water cups being handed to her by the young race volunteers. She pressed the edge of the cup up against her lip and flipped it back to suck up the wetness as quickly as possible. Instead of soothing her, it choked her and she doubled over, dropped to her knees and gasped for air. Immediately, one of the volunteers came to her side and asked if she needed any help. She grabbed his arm and pulled herself back upright.

"No, I'm fine, just took the water in down the wrong tube," Piper sputtered as she tried again to inhale. It took her a few more minutes to regain her breath and her composure and get back to her running pace. Her competitors were gaining on her.

"Thank god, you're here," Piper sighed as Rich pulled up alongside her. "I felt like I was a goner...saw the white light and everything."

"Run your own race, Piper. *Enjoy your achievements as well as your plans; for always there will be greater and lesser than yourself"*, he said.

"Huh? Why are you quoting the *Desiderata* to me right now? She sneered.

The last stretch of the race felt easy for her due to the crowds of admiring and supportive fans. Even the weakest of runners wouldn't be able to give it up at that point where so many people offered inspiring words of encouragement. Piper finished 23rd in the race with a total of 212 runners and she was the 3rd female to cross the finish line. She was both exhausted and exhilarated.

Rich was ecstatic as he rushed towards her and scooped her up in his arms. "You did it babe, all on your own. Sorry I couldn't help you sooner; I lost you just over the halfway mark."

"You weren't just talking to me?" Piper asked.

"No." Richie looked concerned briefly but tried to reassure her. "I'm sure it's just the adrenaline. No worries, Pipes. You did it! And a bronze medal performance no less, for your first one. I'm so proud of you," as he draped the medal around her neck.

~~

"So what did Doc O'Reilly say?" Richie finally asked after what seemed to be several days of him debating whether he should get involved.

"He says I'm fine." Piper assured then added, "He says I look happier and healthier than I ever have."

Chapter Fourteen

That wasn't altogether the truth.

On Piper's last visit to him, Dr. O'Reilly congratulated
her on her running prowess and maintained that the
daily activity was a really good idea in keeping her in
check, emotionally. He explained how the serotonin
levels tested in long distance runners were always
much more balanced than those levels in the general
population. And for someone like Piper who
demonstrated an imbalance towards bipolar, the daily
grind was a good stabilizer. However, running in an
extreme fashion, like what one's body goes through
during a full-length, 26.2-mile marathon, could
potentially tip the balance and do the reverse to cause a
greater imbalance. Piper at that time, seemed to be
suffering from 'runner's high' and she reached out to
him for some emotional assistance.

Doc O'Reilly came recommended to Piper through her
older brother, Jonny. He just seemed to worship the
ground the doctor walked on and that was really saying
something about him because Jonny was no willing
participant, at least in the beginning. Jonny was the
strong and cocky first-born Brown child. He knew early
on that his parents would not define him and he set out
prematurely in his young life to rebel against whatever
ideals the Browns' elders expected of him. He too,
shared a quick temper with his father but he had, on
more than one occasion, demonstrated his innate
compassion and sensitivities, much more like that of
Emily. He also struggled with maintaining commitment
within his early relationships but seemed, in later years,
to feel more satisfied in complacency. He was highly

musical and despite the fact that he dropped out of Music College, he had developed quite a name for himself within the local music scene. Piper adored him. It was for his third drug charge that he was mandated to see a psychiatrist. Enter Doc O'Reilly.

As Piper had an equally strong bond with her older brother, she figured that he'd be the right guy to see. O'Reilly was also Irish and had some obvious insight into the dynamics of the Brown household as well as some knowledge of the idiosyncrasies that came along with them.

"You're a quirky bunch," he stated matter-of-factly, during one of Piper's first visits with him.

"You mean 'you, Browns'?" As she asked for greater clarification, "Or we, Irish?"

The doctor smiled a big wide close-lipped smile that quickly became his signature. Piper loved this gentle-natured physician instantly. "Well, you've caught me on that one, Piper. You seem to have inherited both the 'brown' and 'green' into your psyche. Oh you lucky lady!" Piper wasn't anywhere near as impressed, as she'd roll her eyes with her usual look of distain.

"It's only natural, Piper, when you have this addictive type of personality, for you to get addicted to whatever you're doing. You're passionate and strong and get 'high' on life. Running offers you that. It influences your body by increasing blood flow and excreting toxins from your body. It also stimulates the endocrine and nervous systems that affect hormones. As you run, your hormone flow increases, including special hormones known as endorphins. In as short as a 30-minute jog, endorphins are released and you can feel their beneficial effect. Endorphins cause the natural feeling of a 'high', have painkilling effects and can continue this release for up to one hour after jogging. So what happens after a 4-hour run? It's just too much for most people. You included, because unfortunately, wherever there's a high, there's a low. This is why we must work on balances," he said.

"Well that might account for why I feel so depressed days after running a long race but why do I feel like I ride an emotional rollercoaster after just about everything I do?" Piper questioned.

O'Reilly hesitated for a moment. "Okay, tell me when it is specifically, you feel this kind of distress and what are your symptoms? Describe how you feel?"

"The last time I felt this desperate was when I was in Africa and my father had just passed. The time before that was that fateful night when I got a call from my lover's wife," she recalled.

Dr. O'Reilly just shook his head. "Do you really hear yourself, kiddo? Do you really hear what you're saying? These are traumatic events, not just for you, Piper, but also for any of us. You're putting yourself, and you are being put, into situations that are extreme and expecting everything to be hunky dory."

"I am?" she asked.

"Your expectations, my dear, are exceedingly high. You have to understand that most people live such mundane lives, in comparison. I have a number of patients who merely get on the Go train and get off the Go train, every day. I can't think of an occasion where you actually do anything the same twice. You're always changing it up. You're one of the most diversified patients I've ever come across or really have ever met, for that matter. It's hard to find a balance when you live like that, let alone try to maintain one."

"Well I guess you're right. But what's the alternative? Are you asking me to be boring like everyone else? I just can't possibly do that. I'd kill myself." Piper insisted.

"Well, you're not exactly feeling good about yourself going at this pace either, are you? And what's with the dramatics, Piper? Why is it all or nothing with you?"

"Right again sir," she conceded, "I guess I really just have never experienced the concept of a balance so I'm rather anxious about trying to find it. I'm not that great dealing with unfamiliar territory."

"What? Little Miss World Traveler? You don't like the discomfort of new experiences?" She had shocked him this time, which was a rarity.

"I honestly don't. I realize that makes me a bit of a contradiction sometimes. I love traveling and the excitement of new adventures but it isn't comforting to me; that's for sure. I much prefer the stability and humbleness of my home. It's just that I get caught up in the spontaneous thrill of the moment and jump in before I even ask myself whether I can swim."

"Well that's a great way to set off the balances. You're a tightrope walker and you're walking a precariously thin line," he agreed.

"Just ask me what it's like to teeter on the edge?" She looked at him and he nodded. "There's a certain amount of anxiousness and a feeling of being overwhelmed followed by a thick darkness. It's like there's a big, black cloud hovering over me or a very heavy blanket laying on my chest that I can't push away or lift off and sometimes I think I'm just downright losing my mind. I can even hear voices."

"What are they saying to you?" He asked non-judgmentally.

"It's not so much what they say, it's more of the notion that they exist for me. I get a certain euphoric sensation when I hear them or feel their presence; it makes me feel less lonely and like I'm being guided by some superior being," she clarified. "But that's when I'm feeling good. They have their downside too."

"Can you identify when you experience this or at least try to keep a log for me, of when you go through these sensations? I find this fascinating. I think you're a good candidate to try some of these stabilizers," the doctor said. "Are you interested in doing this for a little while because they work best if you can use them consistently for a few months? They get absorbed gradually into your system so the impact is not as severe and the removal from them is not as great either."

"I suppose, as long as you can assure me that I'm not going to NOT feel anything anymore. I often like the up side of my whacky experiences, real or not, and it's my down side, my pain that tells me that I'm alive. I need it; I just can't handle it being so severe," Piper confided. "And do I have to mention this to anyone? I'm not sure Richie would think too highly of me if he knew I was on anti-depressants nor if I was hearing voices."

"Absolutely not if you don't want to. What happens in our sessions is completely confidential." O'Reilly assured. "And Piper, please rethink your whole agenda on psychiatric medication. Depression and bi-polar are proven as much physiological as psychological illnesses. Would you think lesser of someone who had to take meds to control their epilepsy or diabetes? I think not." She nodded back at him.

"Okay then, go ahead with a prescription and remember what happens in Vegas stays in Vegas, right?" Piper giggled.

~~

"Do that again," Piper oozed. "Whatever you did, do it again. Our love-making sessions just keep getting better and better."

"I really notice a difference in your confidence after you see Dr. O'Reilly. You seem to be better able to trust me. What's he saying to you 'cause maybe I'll say it to you more often?" Richie asked.

"I dunno. I think he just makes me feel normal and like I'm not losing my mind," she said.

"Well that's good. But you'll never be 'normal' Piper. In fact you won't be 'normal' because you work so hard at not." He said.

"That isn't helping me any, Rich." She felt hurt and resented his comment.

"Okay, how about becoming my wife? Will that help?" He asked, noticing that she took his comment seriously.

"Oh Richie, I love you but I'm not sure we're ready. I'm not sure I'm ready."

"What can I do to get you ready?" Rich looked mischievously deep into her eyes. "I'm the right one for you my darling. Don't you forget it," he continued, "and if you ever need reminding..." Again the look of mischief appeared. "I'll be here to show you again and again."

It was sometime in the early morning hours that Piper finally freed herself from his snoring clutches in their bed, tiptoed across the room, grabbed her fluffy robe from the back of the door and crept downstairs. She put a fresh batch of coffee in the coffee maker and reached for the dog-eared copy of her favourite book, *The National Geographic Atlas*. She had taken to playing 'the pointing game' with an atlas, when she felt she couldn't make it to the airport the way she used to do as a younger girl, to choose her next destination. It was that book under which Piper was found when the sun came up.

"Okay. So where are we going now?" Richie said as he snuggled in beside her on the couch with his microwaved coffee.

"Um. Well I'm going but I haven't invited you yet." She answered.

"And where is that?" he questioned.

"I need to go to Ireland. I need to understand my roots. There are a whole lot of idiosyncrasies with the Irish psyche that I seem to have inherited and so I think I'd feel better about myself if I could go there and do some research. Maybe check out my family tree, visit some relatives..."

Richie interrupted "And?"

"No and," she clarified. "That's it." She lied. She wasn't ready to reveal all that she needed to figure out about herself yet to Richard. She harboured deep issues in trust and commitment. Doc O'Reilly, as much of a blessing as he had been to her in resolving some of her insecurities of isolation and abandonment, had also begun to uncover some darkness. She felt it needed to be addressed and going to Ireland might help her deal with her demons. "And with any luck, we could catch a Sinead O'Connor concert? Nothing would be greater for me than to see and hear her live in Dublin."

"Did I hear a 'we' in there?" He teased.

"I'd love for you to accompany me, if you would like? We seem to travel well together, despite some of our 3-round boxing matches," Piper smiled.

"When are you thinking? Maybe we can take the bikes?"
Rich added.

Chapter Fifteen

"Thanks for meeting me, Piper. It's been so long."

"No problem, Steve," she sighed and I pretended not to notice.

"I told you I'd always make time for you," she said, trying to cover up her apparent disinterest. "What brings you to town?" she asked.

"Well. I've been seeing someone and I wanted your..."

"Approval?" she said.

"Advice, really."

"Okay. What's up?" She asked in a very flippant way.

"Well what kinda response is that?"

"What do you mean? I've always told you that we're great friends; we connect on so many levels; we'll always be there for each other, but I've never promised anything more than that. And I've got someone special in my life too. So what?" she questioned again.

"Oh nothing. I just thought maybe things would be different."

"Things?" she said.

"Well yea. To be honest with you, I thought that if I started to play the field that maybe someone would find me interesting and that would make you not jealous but perhaps more interested in me than you seem to be." I confessed.

"Hmm...is that what you want from me? You want me to argue with you about finding someone special?"

"Not exactly," I said.

"Okay then. I'm really confused now. Perhaps you should just tell me what's going on and how I can help?" Piper broke down.

"Nevermind," I said, "She's beautiful. She's smart, athletic..."

"Well thank you!" Piper replied. "You forgot, funny!"

"Everything you are..." I continued.

"Great. I'm happy for you, bud," Piper replied, not allowing me to finish and emphasizing the word *'bud'* knowing full well how much I hated when she called me that.

There were some things that drove me crazy about Piper. She had a way of making me feel really insignificant at times. She had a belittling demeanour when things didn't seem to go her way or when she was caught unexpectedly. She was never good with surprises. That was a bit hypocritical about her character. Always one to appear spontaneous, and the queen of surprises yet she hated it when others pulled the same stunt and gave her the same courtesy.

"Terrific!" I said sarcastically. This isn't really going as I'd planned. She was supposed to be putty in my hands.

"Now what? What do you want me to say to you or do for you?" She asked.

"Do you wanna meet her? It would mean a lot to me." I asked sounding rather desperate.

"Sure I guess. I wouldn't have a problem with that," Piper lied.

"Her plane lands in 10 minutes; can we go over to Terminal 3 and pick her up?" I asked.

"Like now?" Piper asked looking rather horrified.

"Yes," I said.

"Okay, sure?" Piper offered. "Let me get this round. I think it's my turn anyway."

I declined. Piper actually ordered another shot for herself while up at the airport bar. She obviously was struggling with this whole meeting, or was it something else? I wasn't sure at the time, and now with the addition of having to meet the new love of my life, it was something beyond her control and that never sat well with her. The ultimate planner was walking on uneven turf. I could tell she was anxious, as she didn't normally drink so heavily during the day, so I tried to reassure her. "No body can replace you, Piper. I thought you knew that."

"Really? You mean even Stephanie or Kaitlyn or Jessica, right?" She teased. "And what is this elusive woman's name anyway?"

"Deborah. Deb."

"Okay then."

~~

That just didn't go as I was hoping it would. Piper was unbearably adorable and Deb fell right under her spell. *Oh great!* I thought to myself. *Now we're both in love with her!*

"She's lovely!" Piper exclaimed after I prodded her on her thoughts about my future wife.

"Okay. Thanks!" I said.

"Well seriously, what do you want me to say, that I want to hook her up with Richard and we run away together or that you have my blessing? Do you need that?"

I conceded. "No. I just thought maybe you'd... Never mind." It seemed to be a recurring phrase for me with her lately.

Piper just shrugged and turned her shoulder away from me. I had hoped that she was trying to avoid my eye contact but perhaps it was just because she really didn't care. It was always hard to tell with her. Some days she seemed so into me and other days, it's like I didn't even exist in any real form; I was invisible. Today was the latter. I honestly wanted to shake her and ask her if I'd ever meant anything to her at one moment and the next, I wanted to wrap my arms around her and embrace her with my abundant love. Today, neither direction would've been appropriate.

As much as I had opened myself up to be more courageous in my relationships in general, Deb was certainly a new beginning for me in that regard, I still hadn't quite found the way to communicate or express what I was actually feeling at the time when I needed to the most, around Piper especially. I felt so close to her in some breaths, like we were even the same person, sharing the same spirit, and then other times, it's like she'd vanished and the whole scene was an episode of my overactive imagination. We were so similar in fact that I tried often to put myself into her shoes when I came upon a particular dilemma. How would Piper handle this? She had spoken to me about the work she was doing with balances with her doctor, so that's what I was trying to do as well. Find and maintain the balance and life will be better.

"Okay then. Will there be anything else, Steve?" She batted her eyelashes.

"Arghhhh!" I thought; she was so frustrating; yet so beautiful.

Without so much as a few more words, she waved and disappeared out of the terminal.

Chapter Sixteen

Piper and Richie decided not to take their bikes because it would just cost too much in transport but they'd rent bikes as soon as they landed. They'd flown directly from Toronto to Belfast, another overnighter. By the time they had been searched and collected their baggage, they were again, at each other's throats.

"Why do we have to go through this every time we start an adventure?" Piper asked.

"What do you mean?" Rich replied seeming to not notice the obvious irritability.

"Why are you so snarky with me?" Piper reiterated.

Rich shrieked. "I'm snarky? I think you need to rethink that. Did you wake up on the wrong side of the bed?"

"Was there a bed? In fact, was there sleeping involved at all?" Piper reminded him.

"Let's just grab some coffee and breakfast and start over."

"Forget coffee, I'm going for a pint. It's gotta be noon somewhere in the world," Piper joked. The two hailed a cab, tossed their luggage into the trunk and squeezed together into the back seat where Rich snuck a peck on her cheek and reached his muscular arm around her shoulders to pull her in even closer. As much fun as traveling was, it certainly wasn't easy and particularly the way Piper liked to arrange her adventures, opting for mystery and intrigue over comfort and security. It was a bit of an oxymoron when she thought about it like that. She tended to travel as a means to find herself but always felt more comfortable when she was settled in back at home.

"Hey Pipes?" he said soothingly. "We're here. We made it! Your dream destination!"

The little pub the cabbie drove them to was in an old region of what is now downtown historical Belfast. Just as they were approaching the nearest intersection at Main and High streets they noticed a section of the sidewalk and neighbouring road all cordoned off. It looked like an excavation site.

"What are they building here?" Piper asked.

"Oh no. They're not building. They're tearing down. That's a bomb site." The cab driver corrected her in his heavy Gaelic dialect.

"The I.R.A?" Richie asked. Piper looked back and forth from the driver to Rich in curiosity.

"Yes, they continue to blast us when we least expect it," the driver explained.

"Any injuries?" Piper asked.

"Not this time and usually not too many. They do this more to scare than anything else. It's a constant threat." He continued.

"Pardon my ignorance but what's the history behind the I.R.A and what's their status now?" Piper questioned.

The cabbie went on to explain that "Northern Ireland came into existence with the British Government of Ireland Act back in 1920; it divided Ireland into two areas: the Irish Free State, made up of the 26 southern counties and Northern Ireland. It was basically a geographical division but it also separated the Catholics and Protestants. The Roman Catholics, who made up virtually a third of the population in Northern Ireland were opposed to the division."

"So they're 'the green' Northern Catholic Irish that want unification and the southerners are considered to be 'the orange' Protestants who want to maintain the division and the British rule?" Piper translated. "I gather you're a Sinn Fein supporter?" she asked, referring to the oldest political party in Ireland.

"Yes ma'am. But I'm no radical. I honestly believe they are devoted to removing British forces from here in the north and to unifying Ireland but bombing and carrying weapons in general, is just not the way to go about it."

"Will we be safe here?" Rich asked, beating Piper to the punch.

"You American?" the cabbie asked.

"No. Canadian," they answered in unison.

"Then really safe. We love Canadians here. We hate each other but love you. Are you here to investigate your ancestry, your roots as they say?"

"How did you know?" She asked.

"That seems to be a favourite pastime for Canadian people. You should probably call ahead to any of the genealogical registry offices. They generally want you to book an appointment; you'd probably not want to wait hours in line-ups when your travel time is so limited anyway." He advised.

"Thanks so much for the info, bud," offered Rich as he handed the driver a healthy tip.

They had to duck to fit into the doorway of the tiny stonewalled pub. It was as they imagined it to be: dark, rustic yet somehow inviting. They took their time getting their feet wet in the culture of the Irish by ordering several rounds of Guinness and spoke often to the many locals who frequented the watering hole throughout the early afternoon hours. They sat a good portion of the day right at the bar and were amused by the bartender's stories.

"So did you hear the one about the Irish man who walks into a pub?" initiated the barman. The pair just knew that this was going to be the first of many jokes they'd hear over the next few hours. "'Give me three pints of Guinness please,' the man says to me. So I bring him three pints and the man proceeds to alternately sip one, then the other then the third until they're gone. He then orders three more. So I say, 'Sir, I know you like 'em cold. You don't have to order three at a time. I can keep an eye on it and when you get low I'll bring you a fresh cold one.' The man says, 'you don't understand. I have two brothers, one in Australia and one in the States. We made a vow to each other that every Saturday night we'd still drink together. So right now, my brothers have three Guinness Stouts too, and we're drinking together.' Well I just thought that was a wonderful tradition until that man came back into the bar one day and only ordered two beers. I said, 'I'm so sorry sir, to see that you've lost a brother.' He said, 'Oh, me brothers fine…I just quit drinkin.'"

It was probably the Guinness talking but the young pair seemed to fit in rather comfortably in their new environment. The older thick Irish accented fellow never seemed to tire of reciting his tales and offering his words of wisdom to the visiting couple.

"Ah yes! There's nothing like a good Irish pub," he said. "I recall a time when a Scotsman came by and said he preferred the pubs back home in Glasgow, a wee place called McTavish's. In it, the landlord goes out of his way for the locals. When you buy four drinks, he'll buy the fifth. Well the Englishman beside him chimed in at that point and said, 'Well at my local pub in London, the barman will buy you your third drink after you buy the first two.' Not to be outdone, I say, 'Well dat's nothin', the moment you step foot in my joint, we buy you a drink, then another and another and as soon as you've had enough, we take you upstairs and see dat you gets laid, all on the house.'" Richie and Piper exchange looks, then he continues, "And that's just what we do for the ladies." Laughter naturally ensued.

The pair felt good, ate well and laughed continuously. They spent time plotting their next move. They'd have to get bikes and packs. There's no possible way they could have been riding bikes and carrying their luggage too. They had mapped out points of interest and called ahead to the various registry offices in order to do some family tree research. Just as they finished drawing up their plans and emptying their final refills of the day, the bartender said to them, "You won't be driving will ya?"

"Heck no," Richie said taking the bait.

"Well that's good because ya know, the last Irishman we had leave these premises had a little too much to drink and was driving home and weaving no less. A cop pulls him over and says, 'Where have you been?' and he says, 'Why the pub of course.' 'Well,' says the cop, 'it looks like you've had quite a few drinks this evening.' 'That indeed I did,' he says with a smile. 'And did you know that a few intersections back, your wife fell out of your car?' The cop added. 'Oh thank me Lord,' sighs the drunk. 'For a minute there, I thought I'd gone deaf.'"

"My cheeks hurt from laughing so much," Piper cried. "And men, gosh, they're the same everywhere! He reminds me of my father. Wasn't a week to go by where dad wasn't sharing another Irish joke with us. He was funny; I gotta give him that."

Another cab took them to the bike shop where they rented very sturdy street bikes and saddlebags. After the pair went through their luggage to gather just the essentials they'd need over the next 8 days, they filled up their packs to capacity. "Make sure you evenly distribute the weight in the bags otherwise you'll topple, Pipes," Rich said.

"I'm pretty sure I may topple anyway, with the amount of Guinness I have in me."

"Well we won't try to do too much more today. We'll just get accustomed to the ride and then find a place to camp for the night." He said.

The 'getting accustomed' was harder than it seemed. The pair looked a little like street people with their bikes loaded down with gear. They even managed to hook up a kitchen pot to one of the handlebars.

"What on earth?" Questioned Piper.

"We may very well be camping this whole week. We've gotta have a way to cook our food."

"I guess, but then hook it up to your handle bars, please." Piper sneered. They continued riding around Belfast for a while and stopped in at the local campgrounds they came across; they were disappointed to learn that camping in Ireland was far different than camping in Canada. They weren't legally allowed to pitch a tent and stay overnight. All the campsites in Belfast seemed to be just parks, really, and that just wasn't going to work. It was at the third site they arrived to where they were approached by an elderly couple that was out walking their dogs.

"Are you Canadian?" the woman asked.

"Yes we are!" Piper answered. "Do our dazed and confused looks give it away?"

"No! But your accents do," the couple replied. "Can we help you?"

"Not sure. We're looking for a place to camp, overnight. We're traveling around your beautiful country on our bikes and haven't really figured out where to lay our heads for the night."

"You say you've got a tent?" the man asked.

"Yes, in our packs. We've been to several parks and the rules at each one say that there is no overnight camping allowed." Richie added.

"You poor dears. You are certainly welcome to come and pitch your tent in our garden. Right Henry?" The woman offered. The man nodded.

"Are you sure we can camp in your garden?" Piper asked, trying to get her head around sleeping with broccoli and cauliflower.

"Oh yes! There's plenty of room." The couple gave them directions to their nearby walk-up with instructions to meet them there within the hour.

~~

"Oh, this is your backyard!" exclaims Piper with joy. "This will be ideal! When you said garden, we were thinking vegetables or flowers like our gardens in Canada. Thank you so much!" They set up their tent and pulled out their sleeping bags and were just ready to think about what they were going to do for dinner when Henry came out to see they were settled and offered them to come in for some soup.

"Isabelle makes a lovely lamb stew. Please come in and eat before you retire for the night. We wouldn't think of having you here without offering you some hospitality."

"That would be lovely!" said Piper. The modest Irish couple seemed very happy together and content to share what few luxuries they had in their humble abode. Piper and Richie went back to their tent under a starry sky, and slept well knowing that they were welcome visitors in this conflicted country.

Chapter Seventeen

And then the rains came. They had just loaded up their
gear and began to cycle when the first of what was to be
many drops of rain came pelting down from the
heavens. Richie and Piper were beginning to think that
Noah's ark would have been a better mode of
transportation.

At first Piper just sang merrily along with Sinead on her
Walkman, *"I remember it, Dublin in a rainstorm, sitting
in the long grass in summer, keeping warm."* "We better
get used to it," she said out loud. "Apparently it does this
a lot around here. How else could everything get so
green if it weren't for the rain?" They rode in silence for
a while. The roads were far too narrow to have them
ride side-by-side so Richard led for most of the way
while Piper filed in tandem behind. Occasionally he
would pull off to the side to speak to her, as the patter
from the rain while they were riding made
communication too difficult.

"Well this is annoying," she said. "I certainly hope the
weather isn't going to be like this the whole week. It
doesn't really put me in the mood to do much
adventuring."

"Maybe we should be spending these wet days indoors
doing the genealogical work?" Rich said.

"Yea, you're probably right. What's the nearest registry
office we have mapped out?" Piper asked.

"The first one is in Downpatrick. That's another 15 kilometres from where we are now. Can you cycle that far today?"

"Sure. I'm wet now anyway. What's the difference?" They set out at a steady pace, figuring it would take them another hour if they didn't run into any washouts. The rain had collected in pools along the sides of the road and was already beginning to make them feel like they were drowning in it.

By the time they arrived into Downpatrick they were soaked to the bone, cold, shivering and miserable. They had been following the IYT (International Youth Traveller) signs the entire route which took them to the doorstep of the Downpatrick Youth Hostel.

"I don't care what this place looks like. We're staying." Piper sighed. "I need some warm, dry clothes."

"Good luck with that. Everything we have is on us and it's soaking wet."

"Aren't you just a happy camper?" Piper whined and giggled, realizing that, that's exactly what the term meant. They entered the hostel and were greeted in a typically friendly way as Canadian travellers were and asked for a double room.

"We don't have doubles. We have 2 large rooms filled with beds, dry and comfy, I might add. We also have hot showers and a kitchen. You might also want to throw your clothes into one of the dryers in the laundry room to have something ready to wear for later. There are big robes you can use while your belongings are drying."

"Oh thank the Lord." Piper exclaimed.

"You calling for me?" Richie teased.

"Aren't you just a little high on yourself?" Piper continued. "Can the Lord get us some grub now?" Rich smiled.

'Grub' consisted of a can of mixed beans, 2 plastic cartons of applesauce, and several packs of pepperoni sticks. "We don't need to eat like paupers, Rich," Piper proclaimed. "This is all we had in our gear but we should really save this stuff for when we don't have somewhere as nice in which to prepare it."

"Do you wanna go back out into that rain for groceries?" he asked.

"Good point," she said. "Okay, hand me the can opener."

It was not long afterwards that the rain ceased, or at least the torrential downpours stopped. It left a misty, foggy air that was as thick as pea soup. It reminded Piper of her trip to Verona to visit her sister, a few years previously, and then she remembered that, that may have all been part of a dream, or was it? She still couldn't decipher between the reality and the illusion of it, considering her state of mind at the time, and since the image of the fog still remained so vivid in her mind.

"Wow!" she thought to herself but actually verbalized it out loud.

"What's up?" Rich asked.

"Just recalling what I felt like the last time I was in a far away place and felt this 'fogged in'," Piper said.

"Love troubles?" he said.

"You could say that, yes!"

"Well it's different this time, Pipes. You're in such a different place and I don't mean physically, I mean spiritually. I'm here with you; I won't disappoint you. *Be not cynical about love for it is as perennial as the grass.*" He emphasized.

"What? What did you say?" Piper asked shaking her head, realizing that she might have dozed off.

"Piper..." Richie tapped her on the shoulder. "Are you okay?"

"Of course I'm okay!" Piper came into focus. "Why do you ask?"

"Because you had this far away look in your eyes, like you were in a trance, and kept repeating something about being *cynical about love.*" He replied.

"I said that?" Piper asked, looking completely confused. "You said that, didn't you?"

"Oh Piper. Never mind, go back to sleep. I've got a special treat planned for us tomorrow."

"Aren't we doing some digging? Piper asked in regard to her family ancestry.

"You betcha!" he exclaimed. "I really dig you!"

"Ha ha! Well I kinda dig you too!" She answered as she cozied into him for the night.

~~

The first registry office they went to was in the town of Downpatrick, aptly named for the 'downing of Saint Patrick'; basically it was the home of his burial. Piper had been told that as her father Patrick James had been named after the patron saint, much of her family tree stemmed from this region of the country. The office was attached to the very large and ancient cathedral, where weekly Sunday services were still held. Piper immediately checked in with the administration secretary to inform her of her appointment. She was told to take a seat and fill out the first of what was to be many forms that morning. As she was at least 50 percent Irish, father was full Irish and mother was at least half, they would do a full search on her background. Rich decided that he wasn't needed for a while, so he helped himself to the public records available for viewing on the shelves within the building.

"Hmm, Bronwyn…" he said as he sorted through the files. "It is a Welsh derivative and grammatically means 'strong'. *Like many Celtic goddesses, she was once a real person, a princess of the house of Llyr who was wed to the High King of Ireland. An insult at her wedding feast brought war between Ireland and Wales. Her brother was killed during the war to rescue her from oppression at the*

*Irish court, and when she later returned to Wales, she
died of a broken heart,* he read out loud. 'Wow! Hardly
like Piper at all.'"

~~

"So what did you find out?" he asked her after a good
hour of wandering had taken place.

"I've got copies of all the marriage licenses and death
certificates from my father's side. I've got to spend some
time on my own sorting through it all because it looks
pretty extensive but yes, it's going to be helpful," she
replied.

"You're missing one important document, though,
Pipes." He said.

"Really?"

"Here it is, here," as he handed her, what appeared to
be, an official document of some kind. Piper scanned the
title then read further in.

*I, Richard Ivan Sirko, am asking the lovely Patricia Jane Brown, to
marry me as soon as humanly possible.*

She then closed her lips and grinned; she looked up at
Richie. He took her in his arms then kissed her
passionately on the mouth, absorbing each morsel of
sweetness that her lips offered him. There was no place
he'd rather be. He was home.

"You know you have very good timing, right?" Piper
said, still cradled in his arms.

"Umm, really? Why do you say so?" He whispered questioningly.

"Because I missed my period last week and when I didn't get any signs of bleeding I decided to get a pregnancy test before we left for here." Richie pulled her in even closer.

"Oh Pipes, you're going to have our baby. I love you so much." The days following were filled with love and laughter. Due to the fact that she was already pregnant they no longer were afraid of the consequences; they abandoned their inhibitions and made love frequently and randomly. The dark, rainy days continued however, in contrast to the young couple's moods.

"It's so hard to keep unpacking wet gear then repacking it again. I need to feel like I'm on dry land," she said, "and the back of my neck is stinging from where my wet hair keeps chafing it." Piper had just snapped back the kickstand ready to swing her leg over the bike seat for their third rainy day of cycling, when they heard a *'hello?'*

"Oh hi!" she turned around to see a little old woman standing beneath a newspaper.

"Are you Canadians?" the woman asked.

"We sure are." Piper replied. "What can we do for you?"

"It's what I'd like to do for you," she continued. "If you have some time, I would love it if you could join me for tea. We don't get too many visitors in these parts and I would really like the company. Surely you must want some time out of the rain?"

Piper squealed, "You've got that right! I'd love to, Rich?" She asked him but merely as a formality.

He nodded in agreement. "Thank you!"

"How far are you along?" the woman asked as Piper warmed her hands around her steamy cup of tea.

"We've been here for a few days, 3 or 4." Piper answered.

"No, no, I mean with child," she recapitulated. Piper's mouth dropped. "I'm sorry," the woman continued, "are you not aware of your condition yet? It's not the first time I've predicted such a thing." Piper still looked shocked. "It's very obvious to me. You have a beautiful blue glow about you. Your aura is strong and healthy. I'm sure you'll be smiling into the face of a bouncing baby boy in no time!"

"Well thank you, again!" Piper said. "I just days ago, found out the good news. A boy you say?"

"My spirits aren't one hundred percent foolproof but I'm right most of the time. You're carrying a very strong, special young man," she clarified. Piper just grinned at Richie and nodded.

"That would be wonderful!" Rich added.

~~

It was after the 4th full day of cycling in the rain and Richie's tire blow-out that they decided to change their game plan.

"This is awful!" complained Piper. "Can't we just rent a car?"

As Richie got out his repair kit to patch up the wheel he said, "Where are we going to find a rental place out here? You should've decided that in town."

"You hadn't blown a tire back there. Now what are we going to do?"

"I'm going to fix my bike. Maybe while I'm doing that you could flag down someone to pick us up or help us out? Flash a little leg, Pipes, and we'll be outta here in no time."

"Very funny. Are you serious? Hitch hike, you mean?"

"Yep. There's not much else we can do. I did it with my brothers while we travelled through Turkey and we were a bunch of guys. Drivers feel safer when there are women in need; they'll be more likely to help." It wasn't very long before a truck came by, saw the two sitting at the side of the road and pulled over.

"Where are you going?" the driver asked.

"Wherever you are," Rich replied. "We have no set plans and we're tired of cycling through all this rain."

"I'm going over to Ballycastle; it's on the other side of the country. You're welcome to toss your bikes in the back of the lorry and come with me?" the young Irish lad offered.

"We'd love to. I'm Piper by the way," as she held out her hand in greeting. "And that's Richard."

"Seamus," he said. "Piper? Is that short for something?"

"Not really but my birth name is Patricia."

"Irish?" he asked.

"Yes. Irish Canadian."

"I love you Canadians. You're such a friendly lot."

"Hmm. Not sure we're as friendly as you folks. We would've been sitting all day in the rain waiting for someone to help us, had we been cycling in Canada. And here in Ireland we can barely set out on our bikes each morning before someone invites us to 'tea'."

"That's it eh? We all love a stranger but can't get along with our neighbors."

"I'm thinking you're talking about the civil hatred between Northern and Southern Ireland?" Piper asked.

"Yes ma'am, it's such a shame, really." They chatted together as they rode on for what seemed to be just a few hours when Seamus pulled into a gas station.

"Oh let us get this," Rich offered. "It's the least we can do."

"There's really no need. I'm hauling for work so they'll compensate me. No worries. I'm at the end of the road, though, for the day. Ballycastle is just about 3 kilometres from here. It's right on the coast. You've got to see it; pretty spectacular I'd say. A friend of mine could probably set you up in his B & B; you interested?" They hopped back into the lorry and within minutes were face-to-face with the roaring tides of the Atlantic Ocean, where the water was pure emerald, more of the Irish green that they previously could've only ever imagined.

Chapter Eighteen

"Simply breathtaking," Piper sighed as Richie again put his camera to good use. The rain had stopped somewhere along route and the sunset was brilliant against the white cliffs that rose up from the shore. The couple had planned to tag along with Seamus for another ride in the morning. He was headed to Galway before he would make the return trip back to the interior. They could rent a car in Galway fairly inexpensively and could then get to their final destination of Dublin before their return flights home out of Belfast.

Galway had become a rather popular folk community at the time. Rich noticed the posters and signs up all over the city with the names of a number of Canadian folk bands performing in Galway's local pubs.

"Hey, Sarah McLachlan is playing at the Arms Inn tonight and I don't think that's too far from where we are," Rich said. "She's opening for this Irish folk singer named Luka Bloom, wanna go?"

"Sure. I've been a big fan of Sarah's since I interviewed her awhile back at CNDY plus she's Canadian, so a little of the home brew certainly never hurts while you're traveling." They discovered the Arms Inn was also one of the most popular downtown B & B's and when they saw that it looked respectable, they figured they might as well eat, drink and sleep in the same building; it had saved them time and energy.

"Wanna pint?" Rich asked.

"Yea but I don't think I should. Now that this pregnancy thing is all out in the open, I think I'll stick to tea."

"This place is really filling up," Rich concluded after McLachlan had finished off her set and Piper had returned to her seat beside him. She had gone up to the stage to shake Sarah's hand and acknowledge her presence.

"Yes I see that. This Luka Bloom is probably pretty good. I'm glad we got here early enough to get good seats," Piper agreed. "Wow! What a looker!" she said after Luka finished his opening song, "and he makes all those scenarios that he sings about seem so real, *Acoustic Motorbike*. Seriously, was he out riding in the rain with us this past week? It's like he gets me. He makes me feel like I'm home."

> *The day began with a rainbow in the sand*
> *As I cycled into Kerry...*
> *Pedal on, pedal on, pedal on for miles*
> *Pedal on, pedal on, pedal on for miles*
>
> *I take a break; I close my eyes...*
> *In a quiet spot talking to myself*
> *Talking about the rain, talking about the rain*

"*In a quiet spot talking to myself*," Piper repeated in song.

"Well," Rich interrupted, "you kinda are."

Piper grinned, "What, talking to myself? Or home?"

"Both!" They laughed. "Care to dance, my lovely?" Rich asked when Luka began his version of Elvis' *Can't Help Falling in Love With You.*

"Thought you'd never ask," Piper stood up and reached for his hand.

The pair found themselves in their second registry office in the morning. This was the second of three in which they had scheduled appointments. Piper was trying to follow the Bronwyn lineage; she could find family records dating back as early as the 1800s which took them to Galway. "Apparently my great, great, great grandfather Noirin Callanan Bronwen was a spiritual healer and used the voices he heard to help unlock doors to emotional healing. And later in the 18 hundreds a great, great aunt of mine named Tricia Sheehan used the shamanic healing process to predict events and help those who suffered from unwelcome spirits. I find it so fascinating."

"You saying you can do this too?" Richie sounded skeptical.

"No, but I am saying that I think there's more to our inner consciousness than what we in North America give credit to. Even my Mum, Emily, who seems so straight up and can't seem to respond to things outside the box, has always been very 'in tune' with this sort of thing. She talks of how on the day she was robbed, she put on all her most expensive jewelry to go to work in the morning and yet she never usually thinks to wear her jewelry. Or the time she was driving alone and got a creepy feeling so she hit the automatic car lock button just moments before a man approached the passenger side of her car; he tugged at the handle. When he realized it was locked, he made a gesture to her that seemed like he was just going to ask for directions but seriously, would you go to the passenger side and open the door handle if it were just directions you wanted?"

"No, but can't these just be chalked up cases of coincidence and good luck?"

"True they can, but why does it seem to happen more acutely to some people than others? I just really believe that some are more in tune with the spiritual world and I think there's a very good reason for that, yet I don't know what that is. And what happens to our souls when we die?"

"Buried into the dirt with our bones," he said. "But why do I know you're not going to agree with me?"

"I just can't. I think there's so much more to the energy of life than having it end with physical death. What about the child prodigy, a kid of 5 years of age who can play the violin better than a professional violinist whose had many years of training? Or the sensation of a grandfather who has long passed this life yet is watching over us to protect us or warn us? Or have you ever thought about why it is we have the parents and family we do? I believe there are more questions here than answers and I just don't think we're supposed to give up on finding those answers. I think we're supposed to search or at least try to make sense of it all."

"That sounds like you believe in the eternal soul, Piper." Rich stated.

"I'd say I do. I think we're all in this together. We choose our path and we meet people and accept experiences based on for what we're searching. Like a pregnant woman craves the foods that her body seems to need the most, we choose our lives based on what resolutions we need to find. I always hated my father for the mean spirited being he was to us kids and to Mum but do I blame him now for not providing me with a decent dad growing up? No, because I believe that I chose him. I needed to work on aspects of my being that I was only able to work out because he was my father. He in essence, has made me be a better person, a fuller 'me'."

"And I really like that 'me', Piper," he said as he leaned in close for a kiss.

"I'm glad," she replied and returned his kiss. "I certainly don't profess to have all the answers but I know I need to try to find some. I hear it, see it and feel it in everything I do."

"Is your doctor helping you with any of this?" he asked.

"He's been great, yes! And he's given me suggestions as to what I need to research while I'm here."

Richie looked confused, "You mean, because your ancestry is here?"

"That and because of the psyche of the Irish personality. We're very *interesting* people," she said slightly changing the wording that her doctor used.

Dublin was their final stop before they had to return the bikes back to Belfast and catch their flights home. And that proved to be a bit more of a challenge than they had anticipated, namely because Dublin was in the south. Although the security gates were unassuming in themselves and one could have blinked and missed them altogether, the armed guards certainly made the experience stand out.

"I can't even stomach crossing the border at Niagara. With these gun-toting rebel soldiers standing here, it scares me. Why do I always feel guilty when I have to face their inquisition?" Piper shuddered.

"That's their job. Don't let it rattle you," urged Rich, "and besides, keep what Seamus said in mind; they like Canadians." It seemed to be true. The two cars ahead of them had to step out, were body searched, their cars emptied and pilfered. When it was Richie's turn to pull their car forward, the guard leaned his head into the partially open window, noticed Rich's maple leaf pin attached to his shirt collar, something that was suggested for him to do by an owner of a hostel through the IYT agency, and asked if he was Canadian.

"Yes sir," Rich answered politely while Piper nodded her head in agreement.

"Have a nice holiday folks! Come back again soon!" he answered with a faint hint of a smile that parted his lips.

"Wow that was easy!" Piper said. "We could've been packing heavy arms and ammunition here and to them, that tiny flag on your shirt indicates that we're innocent. Thank you Canada!"

"We didn't even have to hand over passports."

Dublin was everything the two had imagined. It was a much more modern city than what they'd previously scene during their ride through the Irish countryside; although there were quainter and more historic sections of the city, it felt like they were closer to home with the more obvious luxuries that the city provided.

"I'm dying to see some of the music studios here," Rich announced. "There's Temple Lane, Westland and Windmill Lane Recording Studios. U2, Bob Dylan, The Cure, and, drum roll please...." Richie imitated the sound of a drum. "Sinead...who...is apparently in town at one of the studios, recording her latest album."

"Wouldn't that be a dream come true to be able to see her while we're here? She's probably performing in a small club somewhere in town; they often do that while they're in recording sessions. Why don't you drop me off at the last ancestry office while you go and see what you can check out? Maybe book us a studio tour or get a schedule for a show tonight and then come back and meet me, say an hour?"

Rich added, "Better make it two. You know how lost I can get sometimes even with a map."

Piper scrunched her face. "I don't understand how you can travel all over the world and have absolutely no sense of direction."

"I find more adventures that way!" he exclaimed.

It wasn't until later that evening when the pair had been reunited and was pressed into a tiny booth in the famous Brazen Head pub that Rich asked Piper about her research at the registry office. "Yes, it was informative...umm...I think I've discovered a lot more about my heritage, my family and roots and even personality quirks since I've been here in Ireland, in general." Rich noticed her hesitation but didn't question her any further.

"I can't really hear you; the band is about to start," Rich lied. *The Hot House Flowers* certainly lived up to their reputation. It was their classic song *Home*, which really got to Piper. She hummed along:

Why is it, we have to run to understand
And why is it that every time we grow close
We fall down, and why is it I break my
Rules to let you in.

"I sure see a theme developing," Rich said.

"What do you mean?" Piper asked sounding like she hadn't known that he was listening. "Shh...shh..." Piper hushed him. "Sinead's up."

It was everything that she possibly could have ever imagined. Piper told me she was going to make sure she got herself tickets to hear her whenever she came to Toronto. "In the bigger venues, she brings a full orchestra," she beamed.

Piper told me sometime later that Sinead came out onto the Dublin stage wearing a full-length white body suit, with a hood that covered most of her face and she was bare-footed. She began with *'Feel So Different'* from her 1990 album *I Do Not Want What I Haven't Got*. I once read a poem from Piper with that same title, and that's

when I saw the connection. Piper had been in awe the
entire hour.

I am not like I was before
I thought that nothing would change me
I was not listening anymore
Still you continued to affect me.

But it wasn't until she hit her final encore and *"Troy"*
when Piper went wild.

I will rise...I will return...
The phoenix from the flame.

Chapter Nineteen

"I don't know, Richie," Piper said when he asked her again to marry him. They were on the plane headed back to Canada.

"Well, you never really answered me," he continued. "You don't love me?"

"I do absolutely! But..." Piper replied.

"But what?"

"I just don't know that I can tell you that I believe in forever after. I don't know that I'm wired that way. I know that I love you and always will but whether we can make things work out on a day-to-day basis and whether we'll always want to be traveling in the same direction with the same values and aspirations, I cannot say that for sure, in all honesty. We've talked about the eternal soul before and the more experiences I have and the greater knowledge of other cultures I acquire makes me believe that we're not necessarily supposed to unite eternally in this lifetime. We're a long way away from the forever after, if it even exists."

"I feel like I'm such a better person when I'm with you and that we're so much stronger together," Rich said.

"I feel that too. We make a good team," Piper agreed and added, "and we're going to make a beautiful baby."

Rich smiled and hugged her but didn't feel satisfied with her response. "My family will be disappointed that we won't be tying the knot, especially with a little one on the way."

"Well I know that my mother won't be pleased either, so we get married to make our families happy? Hmm..." Piper thought. "Just think how unhappy they'll be if this doesn't work out?"

"Can you not for a moment just think positively about commitment?" Rich asked.

"I've seen too many failed marriages, been in one myself you know, and too many unhappy people who stay married just because they cannot deal with the reality of a failed relationship. I feel committed to myself, Rich. I want to be the best person I can be and do my part to raise my level of consciousness to fulfill my responsibilities of the eternal soul."

"That's pretty heavy stuff, Pipes. And you want to do this all by yourself?"

"No, far from it. I want to be with you; I want to have this baby; I want to grow and love and learn with YOU. I just cannot promise you that this will be forever because I cannot possibly conceive of such a concept."

"Okay, I can understand that. Will you marry me under these conditions then?" Rich asked.

Piper looked at him questioningly, "And what are those?"

"That you'll share as much of yourself and your path with me for as long as you can?"

Piper thought for a moment then smiled. "I can do that. I can even promise you that."

~~

The weeks following the return from Ireland were filled with days of morning sickness and general discomfort for Piper. Not a single day passed by where she wasn't throwing up or at least dashing off to the bathroom thinking she was going to purge.

"I thought this was called morning sickness because you felt it in the morning," she said to Finn, who was in training to be a midwife. "It's now 6 pm and I've tossed my cookies at least 7 times today."

Finn assured. "This just means you're growing a very strong baby inside you. History proves that healthier babies fight their way into life by making their mothers ill. You're all developing stamina for a bold life ahead of you, both for the baby and mother. He's going to be an athlete, Piper, *'strong like bull'*."

"He?" Piper picked up immediately on her revelation.

"Don't know for sure but all indicators suggest a boy at this point."

"And *'strong like bull'* too. That's how I always describe myself," Piper added.

"More like bull-headed!" Finn teased. "Have you said yes to that handsome man yet?"

"Argh! Why does everyone think that getting married is the answer?"

"It's just romantic! It's a fairy tale!" Finn grinned and twirled around.

"Whose fairy tale?" Piper criticized. Finn just shrugged her shoulders.

~~

The return to her job at CNDY wasn't any easier. The station had changed hands; it had been bought out by a much larger conglomeration; that in turn, put the 'indy' aspect of its philosophy at risk and it was its independent values which were at the core of why Piper had chosen to work there several years ago.

"This high repeats factor is killing it!" Piper expressed to me on one of the last occasions I saw her, exasperated at the changes the station was going through.

"That's actually a good thing. The employees will begin to see better wages and the recognition you all deserve because it has now gone mainstream and is more accessible to so many more listeners," I advised. "That translates to greater revenue dollars, Pipes."

"You playing good cop or bad cop?" She moaned.
"You've sold out like the others! I never thought I'd hear you say that and particularly never with regards to me. I don't care about how much money I make. I'm all about pushing the envelope; you know that! Are you trying to make me feel guilty?"

"I agree with you and I'm on your side but think of it this way, all your great ideas and creative artistry can be heard by so many more people and you'll be able to continue doing what you do with a better living attached to it all," I compromised, feeling like I agreed with her about speaking from both sides of my mouth.

"Again, it just isn't the way I think and I honestly don't believe that 'the powers to be' will continue to let us be free and program what we want to. It's just a matter of time before we're all squeezed out into cookie cutter radio. It's happening everywhere. And just wait until the Internet and syndicated radio take over. We're only moments away from that now!"

Piper wasn't far off the mark. One by one the best broadcasters at CNDY handed in their resignations or just out and out quit. One of the most beloved announcers at the time even went so far as to recite her resume while she was on-air. It was not in the least way egocentric of this young woman to demonstrate this type of audacity; she wasn't searching for another radio position so much as trying to prove the point that the world was changing and that she had to learn to be adaptable and change along with it. Piper so admired this type of courage. It got her to thinking that maybe she needed to learn to become more fearless. She was carrying around a good many valuable assets in her pocket which she could use to fall back on at any time and now was as good of a time as any. *"Resiliency, adaptability and ever-evolving,"* she thought. *"That's the direction in which I need to grow."*

"And in signing off my news cast today, I'd like to make a special dedication: I want to present both sides of the coin; I feel sad to tell you that this will be my last broadcast here at CNDY yet I'm happy to share with you that life is so full of wonderful experiences. It is up to each and every one of us to take the opportunities presented to us, choose *the road less traveled*, carve our own path through the weeds and thorns and find the silence *amid the noise and haste*. I will miss all of you and this particular journey that I'm on. Know that I'm leaving you only in this form and I do so while I am *Dancing with Tears in My Eyes*. Here is Ultravox. I'm Piper Brown on CNDY fm."

For gutsy broadcasting like that it wasn't long before Piper was picked up by another independent radio station. Several of the disc jockeys that had resigned before she did, had decided to start from scratch and build a new format from an existing community station and thought Piper would be a perfect addition.

"It's not much, Pipes, but we'll have fun!" declared Todd Sullivan, her long-time radio friend and new boss. "And we all know you love to dance!"

"Are you being metaphorical?" Piper smirked.

"No, literal. It's a dance music format! There's a very strong pull towards rhythmic based music from the club scene in the U.K. 'Raves' are igniting and we've got to get on this. How much more 'indy' can one get, right?"

"Well there you go, when a door closes a window opens!" she continued in the metaphorical. "Keep in mind though, that I am preggers and I'm going to be needing some time off when the baby comes."

"We've got lots of time and loads to do before then, no worries," admired Todd. "You are more stunning than ever, Piper. That Richard is one lucky man. Did I ever mention to you just how sexy I think a pregnant woman is?"

"Maybe once or twenty," Piper said to herself and continued ignoring his final question. "Well thanks on both accounts, compliments and a new job!"

"You won't rethink my offer then?" Todd asked.

Piper sounded confused. "Didn't I just accept?"

"I mean my other offer," he teased.

She just shook her head, grinned and said to herself, *"Should I be flirting like this when my wedding is only weeks away? And worse yet, actually even highly considering these propositions? Life is an adventure."*

~~

The first weeks flew by with so much organizing to do. The energy of the new format, her favourite music and musicians at hand to be played 24-7, working with all the most prolific Toronto DJs and announcers and the fact that she had been offered a position of coordinator for music programming and interviewing, kept Piper on a natural high that remained unparalleled. Her upcoming special event didn't even seem to be a priority. Richie outwardly, chalked it up to her new responsibilities at her job; inwardly, he was worried about the lack of commitment she showed to him and the planning of the wedding.

~~

Piper looked as if she'd seen a ghost as she stood waiting for her cue with Emily in the vestibule. Gone was the girl with the confidence of independence. Her spirit had been invaded by fear and apprehension.

"You've got to do this, Piper. Everyone's here for you. He's a good man and he'll be a great father. You've just got cold feet. Let him warm them for you," Emily comforted her as she nervously picked up her train and beckoned her in the direction of the sound of the processional. It was a new beginning for Piper and despite Emily's gentle persuasion, she didn't quite feel convinced that she was headed in the right direction.

~~

Ever since I first laid eyes on her I have known some deeper connection, like we were an extension of each other and that our souls were one. And now it's time again we meet.

She seemed lost amid the crowded terminal this time, a soul perhaps searching for a destination or an overdue arrival companion. It had been some time since I saw her there. Her long blonde hair was pulled back and hidden under a ball cap. Her casual attire looked tighter fitting than usual. Her baby belly was starting to show. She had the glow of motherhood.

She swayed towards me from side to side as the weight from her blossoming belly began to cause some affectation; her arms were open wide yet not wider than her bright white smile that dimpled her face when she laughed. Her friendly embrace was what I had yearned for, for some months now when our long dormant relationship again took a more active and intimate path. She was taller and even prettier than I had remembered. As her grasp loosened with our greeting, my mouth grazed her ear. "I've missed you," I whispered, looking around in fear that I'd said it too loudly. She giggled and leaned back towards me. Her sweet breath and warmth surrounded me and so naturally guided me into the endearing caverns of her soul. "I am home", I thought. This was always the way it felt when I was with her.

~~

BOOK THREE

Take kindly the counsel of the years,
Gracefully surrender the things of youth.
Nurture strength of spirit to shield you,
Do not distress yourself with dark imaginings,
Fears are born of fatigue and loneliness.
Beyond a wholesome discipline be gentle with yourself,
You are a child of the universe,
No less than the trees and stars
You have a right to be here.

Chapter Twenty

Deacon Oliver Sirko was born on Valentine's Day in 1995, brought into the world by the very capable and loving hands of Piper's sister, midwife Finola Brown. From the get-go he was everything he was predicted to be: a bouncing baby boy with big dark eyes, fists the size of pitcher's mitts and cheeks that dimpled when he giggled. He grew quickly and joyfully. For virtually the first time in her life, Piper was in love. And the more she loved her new role and her new man, the more she fell out of love with her husband and her old life.

"I know I promised you that I'd be a stay-at-home mom for the first 6 months, but I just can't keep doing this. Deacon is so consuming for me. He wouldn't even let me get out of my pajamas today," Piper cried to Rich as he noticed the bags under her eyes and the scratches on the hardwood where the incessant rocking of her chair had left marks.

Rich was concerned. "Do you need my mom to come over to help you during the day?"

"Oh no. She'll just take him away," she exclaimed.

"What do you mean by that?"

"I know I sound crazy but every time your mother is here she talks to the baby like he's hers," she replied. "Like she says, 'Come to Mama' or 'Here comes Mama'. Like everything she does will soothe Deacon and nothing I do is right. And I'mmmmm his Mama!"

"You're right Piper; you are crazy. She's just trying to help. Maybe because it's her first grandchild that she's acting a little over-protective?" Rich resolved.

Piper continued, "And like this isn't my first child? Some people need to back off."

Rich raised his palms toward her and said, "You've got to get a grip!" There was a brief pause in the tension then Deacon let out a huge gasp and filled the room with thunderous, agonizing screams.

"Look what you did! You made him all upset. I'm going upstairs to feed him again." Piper felt that the world was closing in around her. The more she wrapped her life around the baby, the more she felt inadequate as a mother and the more inadequate she felt as a mother made her want to go back into the working world faster than she had anticipated. That brought on the guilty feelings she was having about abandonment. Just how could she be considered a good mother if she couldn't handle a few months of maternity leave? She felt trapped by his constant needs yet didn't feel like she could loosen her grip on him either for fear of losing him altogether. She had a classic case of post-partum depression.

"But Deacon is already close to two months old; isn't it a little late to still be suffering from PPD?" She asked Dr. O'Reilly on her next visit.

"Heavens no. Some women experience it for the duration of the first year of the baby's life. Are you breastfeeding?" He asked.

Piper nodded.

"Well then, that's why your chemical balance is still askew. You're not only experiencing new roles and responsibilities as a mother but you also have the physiological changes that go along with motherhood. And it will continue for some time; therefore, it will be something you'll have to learn how to manage in the meantime. Tell me what you're feeling, Piper."

She broke down into huge sobs. "I just feel tremendously inadequate and tired. I just wanna die." The doctor reached his elderly hand toward her and placed it delicately on her shoulder.

"A host of negative feelings may be affecting you. You may be anxious about things that wouldn't normally bother you. You may get no pleasure from being with your baby or even feel hostile towards him. You may be terribly anxious about your baby's health, and think you are a hopeless mom. Or you may worry all the time about your own health. You may feel guilty and ready to blame yourself for everything, exhausted and lacking in motivation. You said you feel trapped and lonely?" Piper nodded between the sobs. "These are all classic symptoms. PPD sometimes makes it hard for you to function in your daily life, as your energy ebbs away. You may not be able to concentrate or remember things, so making decisions becomes a real challenge. PPD often affects sleep. You may find you can't get to sleep, or are disturbed by early morning waking or vivid nightmares. You have suicidal feelings and a low sex drive," again Piper nodded. "PPD affects everyone differently."

"Why do I get ravaged by all these mental issues? I'm always on an emotional roller coaster. What is wrong with me? I feel desperate and despondent; I can't cope and I just feel like it would be better if I were dead."

"There, there darlin'. You don't mean that. Just what would the baby do without his mother? You have to be strong and guide yourself through this because it will pass; you will feel well again, Piper, and you'll find a love in your baby and yourself that you could never possibly have even fathomed," the wise doctor assured her.

"I love my baby. I just don't think I'm good at this."

"Good at what?" the doctor asked.

"Good at being a mother. I stay home because I think that's what's best for the baby and then I can't stand the loneliness and feel like I should be at work because the world is moving forward and all I do is sit and rock in a chair all day afraid to let the baby out of my sight. And...and..." her sobs became uncontrollable. Dr. O'Reilly handed her a box of tissues then left the room momentarily. He returned with a notepad in his hand.

"Here is a prescription for a medication that is very mild and is not considered dangerous to nursing mothers and their infants. It will help you sleep, calm you and get rid of some of the anxiety you are feeling currently. I don't normally like to prescribe meds for post-partum but you've been a patient of mine for a long time and I know what works best for you as you've tried a fair number of them in the past. Remember using St. John's Wort?"

"Yes I do. I think that worked pretty well for me in fact and it's mostly a natural drug isn't it?"

"Yes it's in the Journal of Naturopathic Medicines. It's herbal. There's a small dosage of that in this. And again, like any medication, if overused, it can actually give you more of the symptoms that you're using it to reduce," the doctor explained. "We've got to continue working on building your self-esteem, Piper; you've battled with this all your life. You are such a good person and have such wonderful reasons to feel proud of yourself. And now with this little Deacon, you're going to see that he'll be the one reason, if one is all you need, to hang on, to hang on for dear life."

Piper always felt rejuvenated after a visit with O'Reilly. Rich noticed her change of mood upon her return and offered his mother as a babysitter so that the two of them could go out for a nice dinner.

"No, absolutely not!" Piper refused. "I told you that I'm not leaving my baby with anyone else."

"Okay, okay, but don't forget that he's my baby too!" Rich shouted back. He had been hoping that if he could get Piper away for a few hours that maybe she would have a little bit of wine and start to feel sexual towards him again. It had been months since they'd had any activity, as he recalled. He asked Finn about the lack of sex a man can expect in and around pregnancy and she told him that sadly, the sex drive for women was greatly reduced, particularly after delivery. Not only were the sex hormone levels down but also the pain sensors in the organs and birth canals were still pretty sensitive.

"That's too bad because I think Piper just needs a good lay. She gets so much more relaxed when she can just let her hair down," he said loud enough for Piper to overhear.

Finn questioned, "And I'm thinking that you might get some relief out of it too?"

Richie winked.

"Men!" both Finn and Piper agreed.

Some days home with the baby for Piper, seemed to go on forever, particularly while Deacon was still colicky. Dr. O'Reilly had warned her that the new meds he had prescribed could potentially make the baby irritable.

"Oh my god, this baby just won't stop crying!" Piper wailed into the phone to her younger sister and midwife, Finn.

"Put him in the car and take him for a ride or put him tummy down on top of the clothes dryer. It's supposed to jiggle the cramps out of them." Life as a new mom with a colicky baby was more than Piper had bargained for and eight weeks in she had already called Todd to tell him she was coming back to work.

"No you don't! You've got 6 months; take the time, Piper. You're not ever going to get it back." It was in the third month where Deacon started to show more personality; the colick was gone and what replaced the scrunched face and the heart-wrenching cries was a big, gurgling handsome boy.

"Why do they always do this to you? Just when you think you'd rather be back at work, they make staying home with them so much fun," Piper confided to Todd over the phone on the eve she was set to return to the station.

"Well, you can take more time if you like. But I was really counting on you to help cover the East Coast Dance Music Conference with me," Todd added.

Piper suddenly became very interested, "When is it and where?"

"Halifax, the weekend after next," he said.

"Terrific! No, that's rad! Isn't that what the kids are calling it these days?" Piper asked half jokingly. She had been somewhat concerned that being off for 6 months really took her out of the scene.

"Aw Piper, you'll always be the hippest mom around!" Todd complimented.

"Don't let the mom thing out, please? I already feel old enough as it is," Piper groaned.

"When life gets you down just keep in mind just how sexy I think new moms are," Todd whispered.

"You're a very bad man, Todd!" Piper's voice dropped to match his.

"And that's exactly why you love me!" he replied.

Piper had just put the phone down when she noticed Richie behind her. "What are you doing?" she asked feeling his breath on her neck.

"I was going to ask you the same thing," Rich said.

"I just got off the phone with Todd. They're excited to have me back and I've already been asked to go to the Halifax Dance Music Conference the week after next. I'll have to pump my breasts and freeze a whole lot of milk before I go but I think I'll have time to do that over the next week."

"You mean you've already decided you're going?" Rich asked.

"Well yes!"

"You didn't feel the need to ask me first?" Rich pried.

Piper hesitated, "What's the correct answer here? Umm...I didn't feel the need to ask you first, no, but would you mind if I do this?"

"What's the point, seriously? You've already made up your mind and no isn't an option."

"That's correct. I'm going. I love my job and my baby and my baby will be fine in your care while I'm gone. Right?" Piper repeated.

"Of course, Deeks and I are a team! And he's my baby too!" Rich complied.

Piper gave him a peck on the cheek and dashed up the stairs to get her things ready for her first day back to work.

Chapter Twenty-One

The Beat's entourage consisted of Todd and Piper from music programming, two techies from the road crew, a magazine entertainment reporter, and a label/manager executive and 3 local DJs with their own 'people'. It was a group of 15 in all. They pretty much claimed rock star status and sat silently in first class behind dark glasses and baseball caps. Conversation was meager as it was still pretty early in the day for most musician-types. It wasn't until after the first round of complimentary drinks that the group began to loosen up a little.

"This is so exciting, Todd. Thanks for inviting me!" Piper exclaimed.

"You're it baby! You're my co-host and my sideman and I wouldn't have it any other way!" Todd replied.

"Are these guys staying at the Delta too?" she asked.

"Yep. I think it's where most of the panels are being held and it's the host hotel for the conference itself. We'll be going off site to the club gigs though, tonight and tomorrow. Callie booked us a limo to get us to and from for the weekend. Isn't that swell?" He asked teasingly.

"Very! Who's the guy in the second row beside Cool?" Piper was referring to DJ Cool, the most prolific Toronto DJ at the time.

"That's Peter Stein. You actually interviewed him, maybe a few months ago now. He had a hit dance music song but I think he's got more going on than that and he seems like he's a good friend of Cool's. Why do you ask?" Todd asked.

"Because he keeps looking at me," Piper said.

"Well I told you that you interviewed him. We're stars Piper, don't you know?" Todd teased.

"Yea right! I forgot!" Piper squeezed his hand and leaned into him for added support.

They checked into the hotel and handed out the itineraries to their group members. They had a few hours to get settled in their rooms before they had to check into the conference. *The Beat*'s sponsored night wasn't until the second night, so the DJs were pretty much on their own to arrange their time accordingly until then but Todd and Piper were required throughout the 2-day event as speakers at the various music panels. Todd was a keynote speaker and needed to be at the first panel 15 minutes before it began.

"Do you mind if you do this one on your own?" Piper asked. "'Cause I'd really like to stretch my legs and get a feel for the city first. Running is the most efficient way for me to feel human again after I fly."

"Oh for sure, Piper. I've always admired that about you. And getting to look at those legs doesn't hurt me too much either. In fact, I'd like those babies wrapped around me tonight." Todd responded.

Piper scrunched her nose. "I thought we decided that we could stay in the same room without any hanky panky going on?"

Todd's eyes rolled, "Hanky panky? I thought you said Hokey Pokey. I'm not sure if I can keep my hands to myself, Piper. I think you might be in trouble."

"Argh!" she groaned. "Come on Todd, I'm married with a baby. We're best friends; we can't take advantage of this situation."

"Alright alright, I'm just teasin'! But you're still one of the most beautiful women I've ever known and I want you to know just how important you are to me."

"Which part of you?" Piper asked.

"I'm feeling it in all my parts, baby!" he said, "Can't you tell?" He pointed down to his raging hard-on. *'Lovely,'* Piper thought to herself. *'At least I'm good for something!'* she said but caught her self from continuing, as she knew that her doctor wouldn't be too impressed with her negative self-image.

When it was well past the time that Todd was to return back to their hotel suite and he hadn't, Piper decided to venture down to the conference room to find him. It didn't take her long to see him engaged in a highly flirtatious conversation with some pretty young girls. Piper assumed they were broadcasting students who had attended his previous panel. She didn't want to interrupt so she just sat in a chair at a nearby table and waited until he turned his head to see her there. Some ten minutes later she could finally hear him say, "Oh thank you ladies. Please sign up for the other addresses at which I'll be speaking and I can answer any further questions then."

"Wow! You are a rock star!" Piper exclaimed after looping her arm around his and virtually dragging him out of the convention hall. "I wouldn't be in such a hurry but I thought we should really dine with our guests tonight; maybe do the clubs tomorrow since we are the hosts? Cool and company has invited us out to dinner. They said reservations are for 8:30 and that gives you exactly 40 minutes to shit, shave and shower."

"Are you going to join me?" he asked as he headed into the bathroom for a shower.

"What the fuck is wrong with you?" she replied.

"Just teasing!" he sighed.

The two were fresh and sparkling as they stepped out of their limo and entered *DaMaurizio's.* "We're not too late are we?" Piper asked Peter as she moved towards the empty space beside him.

"No perfect! You're perfect!" Peter said as he stood and gentlemanly pulled the chair out for her to sit on.

Piper heard him correctly but played the modesty card. "Oh good, because Todd drives me crazy with his tardiness. I have to drag him everywhere to get him places on time. He's as slow as molasses!"

"In January!" They both said in unison.

"It's not January," Peter reminded her as they giggled.

That was the beginning of one of Piper's most electrifying evenings. I knew it even before she spoke of him that the connection between them was perhaps even life altering for both. And when I had a chance to finally speak to Todd and to anyone that knew the two and saw the sparks fly, it had been confirmed time and time again, that this was a union that just could not have been denied. But whenever you have this kind of flash electrical storm, it's never likely to last long and it will often leave many casualties in its wake. Such was the case for Peter and Piper.

Cool and his wife and manager left the table after a few hours. They had left an open tab for the others to enjoy the remainder of the evening on their behalf and since they all seemed to be getting along so well and laughter was in abundance, they sat and drank the night away.

"I'm laughing so hard my cheeks hurt!" Piper howled.

"Which ones?" said Petey as he turned to his friend and music exec, Karl, for support.

"Why are you looking at me? I'm embarrassed for you. You don't know her that well," he assured in his strong German accent.

"Aww, but the night is young!" Petey continued, "I'm on a roll!"

"That you are my friend!" agreed Karl. The others shook their heads through bouts of laughter. There was no denying the electricity and even Todd, who often expected Piper to be 'his property' when they went places together, couldn't deny that this couple was a hit. They all felt lit up by the power their passion ignited.

"Hey, Peter Piper picked a peck of pickled Pipers or was it Piper picking Peter's pecker?" Pete was clearly inebriated.

Piper agreed with the latter, "Yep, Piper picked a pecker all right!"

"Pick me pick me!" Pete pushed on with more hoots of insane laughter.

"Wow!" said Todd as he finally pulled Piper through their hotel door, leaving a singing Peter in the hallway. "That guy is persistant! And is he ever talented!"

"I know," Piper agreed, referring to Pete's take-over of the house piano at DaMaurizio's just some moments earlier. The group of them had decided to stay in the lounge at the restaurant rather than trek out to the clubs, as Pete was so engaging.

"Uh oh, I know what that means. You are such a sucker for musicians," he remembered.

"Brrrringgg..." the phone lit up.

"Who the hell is that? It's 3:30 in the morning," Todd asked.

"Oh my God, you are too drunk. Just stop! We've all get to get some sleep. Good night Pete!" Piper hung up and shook her head. She went into the bathroom. When she came out she saw that Todd was hanging up the phone.

"Peter again?" she asked.

"Um no, that was Richie," he replied.

Piper's jaw dropped. "What did he want?"

"Well he asked for you and I told him that he had the wrong room and that I couldn't remember what your room number was but that I'd dropped you off about an hour ago and that you were safe and sound for the night. Hopefully that did the trick?" he explained.

Piper looked doubtful, "Oh god! I guess I've got some things to deal with tomorrow. Nighty night, Todd, today was an absolute blast, thanks for inviting me," she said as she did a flying leap onto her bed.

Todd reached for the light switch and then jumped in beside her. "Get out you silly man! Don't you think I've got enough troubles already?" she screeched.

Piper rose by mid morning and peaked out behind the heavy denim curtain that was draped tightly across the window. "Oh, it's bright and sunny already," she whispered, trying not to disturb the beast in Todd. She gathered her hair back into a ponytail and pulled on her tights then grabbed her runners that she'd pushed under the bed the night before. She tiptoed across the room into the bathroom where she could finish getting ready with the help of some light. She grabbed her room key and headed down the stairwell to freedom.

The morning was perfect for running! She'd mapped out a good route on her last day's run that included Citadel

Hill. It was worth tackling the hill to get to the top. Piper took her time breathing in the sea air and absorbing all the sights the city offered from high atop her perch. She went over to a park bench and began to stretch her quads and hamstrings. She was about 3 weeks out from competing in another marathon so this had to be her last big run before race day. The incline was grueling and difficult and she rather wished she had some one to help with these final weeks of motivation. Richie had sort of cooled in the idea of having her do a long race so soon after having a baby but that didn't stop her; it added another angle of strain that seemed to be growing between them. Things weren't good in their relationship. The race and her trip with Todd to Halifax were certainly not going to make things any better for them, either. So why did she just go ahead with them? It's like she purposefully wanted to create tension.

"I'll just never be happy in the forever. Not built that way," Piper said to herself.

"Not built what way?" She turned around to see a young, thin man wearing a baseball cap bent over tying his running shoes.

"I'm sorry. Did I say that out loud?" She asked.

"Well I heard you. We made it up in one piece; wanna head down?" he questioned pointing down Citadel Hill.

"Sure could use a buddy!"

"Sounds like it," he said as they headed down the same path they went up. "Relationship issues?"

"How'd you guess? I just don't know if I was built for marriage. I just cannot fathom the forever. I feel like there's too much compromise and too much living I have to prevent myself from doing in order to stay married," She admitted.

"Well, we aren't all built the same way," he reasoned.

"But the problem is me. I have this fairy tale idea that I'm supposed to find the man of my dreams and live happily ever after and I rope in the men I'm dating at the time to think that that's what will make me happy forever after, but that's not really making me happy at all. I'm really terrified, actually. My doctor seems to think that I've got an awful lot to figure out about myself yet. What do you think?" Piper squinted into the bright sunlight.

"Do not distress yourself with dark imaginings; fears are born of fatigue and loneliness; beyond a wholesome discipline be gentle with yourself," the voice in the sunlight said.

"What the...?" Piper tried to shield her eyes to see him but he wasn't there. She looked right and left and behind her and still no sign of her running mate.

"Most bizarre," she said out loud again. She was only a few minutes away from her hotel so she continued on her way.

Chapter Twenty-Two

Todd was still in bed when she returned so she
showered and got ready for her first panel appearance
of the day. It was on creative radio programming and
that was her forte. Since she had started work at *The
Beat* she had developed a strong listener base by
combining her eclectic musical tastes with her
innovative writing style. She had been producing and
hosting a show called *Sensual Sundays*, which was a bit
of an experiment for them. Each week she would take a
different topic and create around it then she'd add
suitable music and host it. For example, one week was
based on moods, and then the next was on spirituality.
Due to its very diverse nature it got great critical
acclaim from the industry but never fared as well in the
actual ratings as she tended to stick to the obscure
artists and ideas, so it wasn't a huge financial boon for
them but it did create quite a following. Some of the
artists she used and their independent record labels
were really pleased that she'd put them in the spotlight.

"Well, when else will we have the opportunity to hear
from some of these indies? There's a ton of music out
there that just never gets airplay and it's such a shame,"
Piper admitted to her small panel crowd. She in fact, got
a standing ovation from the group. "Hey, don't applaud
me; I'm just like you guys. I wanna hear cool music and
introduce these young artists to you; it's my station, *The
Beat*, which truly should take all the credit. They're
probably losing money on us, but good for them for
taking the chance," she continued, "and don't hold your
breath that this is going to last forever. I've been
warned that this is just an experiment and I'm so glad
that you've all been able to be a part of it and share it

with me." Again, the small crowd roared with cheers. "I'm taking show suggestions as we speak. Please leave topics with appropriate artist selections in the box to my left and I'll see what we can do to get them spotlighted for you."

"Well that was truly ego-building," Piper admitted to Todd when she met up with him after the first panel was over.

"I knew you'd kill it, babe! How about we meet up for happy hour after the next panel so we'll be good and loose for the last session at 6?" Todd asked.

"Sounds great!" she exclaimed. Her other afternoon session went equally as well. That one was on script writing, which was one of her major passions. She blended her unique imagination with her technically near-perfect writing skills to make for great copy in both programming and advertising.

"Hey! You're Piper Brown," said one of the attending students in the audience.

"Well I certainly was the last time I checked," said Piper teasingly. "What's up?"

"Tell us what it's like to work with Todd Sullivan." "Are you two as close as you seem, in real life?" "Are you two dating?"

Piper was shocked. "Wow! One at a time, um, we're very close, best friends in fact and have been for many years now; he's an awesome broadcaster and friend and no, we both have significant others in our lives, so we're not dating."

"You are so right about us being stars, babe!" Piper exclaimed as they ordered their first drinks at the bar.

"I told you. They're not really here to learn so much as to lean into us to get our energy and live our lives," Todd admitted.

"Okay then, I can share," Piper winked. Their last panel they spoke at together. It was on industry standards, advertising and direct marketing. It was a rather dry subject and something Piper knew next to nothing about, so she let Todd take the reins. She marveled at his wisdom. "You're so sexy on so many levels," she whispered.

"Does that mean I'm in for some special treats tonight?" he prompted.

"Oh dear Lord, is there no end to your bribing?" she teased.

"You started it. I'm just going with the flow," he said. Piper just laughed and shook her head.

"Do you think Pete will be at the club tonight?" she questioned.

"Seriously?" She nodded. "He's a good friend of Cool's and I'm pretty sure he wants to be wherever you are," Todd explained. "Didn't you see him watching you during your panels today?"

"No," she said.

"Well, he was there. I saw him watching you like a hawk."

"Should I be afraid?" Piper asked.

"I dunno. I think he'd be great for you. He's a great catch, very talented like yourself."

"But I'm not looking for someone?" Piper denied.

Todd noticed that her statement was worded in the form of a question. "You sure?" Their eyes locked.

They went back to their room to get ready for their club gig. Todd made a few phone calls to make sure that the DJs were set up and that the sound system was tested.

"How's Cool?" Piper overheard Todd on the phone. "Really? Can't we get someone to watch him? He's so unpredictable. All right. I'll take your word for it. But if he doesn't show I'm coming back for your hide. Do we have a replacement in case? Okay, yep, he's good, won't have the draw that Cool has but, he's got some great mixes, love his style."

"Just the usual pre-show tension, my dear?" Piper consoled after Todd hung up.

"Uh huh, that it is!" Todd agreed.

The limo dropped the pair off in front of The Dome on Argyle St. downtown Halifax. It was a club that boasted 6 different bars and party atmospheres to match. *The*

Beat's show was set up on the main stage. The cages for the go-go dancers were all decked out in blue and gold sparklers, the lasers were shining, and the hostesses were already circulating around with their shooter trays and appetizers.

"Their costumes seem to get skimpier and skimpier these days. Is that pasties they wear or what the...?" Piper's brow furled.

"And where are yours?" Todd mused. "You'd look so dynamite in tassels! Or out of tassels, either way!"

"I wouldn't have any credibility if I dressed like that!" Piper reminded him. They walked in behind the stage to the DJ booth. DJ Ray-Von was already into his first set of the night while his entourage was doing lines on the tables in the back of the booth. Piper looked a bit shocked.

"Get used to it, babe! That's what backstage is like," Todd replied.

"Hmm...not sure if I'm going to like that too much," she said. "The crowd loves him though, wow! He has a way with his mixes, for sure!"

"Hey, let me get you a drink. Loosen you up a bit," Piper heard a familiar voice from behind her. She turned to see that it was Pete Stein. Todd seemed to vanish into the darkness.

"Fancy meeting you here," she said. "How was your day? When you left me in the early morning hours you were rather... er... happy?"

"I'm always happy. That's me, Petey Happy Stein!" he concluded. "Wanna dance?"

She looked surprisingly pleased. "You dance? I was always told that DJs don't dance."

"If you call this dancing," he wiggled around and threw his arms into the air. Piper laughed and imitated his moves. "We're going to rock this joint!"

Peter and Piper took turns refilling each other's drinks and pulling each other up onto the dance floor every time there was a better song that was played. Their union was easy and comfortable and the two of them laughed and joked like they'd known each other forever. Despite the fact that they seemed to talk endlessly about every subject they could imagine, they never brought the topic up about their relationship status. That might have been, Piper thought afterwards, due to the fact that Piper had taken her wedding ring off and put it onto her right hand. Pete did seem to get a bit suspicious every time Todd would come over to her and whisper, but he just continued on with his 'happy' demeanor. Petey also made it very clear to Piper that this was new territory for him. He kept saying he'd never met anyone so tantalizing and that he could barely contain himself. Todd kept coming around, she told me afterward, to tell her to be careful.

"And what was your response to Todd when he said that?" I asked.

"I told him it was too late; I was smitten," she said.

Todd told me he was smitten too. Everybody loved Petey. He was always the center of attention everywhere they went. It was on Cool's final set of the evening where Piper's cake was iced. The two had worked their way toward the back of the dance floor, away from anyone who knew them or had anything to do with them. Cool had moved away from his regular club mix into more of his early morning rave sound and pulled out Chicane's *Offshore.* Pete pulled Piper into him and their eyes met. Then it happened. As Piper retold it to me, several times over the years, this was her 'kiss of death'. She'd never experienced anything of that magnitude. Perhaps it was because she was married and taken herself off the market so it was taboo or because she was really intoxicated, but the feeling she had was indescribable. She felt that her body had separated from her lips and she was standing outside of the embrace watching her self. The world stood still. The sounds of the music, the beats of the drums, the noise of the crowd, all disappeared. She felt like she was in a vacuum, a time capsule, being catapulted into another dimension. She stood motionless absorbing his mouth, his teeth, and his tongue. For a brief moment, they moved apart and he said, "Did you feel that?"

Still in awe she said, "I did. You felt it too?"

"This is amazing! Pinch me, are we still here?" He asked.

This was a moment the two of them kept coming back to for many years afterwards. They even went so far as to think perhaps they'd been drugged because the intensity of their kiss was so strong and so similar in texture they could never have believed it was 'au naturale' and Doctor O'Rurale would use this scenario later for Piper, in explaining to her just how responsive her sensations could be naturally without the use of recreational drugs.

"No, you can't sleep with her, Pete," Todd warned. "She's married," as he pushed him out of their hotel room. Piper gave Todd the 'what the fuck?' look and told him to stay out of her business.

From that moment on, Pete was like a fly on flypaper to Piper. He tapped on their room door in the morning to find out what they had planned for breakfast and how they were getting to the airport. He met them down at the café and kept trying to corner Piper. "It's not over, baby. Don't let this end. We've got to do something about this connection."

"There's so much about me and my life that you just don't know. I'm too high maintenance and it will be too much work for us to get what I think you're after," Piper uttered calmly. He was clearly nearing desperation.

"Can we try? Can I try? Can...can..." Petey begged.

"You've got to get a grip. We'll be friends back home and see where it takes us?"

Pete nodded and bear hugged her. "You mean, a grip like this?" Over his shoulder yet still in his grasp, her eyes met Todd's. She could see him mouth the word, *"Wow!"*

She giggled. "You certainly do make me laugh."

They all hopped into the limo together and headed for the airport. Once there, Todd pulled Piper aside and said, "Man, he can't keep his hands off you. It's a good thing I like him because it looks like he's here to stay."

Chapter Twenty-Three

Not a day went by where Pete didn't drive by her house. She would look out the window as she was doing the nightly dishes and there he would be sitting outside in his BMW 328i convertible waiting for her. On some occasions she found the courage to go out and actually talk to him but usually she just stared straight ahead and prayed that Richie wouldn't notice. And things were deteriorating rapidly with Richie for sure. How could they not? She had a very progressive, talented man at her doorstep that seemed to worship the ground she walked on. He wasn't going to take 'no' for an answer and those days, Piper wasn't feeling much like saying 'no'.

She had been back at the station for just three weeks when Todd told her they were going to South Beach to cover the Miami DJ Dance Music Conference. "Well the timing couldn't be more perfect for me. Richie's basically not buying the 'oh nothing's going on between me and Pete' lines any more and has said that I have to choose between him and the job. If I go, then I guess I won't be married anymore."

"Let me drive you to the airport, Pipes," Pete suggested. "Have fun sweetie! Call me when you get into your hotel room."

Piper and Todd had booked separate rooms this time; he didn't want anything to do with a jealous soon-to-be ex-husband. Piper had just lifted her bag up onto the bed to unpack and get ready for their first set of interviews and evening live satellite radio show when she heard a knock on the door.

Piper's jaw dropped. "Surprise!" Petey exclaimed and swept her up in his arms. "You happy I'm here?"

"Yes! And surprised, you never cease to amaze me; you are relentless."

"Hopped on the next plane after I put you on yours. I just don't want you to forget about me," Pete confided.

"How could I ever forget about you? You never leave my side!" Piper said teasingly and with just a hint of annoyance.

Pete was classic for pulling off these kinds of tricks. Piper had told me about the time that Pete had gone to Texas for a week or so but returned just after a few days, unbeknownst to her. He phoned her while he was standing outside the front door. While she was on the phone with him he rang the doorbell and he told her to go answer the door. And like magic, there he stood. Todd would often say just how conniving Pete was to capture Piper's heart. He said she never had a chance. Wild horses wouldn't keep him from getting what he wanted and that was pretty clear it was Piper.

"We have such fun and get along so well, but I don't think you're honestly ready to handle a wife and a new baby," she said rather questioningly, one day shortly after their Florida trip.

"Sure I am. Regardless of the fact that I'm a late bloomer, I've always told my mama that when I was ready to take a wife, I'd be going for it." Pete was 38 and had never had a serious girlfriend let alone taking on a wife and new baby; meanwhile, Piper had already been through two husbands and had just turned 31.

 "We're a lot of work, babe; are you sure?" Piper asked him for the umpteenth time.

"I've got it!" Pete proclaimed.

The early months for them were refreshing and fun. Pete seemed to take on the role of new daddy as if he were a natural while Piper tried to settle into the balance of motherhood and radio stardom. It took a great deal of effort for her to not allow Pete to 'look after' the two of them, financially and emotionally. As he was a successful music producer by day, he'd be home working on backgrounds and music beds for different productions while Piper would be at the radio station for her usual shifts. Piper would arrive home at the end of a long working day, and a commute to boot, and scoop Deacon up in her arms. He'd giggle and sputter and it seemed her entire world was turned upright again. She felt satisfied with herself that he had a loving place to live while she was out being creative and enjoying her talents. Until one day...

Piper had been delayed arriving home from work due to a late scheduled interview and construction on the DVP. When she pulled up to the side of the house, like she normally did, she noticed that none of the lights were on. Even though she knew she was later than usual, she didn't think that it was late enough to 'shut everything down'. Petey usually worked well into the night when he was working on a soundtrack or a TV theme song, she thought to herself. *I wonder what's up?'* She reached out to turn the knob on the door to the side of the house and found that it had been locked from the inside. *'Okay,'* she thought again, *'I'll find my key'*, as she searched around deep into her handbag. By the time she had the key in place to turn the lock, the door opened from the inside.

"Hi honey," a very large pupiled Petey addressed.

"Hi?" Piper asked, recognizing the signs of drug use.

"No, why do you ask that?" Pete retorted.

"Why am I saying hi?"

"Never mind!" Pete rescinded. "How was your day?"

"Fine. Where's Deacon?" Piper pushed past him and looked around the room.

"He's asleep. He had a good day. We played; he ate well and I drove him around in my car until he fell asleep. Something wrong with that?"

"No. It's just that you know that I always like to give him his last feeding, and spend some time with him before bedtime, especially since I've been away from him all day," Piper reminded as she peaked into his bedroom to ensure that what Pete said was the truth.

"Yep I do, but he was good and ready and I wanted some freedom, so he went down earlier than usual."

Piper looked at Pete suspiciously. "I'm not sure about this."

"About what?" Pete hunched his shoulders and threw his hands up in the air.

"About this," Piper pointed to white residue on the coffee table, a hand mirror and a rolled up five dollar bill. "I may be naïve, Petey, but I know what this means and I don't like it, particularly around my baby."

"I'm sorry Piper. It won't happen again." Pete assured.

"You are so right," Piper threatened, "or I'm taking myself and my baby right outta here."

"I love you so much, Pipes; please don't leave me." Pete took a hold of Piper like there was no tomorrow and he wept and wept and wept. Piper was her gracious self but somehow something had changed for her.

"I know that you're not going to stop on my account. You really have to want to stop and be ready for it but please, please, please, the next time you feel the urge coming on, let me know. I'll take Deacon to his dad's. I won't have him subjected to this environment and childish behavior."

"I promise you, Piper," Pete insisted and kept true to his word. It was just a matter of a few more days; however, when Pete told Piper he'd just bought an eight ball.

"What's that?" she asked questioningly.

"Well...they cut cocaine into a weight grouping to sell it. An eight ball is basically an eighth of an ounce. It costs about $200 on the street."

"Where did you get it?"

"It just arrives at the door," he answered.
"Huh?"

"Wait and see." He said.

"It's Richie's weekend with Deacon so why not?" Piper said flippantly.

"You going to be mad at me over it?" He asked.

"No. I'm just curious I guess."

"Wanna try it?" He offered.

"I'm not sure. I'm already taking a smorgasbord of pharmaceuticals for bipolar. I don't want to get into serious trouble. To be honest with you, I think my biggest fear is that I might like it."

"Well, I can certainly understand that, on both accounts. Let's get cozy tonight, anyway."

Pete decorated their room with candles and incense and pillows strewn about. His dealer arrived about ten past 8 on roller blades. She was a young girl no more than 20 with braids and a Pearl Jam tank top cut off at the midriff. "It's getting mighty easier and easier to buy drugs these days," Piper giggled truly not having any notion of the process.

Pete agreed, "You have no idea what you're talking about, Piper, but I love you regardless!"

Piper had confided in me some time later that Pete's changes in behavior and mood swings were probably on account of his drug use, although she never said that for sure. I advised her to be careful. I was referring more to her dealings with Pete in that state, not so much with drug experimentation itself, because I knew she was always pretty smart and in control that way. Then the popularity of raves began to move forward and into their social domain; anyone associated with that scene couldn't avoid the communal affects and euphoric highs by combining MDMA with house, techno, trance and drum and bass, to create a new era of 'love-ins'. Although many people like Piper, were afraid of what the consequences of this relatively new drug would be, the rave scene provided a relatively safe and crime free place for youngsters to endure their all-night dance parties. Piper often interviewed people involved in rave production for *The Beat* and she was always pleasantly surprised to hear about the very few altercations and repercussions that resulted on account of the drug use at the parties. Toronto police and security said they never minded being on duty for these big events because mostly the ravers were 'peaceful and happy', rather than being loud and belligerent in the clubs where the popular drug was alcohol.

It was a heavenly high time for her, with or without drugs, she told me. Their sexual appetites were large and very demonstrative. When Pete and Piper would go missing for a few minutes at a party, they'd be found soon after, making out behind a curtain or in a DJ booth. They'd just giggle in euphoria. And the parties they'd host! Todd and Piper often went above and beyond their duties at the radio station to organize and manage independent all-night dance events bringing in many international DJ's and musical artists worldwide. It was on such occasions when she met DJs Sasha and John Digweed, BT (Brian Transeau) and Moby, her enlightenment to the *Global Underground*. She loved her job at the radio station, the people, the creative tasks and the energy and added to that, was her passion for this new kind of underground beat-driven music.

Due to the fact that Piper worked as an on-air DJ at a dance music radio station and Petey was a rather successful dance music producer, the stage had pretty much been set for this new young couple to be crowned the king and queen of rave culture. They basked in this glory for several months before it all came crashing down.

~~

"Smile, though your heart is aching
Smile even though it's breaking
When there are clouds in the sky, you'll get by
If you smile through your fear and sorrow
Smile and maybe tomorrow
You'll see the sun come shining through for you..."

Petey belted out the Nat King Cole classic as he sat and played at his baby grand in the house he then shared with Piper and Deacon. "How about this one? Is this more like the way you feel today, sweetie?" Pete was so good at creating something wonderful on the keyboard. He instantly composed a little instrumental for her. He made her day just by playing a little something every morning to make her feel special. Deacon would jump up and down in his walker any time he heard the vibrations of music around.

"That's one helluva special kid you've got there, Piper," Pete said. "My Russian Momma believes he's going to be somebody special some day. She says you can see it in his eyes." Piper didn't want to mention to him that she'd heard a very similar thing from an Irish woman on her trip overseas, as she didn't want to sound too boastful; however, she had heard it often enough now to think that there might be something more to it.

Chapter Twenty-Four

"I haven't seen you in awhile, Piper; does that mean you're doing well?" the doctor asked.

"I think so. Or maybe I've just been busy," she said evasively.

"Why have you decided to see me now? What's going on?"

"My mum actually wanted me to check in with you and I broke down. She feels that I'm just going in circles," she answered.

"Do you think you are?" he said.

"Well, I'm still moving from one man to the next, too quickly for most people to comprehend, and I still find that I'm unhappy a great deal of the time," she sighed feeling such relief from just airing her concerns.

The doctor opened his familiar notepad and began to write. "Tell me about your current boyfriend. How is this going?"

"Well, we have the highest of highs; when things are good, they're great but when he's down, or I'm down, we both cannot seem to help the other. It's all or nothing."

"Hmm," he said. "That doesn't sound like a good match for someone who has bipolar, Piper."

"That it isn't, I'm afraid," she conceded. "But he's so talented and so extraordinary and went to the ends of the Earth to win me over, that I felt so flattered. It's kind of ironic that the men I tend to fall for seem to adore me more than perhaps I adore them. I love that they love me. Does that make any sense?"

"Absolutely, given your lack of paternal love, I'd say so. You're always seeking approval from a man and when you get it, you confuse this with love."

"I become addicted to the attention they give me and I have to admit, with Petey, I feel he's trying to buy my love a little too. I wouldn't normally fall for this kind of treatment. He lavishes me with all kinds of luxuries and right now, feeling like a princess is a pretty great trip as a single mom."

"That's it exactly! You're addicted to each other, the way you make each other feel, and so you're not dealing with reality here; you're both creating an illusion, which ultimately ends in a disappointment when reality decides to rear its ugly head."

Piper added, "And I don't think adding drugs into the mix is going to help too much either."

"No. Right again; that just makes it a more powerful addiction. I thought you said that you weren't really interested in recreational drug use, so what about the prescriptions you're already on then? Are you not concerned about over-medicating?" the doctor advised.

"I am but as I have been feeling really happy and under emotional control, I figured that I didn't need to be taking those anymore."

The doctor frowned. "You can't just stop and start your meds any time you think you feel well. That's not how they work." He looked rather sternly at the face he had known for so long. He had a way of seeing very deeply beyond her façade. It was not the angry look of a man like the way her father would see her, rather it was a genuine and heartfelt concern that flickered in his eyes as he spoke. It had been a gentle reminder that she had been wrong in not keeping up with her therapy.

"I have to admit that I've learned a great deal about how my own system can get so high and low without drugs that I don't need to add to the complication anyway," she agreed.

"Love is complicated enough; add drugs to the mix and you have a cocktail headed for disaster. Psychologists often study the feelings described by people who say they are in love; they find it, interestingly enough, comparable to that of a drug-induced high and love isn't always healthy if the proportions aren't right. Again, it's a lesson in finding balances. Why do you think they call it 'lovesick' rather than 'love-healthy'? There are virtually so many ways to define love because for every person, it is experienced in a completely different way. Speaking of different relationships, how's motherhood and baby Deacon?" he changed the subject.

Her eyes lit up, "Oh doc, he's just the best!"

"Glad to hear that, Piper. You deserve this wonderful gift!"

"Without sounding unappreciative, I wanted to pass this one by you to see what your thoughts are. As you know, I've been doing a lot of research around my heritage and the belief in the eternal soul. That was one of the reasons why I went to Ireland." O'Reilly nodded and winked as he always did when she spoke of the Irish, to acknowledge this commonality between them. "I've always believed that we choose our own paths but I'm now starting to see that these choices perhaps were made by our eternal souls long before our physical bodies arrived here."

"So you're saying that you chose Deacon to be your son?" he questioned.

"No, the other way around. I believe he chose me as I chose my parents and they chose their parents before them. We choose them on purpose to work out something that needs fixing or adjusting to make us better beings."

"That's very good, Piper, and certainly very plausible. I also believe that that's a good theory for someone like you to honour because it can only build up your self-esteem. If you feel that Deacon has chosen you, then that must make you feel really loved and really worthy, the way you deserve to feel."

Piper smiled her big white toothed, dimpled smile. "I'm thinking that I obviously knew nothing of love before because I know what it is now, and this is very different, very wonderful."

"It's unconditional, Piper. Your father let you down and so you've spent your life trying to find a man who won't disappoint. That man may not exist because your expectations are so high and it's that one particular element you're looking for in a relationship. You've decided that's the most important asset to you."

Piper shook her head. "But I've been the one to walk away from my relationships. Isn't it I who is a disappointment?"

"On the surface, yes. People see you as the one who disrupts the flow of the union but the disappointment occurs before the leaving. It has a great deal to do with trust, which is not your forte. You don't know how to trust people because you fear they might hurt you. They have in the past and so you feel that they will disappoint you or hurt in the future. You're reactionary and have a rather powerful ego, so you don't want to stick around to be the one left behind. That would be ego crushing for you. You're going to be the leave-taker; it's something you can control; it's a disappointment that won't surprise you thus won't cause you as much pain. You walk away too soon, though, Piper. You're a real poster child to the adage, 'When the going gets tough, the tough get going.' Every time someone gets close enough to you to possibly disappoint you, you do something to push him away or you walk voluntarily. You're not really even giving them the chance to try to be the partner you want them and need them to be. But it's probably because you're still not ready.

You've got a lot more to figure out in your life yet. I've helped you battle with all kinds of relationships and whether they be with male, female, older or younger, friend, relative or co-worker, you cannot seem to open yourself up enough to let people in, for fear they will disappoint you. The irony of all this is, that's far more like the personality you've expressed to me about your mother rather than your father and you've always thought you were your father's child."

"Hmm. I guess that means that history is not doomed to repeat itself?"

"Certainly not for you, Piper. You are so much more in tune with which you are than your parents were. It's a fairly common asset with the younger generation, in fact; the more complicated the world gets, the more reflective in general, people get; consequently, your generation seems to be much more on the ball with internal insights than the world in which your parents were raised and better still, you don't have to play your life out in the fashion that they expect of you. You have much more power of control."

"Well that's entirely positive but scary too!" Piper exclaimed.

"Scary because you have control?"

"Scary because it means that I have to be responsible for my own decisions and my own lack of trust. There's no one else left to blame," she admitted.

"Aye, there's the rub!" He said quoting Shakespeare.

"Wow! I see you've got me figured out. Maybe it's time I move on?" Piper's eyes widened in recognition of what she just said.

"My point exactly," he said matter-of-factly. "The first steps in learning to trust someone is by becoming someone trustworthy. Do you want to be trusted?"

"I'm discovering about that desire. I've never thought about it before I had Deacon and now it's all I really want to be, trusted, loved and respected. I want to be dependable for him, unconditionally."

"Sounds like you're on your way," he smiled.

"You're a very wise man, doctor. I guess that's why I pay you the big bucks?" she giggled.

"There will always be people of value in the world and you are very perceptive in knowing how to find them. You've had wonderful men in your life and that's no accident; it's by choice. You clearly know how to pick them. However, don't feel pressured by society to feel that once you've chosen someone to have in your life on a day-to-day basis, that they are supposed to be there forever, in the physical form. It's not necessarily the way of the world. You're a growing, thriving person with many talents and diversified needs; sometimes that means we grow in and out of our physical need for these people too. Have you ever studied Buddhism or done any research on Buddhist philosophies for any of the stories you've covered for the news?"

"No, very minimally, but everything I hear about this spirituality really makes me think I'd like to learn more.

It seems like a very 'balanced' way to think and live," Piper agreed.

The doctor nodded and turned toward his laden bookshelf and thumbed through the rows until he pulled out a copy of one of the latest Buddhist publishings, *When Things Fall Apart* by Pema Chodron. It had recently been dog-eared and bookmarked to indicate different spiritual passages that he had found helpful to some of his other patients. "Listen to this," he said, as he began to read, *"To be fully alive, fully human, and completely awake is to be continually thrown out of the nest. To live fully is to be always in no-man's-land, to experience each moment as completely new and fresh. To live is to be willing to die over and over again".*

"If that's the case, then I think I've died a thousand deaths already," she teased, "But actually, that sounds rather nice. I think I might like that," she admitted.

"This is really how you live and think now. You're already there. You just hadn't identified it yet. Accept these beings for the love you have to share with them and don't regret having to move on. Love is eternal; our physical bodies are not. You'll always have a place for them in your heart. That's a good thing, Piper. You're a good, kind and loving person. Deacon chose well. *Be gentle with yourself, you are a child of the universe, no less than the trees and stars, and remember that you have a right to be here..."*

"Piper?...Piper?" She looked up to see O'Reilly's secretary tapping her on the shoulder.

Piper let out a little gasp. "I'm sorry, did I startle you? The doctor will see you now."

She must have dozed off. "Thank you," she said, rose gently and made her way towards his office door.

Chapter Twenty-Five

Deacon just blossomed under Piper's care and didn't seem to be affected at all by his parent's split. He went back and forth seamlessly from dad to mom without even much noticing which parent was absent at the time. Many people told them that if they'd waited too long to separate then it would begin to play havoc on the child's self-esteem; Deacon was still young enough that it didn't affect him. He never remembers a time when his parents were together so the dual life and dual homes were always the norm for him. That was probably Piper's impetus to end the relationship with Richard so quickly, that and the fact that Pete was ready and waiting not-so-patiently in the wings. He really had no idea what he was in for. If Piper was led by her passions then Pete was that ten times over. He seemed to have boundless energy to support whatever she and Deacon needed.

Piper discovered some time into their relationship that Pete had been very near closing a deal to move his music production company into the states. He'd also wanted to live somewhere warm and California seemed to be the best fit for his career, music and lifestyle but when he'd met Piper and she turned his world on its ear, he settled back into the notion that he'd be fine staying in the country of his birth and to remain close to his aging mother.

"There's no possible way I can move away now. It'll be at least 15 years before I can even entertain that idea; my boy comes first and his dad's relationship with him is a close second, absolutely."

"No worries, Piper, it's taken me this long to find you; I'm not about to desert our little family now," he said. Although she believed him, it never seemed to sit well. She worried about whether she had straddled him with too much responsibility too soon in their relationship. And she rather thought that his increased drug use seemed to demonstrate the point that he carried around too many burdens. Where drugs were his escape, hers was work.

She spent increasing hours at the radio station, writing scripts, biographies, and interviews for the various artists that came around and were added to their playlists. She took on double and extended on-air shifts and booked another night or two weekly hosting at the clubs. So that she wouldn't spend too much time away from the baby, she often brought him in. As it had been a relatively young staff, they all took turns playing games or watching Barney videos with him. It was about at the same time when the *Teletubbies* became popular with the ravers, that Deacon fell in love with the TV series as well. In fact, some of his first words were, 'LaLa' and 'Po', the names of the cute telekinetic cartoon characters. Piper's work buddies would often spend hours joining Deacon in his sing-alongs with the show characters. Piper used to say that she was never sure who the real kids at the station were.

"We've got a DJ show lined up in San Francisco. Wanna come with us?" Todd asked referring to him and his best friend, DJ Ron 'E'.

"Absolutely! I was sure hoping you weren't going to cover this without me," Piper responded assuredly.

"And what's with every DJ shoving an 'E' into their name? Is that the influence that ecstasy has in everyone's lives these days?" She had never heard Ron Herman being called DJ Ron 'E', before.

"Yea, it seems to be the 'thang'," he answered.

She had arranged for Richie to take Deacon for the few days they'd be away, so leaving him was easy. He was a great dad and had a ton of support from his rock solid family. If anything, she was more afraid to leave Deacon because he would have it so good with his dad's family that he might not want to return to her. *"I've got to stop thinking like that. O'Reilly would be upset at how little self-confidence I feel sometimes,"* Piper thought to herself.

"Everything will be just fine," Pete assured her. "Richie's a great dad but you're a great mama and Deacon loves you to bits! Boys always need their mamas," referring to his own love and needs.

"And this is the way you'd prefer it to be, so you don't have to look after him yourself?"

He shrugged. "Geesh Piper, I didn't say that. I'm just trying to ease your mind so you can get away for a little fun."

"Sorry. My guilty conscience is making me snarky." She actually felt relieved that Pete didn't suggest babysitting Deek. She trusted her ex in that regard, much more, and she would have had bigger issues on her hands had things happened contrarily.

Ronny, Todd and Piper were the three musketeers for the week of clubbing and sightseeing in San Francisco. I remember seeing a ton of photos she took from inside their hotel room to, *hippieville* at Haight and Ashbury, the Golden Gate Bridge and Alcatraz.

"You ran this far?" Todd was always amazed at how strong Piper's running skills were. They had jumped into a cab to get an hour tour of the city between engagements and even before the driver could explain where they were, Piper would point out that she had already been there earlier in the day.

"You're a beast!" Ronny exclaimed. "Check out these hills!"

"Quit looking at her chest, Ron; that's my property!" Todd punched him in the arm.

Piper had made eye contact through the rearview mirror with the cab driver and shook her head and rolled her eyes. Their harmless flirtations just weren't about something she was going to be concerned. They were all such really good friends.

"Would you folks like to see the house where they filmed much of the movie *Mrs. Doubtfire*?" the cabbie interrupted the teasing.

"For sure!"

Ever since the 1993 blockbuster movie with Robin Williams came out, flocks of tourists asked cab drivers within miles of the city, to take them to the famous Victorian house at 2640 Steiner Street for picture-taking purposes. The trio did as so many others did before them and posed in various positions on the front steps, along the side street and in view of the windows.

"I feel like a peeping Tom," Piper said as she peered into the darkened front window.

Todd agreed. "So much for privacy, eh? But I bet if anyone actually lives here now they'd have to be used to it."

"I'm sure they were good and warned, at least, about the attention they'd be getting either before they bought the place or after it was used for filming, anyway," Ron concluded.

"Let's just walk for awhile. We look like we're in a funky, boutique neighbourhood," Piper pointed to a shop window across the street and grabbed Ron by the arm to accompany her. He was a good ten years her junior and was thus, she thought, much more interested in the latest clothing trends.

Piper picked up a fedora and threw it at Ron. "See what that looks like on you."

He placed it on his and stood in front of a mirror. "Pretty spiffy," he said with an affected accent. They were only in the tiny shop for a few minutes before they noticed the exorbitant price tags, and the stuffy looks they were getting from the store's personnel; moments later they were being ushered out by an equally arrogant plain clothed guard hovering over them to expedite their exit.

Piper screeched angrily, "What the fuck is wrong with some people?" She didn't usually swear unless she needed the extra emphasis. "Whatever!" she said again to everyone and no one in particular.

"Hey, what happened to Todd?" Ronny asked, changing the mood.

"Beats me!" Piper exclaimed. It was at that moment when they heard the electric sound of the trolley car charge up the middle of the road behind them. They both moved swiftly to the side of the road to watch it go by and as it passed them, there was Todd standing on the back rail of it, holding the hand bar above his head while the other hand he used to wave to them. Once he knew he had their attention, he turned his back to them, dropped his pants and bent over. His pasty white butt shone brightly just above the large advertisement on the back of the streetcar that read, "Rice-a-roni, the San Francisco treat".

"Speaking of some people, what some won't do for a laugh!" Ronny howled.

"What a character!" Piper snickered. The three of them were reunited shortly afterwards and were still giggling about Todd's stunt for hours into the evening.

The DJ showcases were held in different nightclubs throughout the evenings. Todd and Piper were decked out with their DAT recording devices so they could interview the artists backstage before and after their performances then spend time during the day to splice the audio and edit in their own material, sound bytes, and mixes. They did their hosting bits 'live' from their hotel room.

"That Martha Wash is so amazing!" Piper broadcast, "She's certainly known for the famous 'It's Raining Men!' but I truly think her 'Everybody Dance Now' and 'Everybody Everybody' are equally as strong."

"After her solo album in 1993, she came back into the spotlight with Jocelyn Brown on Todd Terry's cover of Musique's 'Keep on Jammin' this past year," Todd continued to colour the commentary.

"She's had a career spanning over 5 decades and she's a native San Franciscan," Piper added. "We'll be back tomorrow to highlight Moby. He's in town tonight; we hope to get an exclusive with him for the show tomorrow."

Todd continued, "Moby's performing tonight at the Ruby Skye. That's where we'll be. Hey Piper, couldn't you just imagine a collaboration between Moby and Wash?"

"I wonder if they've done anything together already? It would be great, regardless." Piper answered her own question.

"The afterhours scene is pretty big right now in Frisco. DJ Carlos has played every weekend rave here all year and now he's starting up his own parties called *LOVE* and will spin with Dubtribe and a host of other big named DJs. It was last year that he teamed up with Josh Wink at Area 51, so he's something to see and someone to watch as well," Todd declared.

"Speaking of up and comers, the latest studio duo, is a pair out of France, Guy-Manuel de Homem-Christo and Thomas Bangalter. They go by the name of *Daft Punk*. They've got a really unique sound that may be the wave of the future," Piper added, "sort of synthpop flavour".

"And I don't know whether you know this, Piper, but they've got an interesting marketing schtick too. Visual media never sees them. Whenever they're interviewed or spin live, away from the studio, they wear masks or head pieces to keep their anonymity. Their deal is that they want the music to sell itself," Todd explained.

"That's rather fascinating. I wonder if when we bring them into the station whether we'll get to see the real deal?" Piper giggled.

"We'll check back with you again tomorrow. Live from San Francisco, this is Todd Sullivan and Piper Brown. Thanks for tuning into *Spin Me Round* on *The Beat*."

"Another stellar performance guys!" as Ronny high fived the two of them.

"We'll get you in there for a set on the last show, okay?" Todd promised.

Ron grinned. They cleared up their gear that had been strewn about the bed for their broadcast.

"I'm going to need a nap if I'm covering the afterhours tonight. I didn't sleep in like you guys did. I was out pounding the pavement for a few hours before you even saw the sunlight," Piper teased.

"Well let's eat now then, grab some grub and come back and chill for a bit before we head out, say 11 pm?" Todd arranged.

It was already 8 o'clock and the sun was slowly slipping beneath the horizon as she watched it drop from her hotel room window. Piper felt a rare moment of peace amid the noise that seemed to travel steadily through her mind. She'd had a comforting phone conversation with her 2 year old, a few hours earlier; Richie had put Deacon on the line so she could hear him say, 'Mama'; she had a great job where she was respected for her wit and intelligence, good friends and health, and even her relationship with Petey seemed to be on solid ground. She recalled the last time she felt so in tune with the moment; that was when she sat silently and motionless on top of the rock ledge in Zimbabwe. She felt blessed.

Chapter Twenty-Six

As is the way with bipolar disorder, settling into the mundane of life presents the greatest of challenges. Piper, as hard as she tried, could not seem to balance being a new mother, a new wife and a thriving career. When her days at *The Beat* were good, her home life seemed to suffer and when she felt she wasn't present enough for Deacon and Pete, she became frustrated and angry and took it out on Pete.

"You've just got to stop blaming me, babe," Pete said. "I've told you a million times that you can quit your job and just stay home. We certainly can afford it. We'd love to have you here full time and dote on us, wouldn't we Deek?"

"And I'd love to be here all the time too but I don't think I can do it. I'm just not the Suzy homemaker kinda person and I'd begin to resent you with all the exciting things you get to do and the people you get to meet."

"Stop treating our life like a competition, Pipes. We're on the same side. We're a team and staying at home would only be temporary. It would just be for a few years until he starts school."

"I'll think about it and talk to O'Reilly too," Piper said but not with too much conviction.

~~

"Absolutely not, Piper. You need your own identity and especially now that Deacon is at such a demanding age and your partner is so prolific. You can't give up what's entirely yours. A career is something one carves out for themselves. It's a path you've paved entirely by your own volition," the doctor explained.

"Well what can I do to feel better about all this?"

"Let's look at other areas of your life to see what needs fixing because your career can't be the only thing out of check. How is it going with Pete?"

"I guess I just feel guilty. When he works from home, I feel he becomes very intense and treats us as if we're in the way. I start feeling guilty that I've put so much responsibility on his plate. I mean he was this single, free-spirited guy for so long until we came into the picture."

"But that's not your fault, Piper. He made it quite clear to you that he was ready and wanted this. As you have told me, 'he moved Heaven and Earth' to get you." Piper sighed so O'Reilly continued. "Well if that's the case then, that's another good reason why you and Deacon shouldn't be staying at home so much. You might be cramping his style."

"So then there's that issue too," she said.

"What's that?"

"His style. I really feel uneasy about the lifestyle he leads. There are always so many... um...interesting characters that come in and out of the house."

"You stuttered on 'interesting'. He is a musician so what exactly do you mean by that?"

Piper hesitated again. "I really think the musician aspect is cool. He's very creative and so too, is his clientele, but with it comes a host of 'groupies', sexy, carefree even loose women and men too, 'cause I don't think it matters to most of them with whom they have sex and I'm just not comfortable with that. I guess one really has to be secure within themselves to be able to handle this kind of comparison all the time but I'm just not. I never feel like I can live up to these expectations."

"What expectations are those exactly?"

"I know that I give off this very casual air, like 'I'm good with whatever goes down' but I think, to be honest, that's just my façade. I really have some deep concerns about living so vicariously. I'm an old-fashioned girl at heart. I married Richard, for God's sake, mostly because he's such a moralist. The Sirkos are the most salt-of-the-earth kind of people and that's the kind of boy I want to raise."

The doctor agreed, "I know you do and I know you are, Piper, and that's such a wonderful thing. It makes you who you are. You can't compromise this on account of what others think about you or what you think you are supposed to be. The only person, who is going to be hurt in all of that, is you, and that's about whom I'm concerned. Again, that's another reason why you can't quit your job. You need to stay independent. Being a new mother in a relationship with a very controlling and strong individual will test your wits. Deacon and Pete have the potential to take you over and you can't let that happen for anyone's sake; what kind of mother would you be for Deacon, if you are no longer in charge of yourself, if you let him rule you?"

Piper nodded, "But that takes such strength. I just don't know that I have it."

"Yes you do. It's just gone into hiding temporarily. How are you for meds?" He asked.

"I could probably use a top up. Paxil in particular has worked pretty well for me."

The doctor cautioned. "Yes, I hesitate to prescribe Lithium again to you, but you should be pretty safe with Paxil. Remember that you shouldn't be taking any other meds with these already high doses and really limit your alcohol intake."

"You mean even wine?" Piper knew the answer to that question.

Piper left Dr. O'Reilly's office invigorated as usual but she did wonder why he hadn't asked her about the strange series of coincidences that had been happening to her. Maybe he figured it was just a side affect from the meds? That answer didn't really sit well with her though, as she thought these had happened even prior to her being prescribed the medications. She intended to pursue this with him at a later appointment and to also ask him about the research she had given him upon her return from Ireland.

Piper picked up Deacon from Richie's mom and took him home to get dinner started for them. She thought she might do as the doctor suggested and feed Deek ahead of time so that she and Pete could dine together later, more romantically. Deacon wasn't really in a good mood, felt a bit feverish, and so what was supposed to be an easy evening of feeding him wieners and Mac and Cheese, while she tried to prepare a gourmet dinner for Pete, turned into a kitchen frenzy. She had barely bathed and bedded the little guy when Pete arrived home. He went straight downstairs to his home studio, shut his door and cranked up the beats. Piper just sat at a chair at the table she had especially set up for the two of them, cloth napkins and candles and all, and stared. Some hours later Pete finally came upstairs to find Piper asleep at the table with her head resting on her arm.

"Hey, Pipes. Have you been waiting for me?" he asked as he kissed her cheek.

"No," Piper said groggily and flippantly, "I was really waiting for my other boyfriend."

"God, I'm sorry. I ate with the guys hours ago, before I came home. Actually it was more of a late lunch."

"Oh that it explains everything then," she said sarcastically. Pete looked puzzled. "You clearly only had several hours then to fill me in on these minute details?"

"Sorry on both accounts then," he said.

"This just isn't working out very well, is it? You say you want me and the baby and this little family but your actions really prove otherwise."

"Piper, please. One dinner I mess up and you're on my case."

"It's not been just one dinner. You're never home and when you are it's like you really don't want to be here anyway. You don't even say 'hello' to me upon your arrival; you never include me in any of your functions and never invite me to the studio. I mean seriously, we kinda even work in the same industry. You don't think that I might benefit from meeting some of the people I interview on a personal level or while they're making music? It always makes for a more intriguing interview when the host and interviewee are familiar."

"I used to include you more but it got really stale having you upset with me every time I had a 'sexy' singer downstairs or was entertaining some 'dangerous' DJs." Pete raised his quotation fingers to emphasize that the words he used to describe his clients, were hers.

"I'm sorry, Pete. I don't know what's happening to us. We used to be the dynamic duo everywhere we went and you were like fly on flypaper to me. 'Member Todd teasing you about that all the time?"

"Well, things change, Piper yes! But my feelings for you haven't. I just am swamped and business right now is not so great, at least not as great as it has been. The glory days for dance music and the dance music industry may well be over. You probably know about that as much as I do." Pete advised.

Piper nodded. "It's true, *The Beat* is certainly feeling the crunch as well. I don't know if it's people's fears over the Y2K thing or what? But yep! We're certainly in a paradigm shift. Apparently South Communications has been interested in a take-over and that naturally has people concerned. They're trimming the staff, kinda non-essentials first, so I hear."

"Well, that could be good," Pete offered.

Piper sneered. "I'm an indy all the way. I don't want some big conglomeration coming in and telling us what we can and cannot play. Look what happened over at CNDY. That's why I left, remember?"

"Well I didn't know you then and they sound great now but I'll take your word for it. You don't think you'd be paid better with South on board?"

"Paid better. Since when have I EVER been doing this for the money?" Piper was adamant.

"You've got to at least understand the principles of working for money, Piper, or you'll never have enough to pay the bills and you'll always be leaning on people like myself to bail you out."

Piper's mouth dropped to the floor. "How dare you say that about me? I don't want your money and NEVER have. You came into my life flashing your big bucks trying to buy me when I was desperately trying to keep my head above water. It made me physically ill to see you waste money by tossing it around. The time you took me to Vegas and pretended to be some hotshot gambler to what, try to impress me? You lost a grand in a matter of 30 seconds and I had to rush to the bathroom to puke. And the thousands of dollars a year you spend on drugs? That doesn't impress me."

"Have you been spying on me?" He looked hurt.

"You are so cavalier about your lavish lifestyle that no spying is necessary," Piper conceded. She began to cry.

"Don't cry darlin'; I'm sorry; you're right. I too just feel way over my head. I've just sunk a hundred thousand into a reno of a new downtown studio and my royalty cheques are down. The networks are going with library instead of hiring composers for original music. I'm feeling the heat."

"I'm on your side. Why are you taking it out on me?"

"I'm not. That's why I'm not coming home so much. I don't want to take it out on you. In addition to that, it's so much more competitive out there now; I've got to spend all my extra time and money on schmoozing the appropriate people."

Piper whispered, "It appears more like you're trying to buy people with drugs in order to win them over."

"Whatever!" Pete resigned and went back downstairs.

What Pete said was probably the truth but he just reeked of suspicion to Piper and she just didn't have the self-confidence to let it alone. She worried herself sick. The last time I saw her, she was a bundle of jealous insecurities.

"You've got to let this go, Piper. If you love him and you say you wanna stay, then you've got to trust him," I said.

"Yep, that's what my doctor said too. I'm sure it will be the death of me."

Chapter Twenty-Seven

As Piper suspected, *The Beat* was next in line on the chopping block. Rumours were that the company was coming in and weeding out non-essential or extra personnel. Anyone without a steady role or defined position was going to be eliminated. That rather put someone like Piper in jeopardy as she was the kind of employee whose role was more that of being the glue or the cement which solidified and made other people's jobs possible.

"It's not really a good time for you guys to be going away right now. The GM of South will be here on Tuesday and that means you won't be here to state your case," Todd pleaded with Piper.

"Can't you plead for me? After all I've done and the inroads we've made together?"

"I can certainly try but they don't even know us, so it'll be tough," Todd explained.

Piper continued. "Petey and I really need to get away together. Rich has offered to take Deacon for a few days and Pete's got a bit of a break in his recording sessions, so we thought we'd whip down to Orleans for a jazzy break! I can feed you interviews with our artists and interesting musical bytes, if you like?"

"Okay. That works for me, but as I say, it's not about me right now. Just warning you!"

Piper was full of smiles when the limo that Pete hired dropped her off at the airport. It was, after all, one of her favourite places to be. Petey told her he'd meet her there because he had a late session and had to go straight there from the studio. She thought she could see him at the bar so she went bounding in towards him. When she got closer she realized that he wasn't alone. He was standing having a drink with a man and two very attractive women. Although she felt nervous and insecure, she pretended not to be.

"Hi honey!" She said and tickled his back. When he turned to her, Piper thought he looked a little flushed.

"Hi!" He said sheepishly. *'No kiss or hug,'* she thought to herself. *'Hmm, wonder what's up?'* She waited for a moment longer to be introduced and when she thought that it was just a moment too long, she heard him say, "Paul? Sandra? Heather? This is my friend Piper, Piper Brown."

"Oh, Piper Brown the radio lady?" Paul asked.

"That would be me," Piper responded still in shock that Pete introduced her only as his 'friend'.

Pete said, "This is DJ Paul E and his beautiful entourage!"

"Nice to meet you!" Piper shook their hands and avoided eye contact.

"Since you're here for *The Beat* we thought you might be interested in interviewing him," Pete offered.

"Right. Sure," Piper repeated herself. "Are you going to New Orleans too?"

"Pauly is the DJ spinning for the headliner at Ampersand's on Friday night."

"You don't say," Piper said mockingly. One of the chesty women grabbed her arm and escorted her up to the bar.

"Sounds like you need a drink. You have some catching up to do, dawling." She said already sounding inebriated. She leaned in closer to Piper pressing her large breasts into Piper's much smaller ones and she whispered. "Do you want a little snort to get you going?"

"Ah, no thanks. This glass of wine will be fine, thank you." Piper was wishing that she'd ordered a double shot of whisky at that moment but she didn't want to have anyone see her dismay. *"This is going to be one helluva long trip,"* she thought to herself.

"Why the hell didn't you introduce me to your friends properly?" Piper asked Pete when she finally got him alone.

"So what do you mean? How did I introduce you?" He pretended not to notice.

"As your friend?" She questioned.

"Aren't we all friends?" Pete changed the subject. He certainly didn't want to get into it with her, especially in the company of others. "Come here," he pulled her into him from the plane seat beside him. The flight and subsequent shuttle and hotel check-in went smoothly.

"We're going to have lots of fun, Pipes. There's a DJ party in the Penthouse tonight. We'll go tour Bourbon Street for a bit and settle in. How's that?" Pete suggested.

"That sounds fine. I'll walk with you for a while, but I'd like to come back to the room and change into my running gear soon. You know how I like to get a feel for a place right at the beginning of the trip, to make it feel like home?" Piper said.

Pete's eyes questioned. "If you like home so much then why do we go away?"

"I think we really needed to get away and spend some time alone together," she replied.

"We won't be alone, though. This is a DJ conference, you know that right?"

"Well yes and I'll be filing my reports and doing interviews but mostly it'll be just the two of us, unless of course we stay glued to the hip of 'Thing One' and 'Thing Two'. Is that what you're thinking?" Piper asked.

Pete turned his nose up at Piper. "They're not that unpleasant." Piper didn't respond and thought to herself, *"They're certainly easy to look at but that's what makes it unpleasant!"* Her insecurities were mounting.

"Let's get a few drinks in you and you'll loosen up," Petey offered a few hours later.

She'd had her run, showered and met Pete down at the corner of Bourbon and Bienville. She had just been seated when Pauly showed up with his beauties.

Piper let out a gasp, "What was that for?" Pete asked.

"Oh nothing. I think I may have twisted my ankle during my run because I felt a little pain," She lied trying not to show her obvious disappointment that she and Pete weren't going to be drinking alone.

One of the women grabbed Piper's arm to get her attention. "Hey look at all the beads I have!"

"I see and what does that mean exactly and where did you get them?" The woman's breasts were so large that Piper naturally couldn't do anything but notice what adorned her chest. "Is that the 'beads for boobies' thing they do at Mardi Gras?"

"Yes ma'am!" She exclaimed.

"But it's not Mardi Gras," Piper corrected her.

"Close enough; hell, it doesn't matter to me. I wanted to enjoy the fun regardless," she negated. The men were laughing hysterically and probably mostly at Piper's shocked expression.

"I'd be willing to show off my tits for a lot less!" She said. *"Really?"* Piper said under her breath. *"One would never have guessed."*

Pauly added, "And what gems they are, babe!"

"Oh fuck!" Piper again said under her breath and sneered directly at Pete.

"What did I do?" He asked.

Piper just shook her head giving that, *"Well if you don't know then I'm not going to tell you look!"* The evening got better as Piper was plied with more alcohol and as Pauly started to pay more attention to her as well.

"I'd really like you to interview me, Piper. I've got some new mixes that I think you'll really dig. I gave them to Pete to have you listen to and see if you think the station will want to spin them," he said.

"Sure. Let's arrange something for tomorrow then, before your gig."

"That would be awesome!" Pauly asked for the check, left some cash to cover his portion and tip, and escorted the girls back in the direction they came. He called over his shoulder to Pete, "We'll catch up with ya later, man."

"Finally, we're alone," Piper sighed.

"Want to go shopping? Dancing? Both? The night is yours, plum cakes," Pete teased. They spent a few hours wandering along Bourbon and stopped in to have a drink here and there. Pete was always so much fun to shop with because he loved spending money and would buy her whatever she looked good in, which was just about anything.

"You can't buy me that dress!" She exclaimed, "It's $1000 and where the heck would I wear it? I'm sure I can find something almost equally as nice back in Toronto anyway, for less than half."

"Why do you worry so much, sweetie? I like spoiling you!" Pete squeezed her. She felt more like it was buying her. *"Arm candy! That's all I am."* Again she was alone in her thoughts. Why did she worry so much? She was always in a paradox in this relationship. She wanted to be treated like a princess but she blasted him every time he did that, thinking he wasn't taking her seriously enough. At least she had Pete all to herself. But it was only a matter of a few moments later when he mentioned that they should probably make their way back to the hotel for the Penthouse party.

"I guess so," Piper agreed.

"Why do you look so glum?"

"I'm not. I just feel like I'd rather be with you and not so much hoopla."

"It's an important party tonight, babe. Maybe we'll find another time to do it upright, me, you and that new dress!" Pete winked.

"Actually, I was thinking of wearing that tonight. What do you think?" She asked.

"Yowza, hot mama!" He replied but somehow the connotation to her with hotness and mama-hood, didn't really sit well. She gave him a half smile.

"Good Lord, nothing I say to you is the right thing," he conceded.

She looked dynamite in the new powder pink sparkle dress that Pete had bought for her. It was a sleeveless and tight bodice with a skirt that had a side split that went almost up to her hip. It showed off her long, very shapely legs.

"You sure rock it, Pipes!" Pete said out loud after several hours of partying. There were many in agreement that evening but it was Pauly who shouted out, "She rocks it in it but I bet she rocks it better, out of it." He winked at Pete who nodded.

The place was packed with beautiful people: tall gorgeous girls with mini skirts and up-dos, guys in trendy suits and leathers, all the money and toys anyone could ever ask for. The highlight of the night for Piper was being introduced to the guys from "The Exemplar", a band with a really innovative sound for the time, infusing rock and dance. She booked an interview with them for the following day.

It was a swinging evening that went to at least the next morning when Piper had to call it quits. She stumbled back to her room with her pumps in one hand and her new dress in the other. She spent most of the evening wrapped in the robe she was given after Pauly unzipped her and carried her into the hot tub in her undies. *"Well it looks like I made someone happy tonight. He was bent on getting me out of my dress"*, she thought. *"Not sure that Deacon would be too impressed with me right about now, though, and not sure even Piper is proud of Piper right now,"* she continued thinking to herself in the third person. It was within minutes she had set her head on the pillow and drifted off.

She slept for hours and when she awoke about mid-afternoon, there was still no sign of Pete. *"Oh Lord! I've got to get that interview for the show with Paul and the others and send some backgrounders for Todd all before 6 o'clock."* As much as she didn't want to be seen heading back to the penthouse, there wasn't much else she could do about it. She bit the bullet, showered and changed into fresh jeans and a tee. She knocked softly on the door of the suite and when no one answered, she tried the knob. It turned and she went in as unobtrusively as possible.

Chapter Twenty-Eight

There were bodies strewn everywhere. She thought it rather looked like a scene out of a 70s rock and roll movie. There were several people flaked out on the couches in the main room, more bodies splayed out in various stages of dress on the plush carpets in the hallways and she thought for sure that the bedrooms would be much more of the same. She didn't really want to go sneaking around to look for whom she needed to interview, so she was thankful that Bernie Howler and Tom Hallett were up seemingly ready and waiting for her on the balcony. That's where she found Pete too. Although she wasn't pleased that he looked like he'd been up doing lines with the band all night, at least she didn't catch him fucking the groupies in the bedrooms, which is where she believed she'd find Pauly and the girls.

"Hey Bernie, thanks for taking the time for us. It's me, Piper Brown from *The Beat*. Didn't know whether you'd remember promising me an interview from last night so I can come back later if you'd prefer?"

"Hell no. The chaps are here. This is just as good a time as any," he said in his Liverpudlian accent. "And I never like to pass up a pretty girl." Then he belched out a big raw guttural sound that was so powerful that Piper thought it might even shatter the glass in the sliding porch doors.

"Yikes! You ill?" Piper asked naively.

"That's my fault. That's a rock' n roll cold, dawlin'! But you stay away from that shite. It's a bugga. It sucks you in pretty quickly and spits you out again even fasta. You're never the same again. You are fresh meat, dawlin'; let's keep it that way. You look like you've got stuff going on. No need to come down to our level."

She always felt conflicted with comments like those; just what club did these people belong to anyway and why wasn't she allowed in? Was that really a compliment or a put down? Were those club-members honestly trying to advise her in a positive way or did they just not want her to 'join'? At the time, she never fully understood or sided one way or the other, but she was a curious person and although there was never any real proof of her partaking, she had often said that she had experimented; however, she always seemed in enough control over her temptations to keep her out of any serious troubles. When I talked to her later in life, she chalked up her good behavior to the power of love that Deacon had over her.

"*Sungrazer* has done amazingly well," she said, speaking with regards to the band's first single from their *The Armed and Dangerous* CD, "and what are your thoughts about this track? Did you know it would do so well? Is it a favourite of yours or a publisher's choice?"

"Yep, me blokes are in agreement. We definitely enjoyed our freedom on that one."

"Are we going to get you out to Toronto some time for this new album?"

"That's in the works, dawlin'. You'd need to check with our scheduling manager for that."

The interview continued for another few minutes during which Piper was trying to think of ways that she could edit out the chopping sound of the drugs in the background so no one could hear it on the radio. As Todd often teased her in the days ahead, "Well, that's what'll make you famous, Piper, doing lines with 'The Exemplar'." *Lovely, Deacon will be so proud!* Was always her response. She grabbed her microphone and started curling up the cord when Pete came up behind her.

"I'm sorry, babe. Do you hate me?"

"No. I don't hate you. It was a fun party. Let's go back to the room now, though," she encouraged. He sauntered behind her sheepishly, defeated, rather like a dog with its tail between its legs.

"I'm going to bed," he said.

"Oh no you don't; you're not getting away that easily, not yet. You've got to help me with this show going live in a few minutes, babe." She set up her notes and tape recorder in the order she'd need them for the broadcast.

"Well what do you need me to do?" Peter asked.

"Can you give me some background songs or provide some colour to my bytes?" Peter thought for a moment and scurried around the hotel room looking accomplished.

"Give me a sec," he said.

"Well that's pretty much all you've got. We're going live 'in 3...2...1...', they heard Todd say through the satellite feed.

"Welcome to another edition of *Spin Me Round* on *The Beat*; I'm your host Todd Sullivan here in Toronto while Piper Brown is jazzing it up in New Orleans. Pipes, how's it going? Where are you exactly?" Just as he asked that, Pete began playing the harmonica that he'd picked up at one of the shops the previous day.

"Well as you can hear in the background, Todd, lots of merriment, for sure; there's never a dull moment on Bourbon Street with all the 'beads for boobies' and 'live sex shows'. We walked from one end to the other stopping in for a drink at each club we came across and by the end, we pretty much were the live sex act." Piper and Todd laughed simultaneously as Pete played the final notes of his harmonica solo.

"Thanks babe!" Piper kissed Pete on the cheek during the first commercial break. "You make me sound so good!"

"It's all you, baby," he said as he made his way into the bedroom.

Once the broadcast was completed, she joined Pete for a nap. They had promised Pauly that they'd be at his club gig that night, so she asked for a 'wake-up call' for 10:30 pm. The phone rang far too soon. They both felt groggy and weak.

"This has got to be the best diet ever. Never eat, sleep and party all the time. No wonder celebrities are so fucking skinny. I literally feel sick to my stomach with the thought of food but I've got to eat something or I won't make it out tonight," Piper said.

Pete agreed, "We'll grab something on the way."

The club was not in the famous French Quarter where they had been staying so they thought they'd ask the cabbie for some fast-bite recommendations in the vicinity.

"There's a Johnny's Po-Boys nearby. So close I can drop you there and you can walk to the club. How about it, sir?"

"Make it happen," Pete replied.

DJ Paul E was good, nothing special really, but good. Piper thought their lack of enthusiasm though, probably stemmed from being over-tired. They didn't stay too much longer than his full set and caught a cab back to the Quarter.

The next day was the couple's last full day in the city and so they did all the sights: the waterfront, the horse-drawn carriage ride through Jackson Square, Saint Louis Cemetery, and Preservation Hall. They thought a dinner at the famous Brennan's Restaurant would be a perfect cap to their holiday.

"Pinch me, I feel like I'm dreaming" Piper gasped as they entered the renowned and historical dinner house. Piper stopped in front of a plaque with the building's history embossed onto a metal sheet. She read, "It was built in 1795 and it had changed hands several times over the years. Its founder, Owen Edward Brennan and his wife, Nellie, opened the actual restaurant, in 1943, which at the time was called the Old Absinthe House, the secret hangout of pirate Jean Lafitte. Brennan as the newest proprietor, once staged lifelike mannequins of the notorious Lafitte and Andrew Jackson in what he called 'the Secret Room' - the very room in which the pact was supposedly made in New Orleans' defense against the British at the Battle of New Orleans. Some of the early dinner guests were Presidents Franklin D. Roosevelt, Dwight D. Eisenhower and Admiral Earnest King."

Piper moved further into the grand mezzanine and saw that the walls were adorned with photographs of one famous person to the next, signed and framed. Countless movie stars from Bob Hope, Anthony Hopkins, Paul Newman, Robert Redford and Elizabeth Taylor considered Brennan's their home while visiting the Crescent City. Pete took a hold of Piper's hand as they were escorted to their table.

"This way madam, monsieur."

As they walked through the gallery they saw a variety of dining areas with courtyard seating to second-floor balconies. Piper was still in awe by the time Peter pulled a chair out for her at their table in the grand ballroom.

"Wow!" Piper sighed, "This is the ultimate dream for me!"

Pete grinned, "And we haven't even had the dessert yet." Pete was right, the famous *Bananas Foster* was unlike Piper had ever experienced.

"Thanks Pete!" Piper couldn't say it enough. "From soup to nuts, that's the most delicious and elegant dinner I've ever had and it was so great to share it with you. If only we could stay in this moment forever!" Piper wished, in irony of the events that were about to unravel. And as all good honeymoons must come to an end, it was just a matter of weeks before theirs came to a crashing conclusion.

~~~

"Oh Deacon! You grew! You're such a big boy now." She bent down, lifted him into her arms and swung him around. They pirouetted and landed together softly on the plush family room carpet.

"I'm four, mommy!" He said indicating two chubby fingers on each hand. He'd actually turned four just before they left but it was still new to the toddler.

"You're how many?" She teased as he repeated the action as children do.

"I missed you so much, sweetie. I don't think I'll ever go away again without you."

"I missed you too, mommy. Did you bring me back anything from 'Nodeans'?" He asked sounding very sophisticated despite the mispronunciation.

"As a matter of fact, check my pockets. Something may have slipped into one of them."

Piper had purchased a replica harmonica for Deacon to imitate Pete's figuring that he'd want whatever Pete had anyway, and besides, there wasn't anything better than having her two most favourite men serenade her. Even badly played harmonicas can be sentimental given the proper circumstances. When his hand found the toy he pulled it out and began to blow and gurgle to his heart's content.

"That's a good toy. I'm going to show Pete how I can play it," he said between big puffs of breath.

Piper bent down to his level again and gave him another hug. "I think you should just wait for a little while. Pete's gone down into his studio to catch up on the work he's missed from our trip. Maybe you could practice a little more and you'd really surprise him later with just how good you are at playing it?" With that, he nodded, readjusted the toy to his lips and marched and blew back and forth across the floor.

~~~

When Piper got back to the station the day following their arrival, she was issued a pink slip. Her heart sank.

"I'm so sorry, Pipes," Todd said as he hugged her. "I really don't know what I'm going to do without you around here. We're a team and we've been a team now for like 10 years."

She didn't say much other than to ask him if they could do a 'farewell' show together. "Afraid not; that's not allowed. Once they let you go, you're gone, no goodbyes. They're afraid that you'll use the power of the airwaves to do something crazy like..."

"Like asking your listeners to plead your case to the owners?" She asked.

"Yea, maybe something like that or worse, make threats or hold them hostage."

"Hey, now there's an idea!" Piper perked up. "Just kidding!" Todd hugged her again while big, juicy teardrops streamed down her face.

"Love you," he said.

Their bodies began to sway as they sang what had become 'their song':

"Dancing with tears in our eyes,
Living out a memory of a love that died."

Chapter Twenty-Nine

"Where are you, Piper?" She heard Pete say on the other end of the telephone line. He seemed to be trying to keep tabs on her a lot lately, she mentioned to me the last time we spoke. What this new interest he had in her, she wasn't sure, but ever since she lost her job at *The Beat*, it seemed to her that he never let her leave the house without notice. "I asked Julie to come and sit for Deacon when you hadn't returned. You knew I had to be downtown for a recording session. I'm worried about you. What's up? Where are you?"

"I'm driving home from the airport. Didn't I tell you I was meeting an old friend there today?" Piper sounded confused.

"No, otherwise I wouldn't have been waiting for you. I would've called Julie in right away. But there's no worries now; you're almost home right?" Pete resolved.

Piper was pulling in the driveway. "Yep. Will you be late?" she asked.

"Probably another all-nighter, sweetie," he said as he hung up. Although he was always keeping track of her whereabouts, he was much more evasive about his. So Piper had to get used to living like two ships passing in the night, and she didn't like it very much. She believed what Pete had been telling her. He was the best recording engineer in town and he ran a very busy studio in the most prolific area of the city. And in that particular project, he had been hired to keep DJ Cool on track, literally. He had to master the final cuts on TMC Music's latest *Hot Traxx* Album. As talented as Cool was, he was renowned to be a bit stubborn in getting down to business. He would come into work already as high as a kite or surrounded by 'a bevy of beautiful creatures', to which Pete, of course, was no stranger. If Piper's propensity to jealousy was bad before she lost her job, then it became insurmountable afterwards. Her self-esteem was at an all-time low. She continually found it unnerving, to even be reminded about his 'work environment' and her lack of one.

"Hey look Pipes, if I wanted that kind of life, I could've had it, but I chose you!" He said to Piper on a number of occasions. That seemed to appease her only externally. Piper was beginning to mount miles of suspicions between them but continued to hide her genuine insecurities. She decided she was going to pop into the studio later once Deacon was fast asleep. She'd call Julie in after 8 to sit for her while she went out.

She prepared another plate of mac and cheese, which Deek ate in fistfuls, while she managed to nab a few straggling noodles for herself, before she cleared the dishes away. *"I'm feeling rather anxious. I wonder if I've forgotten to take my meds?"* she thought and went to the cupboard to retrieve her pillbox. She popped the last remaining ones into her mouth and flung her head back with a gulp of water to ease their ride.

"I'm going to have to talk to the doctor about either upping the prescription or changing meds because I just don't feel like they're having much of an impact lately," she thought to herself.

After her third and final reading of *Goodnight Moon* with Deacon already snoring away beside her in his 'big boy bed', she slipped out of it, covered him up, turned his night light on and flicked off the main switch. She then went into her own room to fix her hair and reapply her make-up. She stared at herself in the mirror.

Who was she really? Patricia Jane Brown, christened by her Irish parents, PJ, the Irish school girl or Piper Brown, the once successful radio broadcaster. Was she a mother, a wife, or a professional career woman? She felt like she was outside herself looking in. Her vision became clouded and foggy so she blinked to clear the reflected image. The face in the mirror disappeared and she gasped. She blinked again and it returned all distorted. The third time, her vision doubled. She sat staring at two faces in the mirror. She shook her head then closed her eyes.

There comes a time in everyone's life when they look in the mirror and they see something different, someone different. She felt weathered and worn. Her eyes were tired, maybe even sullen. The luster in her hair had gone and her normally tanned skin appeared hollow and pale. Was it possible to be the same person she once was, with all the things in life she'd experienced? And with all the people she'd met and all the wisdom she'd gained from getting older? Can one gaze in the mirror and convince themselves they can still do the impossible, still be fearless? She was filled with doubts. She slid her make-up bag into her purse, grabbed her keys and sat on the easy chair nearest the front door to wait for Julie.

"I won't be too long, Jules," she promised. "Sorry for calling you out on such short notice but I'll make it worth your while. Please help yourself to whatever you'd like."

"It's never a problem, Piper. I like being here."

She sped away in the two-seater Del Sol that Pete had bought her, a little anxious at what her surprise visit was going to uncover. Within minutes she was on the Gardiner and off at the studio's exit; when she pulled up to the intersection of James and St. Paul and stopped at the lights, she felt a really uneasy feeling, like something bad was going to happen. Her stomach was churning and all tied up in knots and her skin became pocked with goose bumps. She brought her hands up to her face because of the pressure she felt in her head...

~~

"The Stein Way" studio, named after Pete and his favorite piano maker, was quaint and elegant. It was well appointed and trendy in keeping with the area and Pete's eclectic tastes. As it was well after hours, there was no receptionist to greet her and the lights had been dimmed to conserve energy. She noticed flickering beams down the hallway and recognized the heavy electronic drum beats from Pete's Pro-Tools mixing program.

"Hey Pete!" She called out towards the music. "Petey?" She asked as she walked closer. When she got to the doorway of the interior mixing room she saw Pete and DJ Cool and a few other familiar faces, as well as some scantily clad go-go girls, in the throes of a studio rave. She stuck around long enough to make eye contact with Pete. She'd seen enough to know that she didn't want any part of it. It made her physically ill to think that she'd trusted Pete with her love and devotion and had brought Deacon into this mess as well.

She turned as quickly as she came, bolted out the studio's front door and sped away. It wasn't long before she was back at that same intersection, with that same uneasy feeling; her stomach was churning and all tied up in knots and her skin became pocked with goose bumps; she brought her hands up to her face because of the pressure in her head; this time it was a pounding headache and a crushing heaviness into her chest. It was so intense that she let out a blood hurtling scream. She was powerless to the menace that was preying upon her soul and ripping her heart in half. The pain was so severe that she felt nauseous. The part of her that she still controlled rocked back and forth behind her seatbelt to help eradicate her compulsion to vomit.

~~

It was some time later that she had found her way back. She hadn't wanted Julie to see that she'd been crying, so she tiptoed in through the garage door and kept the lights turned low. Thankfully, Julie had fallen asleep on the couch.

She nudged her gently and said, "I'm home now. You're welcome to stay. I really don't think Pete's coming home tonight and I've got the day off so I'll be sleeping in. The spare room is free. Do as you please. Thanks again, eh?"

Julie mumbled a gravelly, "Oh thanks. I'll stay but I'll be up and gone early."

Piper didn't even have the strength to pull her clothes off and hop into bed. She fell face first onto the bed and pillow and cried again until she had no more tears left to cry.

"Mommy. Come and throw the ball to me!" 4-year-old quarterback-bound Deacon exclaimed with glee as he pulled at her jeans belt loop. "Didn't you get in your jammies last night? Can I sleep in my clothes too?"

She rolled over and pulled him into a bear hug. "You're my sweet angel boy! I love you so much!"

"I love you too, mommy! Are you my girlfriend?"

"You betcha and we're gonna have a date night, really soon. Okay?"

He moved close into her face and despite her efforts to avoid his eyes, he said, "Have you been crying? 'Cuz your face is all dirty."

The floodgates opened wide with his innocent concern and she began to weep uncontrollably. He held her close, patted her head and said, "There, there, I'm here now. We'll be okay, mommy. I'll look after you."

Before long the two were giggling and pillow fighting. There was no sign of Pete all morning and despite her anger, she also felt relieved. She didn't want to have to deal with him while Deacon was in her care. Just after lunch she phoned Rich to see if he was still good for their switch at 2 pm.

"Looking forward to seeing him again, Piper! For sure, I'll be there, with bells on!"

She made a quick lunch for the two of them and took him into the backyard to throw the ball around. They weren't out for 15 minutes before Pete pulled up in his convertible, looking sheepish and hung-over. He managed a meek, "Hi kids!" and went inside. Piper grabbed Deacon by the hand and walked him over to the park across the street.

"Do you want me to push you while you swing?" She asked him.

"Sure, but I'd like it better if I could sit on your lap while you swing," he said.

"Oh Deek," she complained. "You're too big now. And I'm not strong enough to hold you and push us both." He looked sad with his lower lip flipped over.

"Deacon, you sure know how to get to your mommy," Piper said. "Okay, we can try!"

She grabbed the chain for the nearest swing and sat her butt down on it. Deacon crawled on top and placed his chubby hands on both chains like how she told him to do it in the past. She then placed her left hand on top of his and held him around his waist with her right; she walked him back as far as her strength would carry them, pushed off and let them go.

"Weeeeee!" Deacon screamed for joy.

"Okay Deeks, help me pump!" Back and forth they went further and higher each time. Within a few minutes she started to feel like herself again. She had hoped that, that moment would last forever. She wanted time to stand still.

"You are definitely my special angel! I don't know what I'd ever do without you!" With their final ascent, she said, "Are you ready to jump?"

He gleefully replied, "Whenever you are!" And she let go of the swing. They flew into the air together with hoots of laughter. Piper threw her body in front of his to break his fall and he landed with a thud on top of her head.

The last thing she remembered was his sweet, little boy giggles as everything around her went black.

Chapter Thirty

There were sounds of sirens and beeps and horns and bells. Piper had no idea where they were all coming from and where she was. Her vision was blurry and her body felt that it was being suffocated under a heavy weight. She tried to blink away the confusion but her eyelids seemed to be glued shut and all she could see was a dark red. She tried to swallow and her throat was tight and dry and her tongue felt foreign to her teeth. She tried to reach her arm up to touch her face and nothing happened. She had no strength. She could not move. She could not speak.

Amid the confusion, she tried to focus on a few recognizable vibrations. The first one sounded like a beating of a heart. *Yes it was! Was it hers? Was she alive?* Then she thought she heard a breath but it was very mechanical; it sounded more like an inhalation made by a fictitious monster. *Was she on a breathing machine?* Everything was so dark and so hollow. She stopped trying to focus for a moment and the noises ceased; all was quiet, even the heartbeat. She felt a warm glow and the darkness seemed to lift. Her body, once heavy and crushed, became ethereal and weightless. The sensation was so pleasant that it almost made her want to smile. She began to float upwards with her head and shoulders being raised higher than her hips. She imagined herself to be an astronaut in zero gravity. She allowed the force of the white light to guide her. When her body stopped floating, she again, tried to open her eyes. This time, they flickered and opened. Beneath her was a woman's body, mangled and bloody.

As much as the sight was physically horrible, she had no abilities to react. She felt neither pain nor anguish. She watched from her perch, the surgeons and assistants work away to try to bring back some life into her motionless body. Spoken words began to become audible.

"Her heart was beating when we brought her in here. We can get it going again; she's young and strong. Bring the defib, stat!" urged one of the chief surgeons of the trauma team.

They intubated her and hooked her up to the ECG monitor to keep tabs on her vitals: pulse, breathing and her blood pressure. Her heart, although was beating however faintly when they brought her in, had just ceased. The team of emergency personnel worked quickly to set up the defibrillator paddles and administer CPR. With one shock, there was nothing.

"I know her. She's a friend of my wife's. She's got a young boy," said one of the E.R nurses. "C'mon baby, you know it's not your time yet. Come back to us, do it for your son!"

The particular difficulty in Piper's case was that the chest cavity had appeared to be smashed in with the possibility of a collapsed lung or broken sternum. The doctors had to be extra cautious in the placement of the electrodes so as not to create further stress while still focusing on the return of the heartbeat. They would have to perform surgery to repair the damaged lung but not until her heartbeat and breathing were restored.

The second shock riveted her body and within milliseconds, her heartbeat came back into arrhythmia, sending the lines on the ECG graph scattered randomly in both the northerly and southerly directions. It was several seconds later before her scan stabilized and resumed into its more normal pattern.

"Ok, we got her back."

Piper felt her spirit start to descend in the same manner that it raised, like a balloon losing its helium, and within another second or two she felt the weight return to her body as it was pressed firmly down onto the operating table. Then everything went black.

~~~

"We're interrupting this broadcast this evening to report a serious accident involving our much beloved Piper Brown. She's in Toronto Grace Hospital fighting for her life. She was involved in a head-on collision at the intersection of James and St. Paul downtown just after 8 pm tonight. She was the lone occupant of the vehicle she was driving. The driver of the other vehicle was pronounced dead at the scene. We've been told she has had severe head trauma, broken ribs, a collapsed lung, and multiple contusions and lacerations. We ask that you all pray for her tonight as she undergoes emergency surgery. We'll keep you posted with news as we hear more. This is Todd Sullivan reporting for *The Beat.*"

Ironically, I heard the news broadcast in that very way while I was driving. I rarely listened to *The Beat* after they let Piper go. I worked for a competing network just outside the city so it was a bit of a conflict of interest in the first place for me to be a regular listener but I had been willing to make the sacrifice on occasion to hear her voice when I needed to feel closer to her.

My heart jumped into my mouth and I let out a guttural cry. *"Oh my God! I've got to go to see her, pray for her. C'mon baby, pull through. You've just got to hang on!"*

By the time I arrived to the hospital, most of the Browns were already there; Jonny and his wife Annie, Emily, and Finn, as well as Peter Stein, an elderly woman who was probably Pete's mother and several others I didn't recognize from Piper's descriptions; they were all huddled together in the waiting room to hear further word from the surgeons. Todd arrived shortly thereafter with the largest bouquet of sunflowers I'd ever seen. Piper would've been touched to see so many come to her side bearing her favourite flowers.

Without having been properly introduced to the family, I just watched from the sidelines. I didn't want to be intrusive but I needed to be nearby. It was 2 in the morning by the time there was any word from surgery. At 2:03 am, two surgeons came out of the emergency room and walked stoically toward Jonny and Emily. They pulled their masks down and one gave the other a nod to begin. I moved in closer so I could hear what they had to say.

"After 4 hours of surgery, she is now stabilized. Her heart had stopped for a brief moment while we worked vehemently to repair her collapsed lung. We're hoping that it was not long enough to do any permanent damage. It was touch and go there for a while, but we think she's out of immediate danger. She needs to stay in an induced coma while we see whether the repairs we've made are sufficient and to prevent her from getting any infections. She's a very strong lady and she's very fortunate to have so many people here to support her. That always helps in the healing process."

"Thank God! And thank you doctors!" Emily said as Jonny held her up from the waiting room chair in which she had been sitting for the past turbulent hours. She seemed frailer than the way Piper had often described her to me. But given the circumstances it's no wonder she looked nearing her 70 years of age.

"Can you tell by her injuries, how and when this happened?" Jonny asked the doctors.

"You'd really have to talk to the first-response team to make this conclusive but she was brought in just minutes past 8 o'clock and it appeared she was heading eastbound towards town rather than westbound towards her home when she was hit head-on by another vehicle. The lone occupant of the other car was pronounced dead at the scene. Although badly bleeding Piper did have a pulse. Her vital signs were present but weak."

Pete interjected. "I can pretty much verify that she was on her way to my studio for a visit as I've spoken with our babysitter and she confirms that Piper had just left the house a few minutes prior to the accident and that's where she had claimed she was going. And I was in the studio by myself at the time and didn't see her. I had a client in with me earlier but he was out getting take-out for us just before 8 o'clock."

"She will be out for a while; you'd all be better off to go home and get some proper rest. We can have the nurse on duty take your number and call you if there's any change. We don't anticipate that however, for at least another 24 hours. So go home and rest and come back tomorrow."

The doctors turned and walked back down the long corridor to intensive care.

Pete left his mother's side and moved towards Emily. He reached for her hands and knelt down in front of her. "I am very sorry for all of this. I feel like I'm to blame. She was coming to surprise me and she didn't make it. I am so sorry. I'm going to do whatever it takes to get her through this. She and Deacon are my angels. I feel your pain. Please let me know if there's anything I can do for you and I'll be there." Pete's mother smiled at him and nodded to Emily, demonstrating the pride she had in her son. He stood up and let go of her hands.

I stood in silence down the long hallway between the waiting and operating rooms so that I could listen to what was being said without being too intrusive.

"I'd like to add to what Pete has said for you folks; whatever you need, I'll be here. Piper is really important to so many people, more than even she realizes. I think we all need to stay positive. I overheard the news from the surgeons and that sounded pretty hopeful, so we should all go and do as they say now and rest up for her recovery. She's so strong..." Todd said.

"Strong like bull!" They interrupted and said in unison.

"...that when she's ready to face the future, we're going to have to be one step ahead of her to even try to keep up!" He continued teasingly. *"Gee that really worked!"* I thought, after seeing some smiles adorn their faces. *"It helped to put her spirit back into the room."*

"Where's Deacon?" Todd asked, knowing full well he must be sleeping somewhere; after all, it was the middle of the night. Pete added that he was still in his bed at his house and that Julie would be there until Rich gets there to pick him up in the morning.

"I'll leave my number with you folks. Please let me know if you need me. I'd really like to stay connected with Piper's progress."

I turned and walked down the hall and out to my car. It was going to be a long, painful drive home at this hour so I turned on the radio. And as I was beginning to believe ever since I met Piper, there was no such thing as coincidences. Things all happened for a reason. The song playing on the station that I had not purposefully selected before I got out of the car, was Robert Miles', *Children*, Piper's new favourite song. I wondered what it all meant. When I finally pulled the car into my driveway, gathered my belongings from the back seat and headed toward the house, the sun was already starting to peak up along the horizon. I sat on the front porch and gazed up toward the heavens. I thought to myself just what did the big guy have in store for our beautiful angel? She had so much life left in her, so much spirit; *she was a child of the universe, no less than the trees and the stars.* "Where did that come from?" I thought to myself. That had to have been from Piper. She was always reciting *The Desiderata. "She'll be all right"*, I thought. *She has a right to be here.* More *Desiderata.*

Chapter Thirty-One

"Morning sweetie," my wife Deb said as she rolled over to me and tucked her head under my chin the way she so tenderly does.

"Morning," I echoed.

"Did you hear anything more about Piper?" She asked.

"Just what they've announced on the radio. I believe she's out of immediate danger, but they have to wait and see what damages have incurred," I said matter-of-factly.

"And the boy?" She asked.

"Well, he's not been included in news about his mother so far, and I don't get the feeling that the Browns would include him in her recovery, from everything that Piper had mentioned to me about Deacon's father. My belief is that they don't want to upset him. Why do you ask about him?"

"Well, you were talking in your sleep rather mumbling fitfully and kept saying something about children so I figured that you were concerned about him. They really need to include him in all this. I'm sure that she'd respond quicker and heal faster with the aid of that special boy. Any mother would."

"I realize that," I said.

It was in the evening on the second day when I heard Todd on the radio with an update on her condition.

Apparently they moved Piper out of surgery into the long-term intensive care unit and she was now allowed visitors. "Has she made any progress or come around at all?" Deb asked me, hopefully.

"Not that I've heard. But it is good news that the doctors have moved her into the I.C.U," I replied.

"Have you been in to see her yet? She asked me, "Because I'd like to go if you want to?"

"Well. Her family is there and as it is now, they'll only let 2 visitors in at a time so I think we'd probably just be in the way. If she continues like this for a bit, they'll need some spelling off in the evenings, particularly her mother Emily; she's not strong enough to withstand the stress of this for long periods of time, so I don't want to create more problems, just be there to help them out."

"I'll keep my ears open for more broadcasts, Steve," she offered.

~~

Todd arrived to the hospital rotunda on her fifth day post-surgery. He had been told that she had remained unresponsive but her vitals were strong and stable. He was to follow the yellow lines marked along the walls and floors to find his way to the I.C.U where Finn was waiting in the room just outside the nurses' station.

"Hi! Thanks for coming in. Did you bring any music?" Finn asked and Todd nodded.

"I brought a Discman. They say this often helps to bring them back." She handed him the player with headphones.

"They're still only allowing 2 in at a time and Pete's in there now, so you go ahead with the nurse and I'll wait for you out here," Finn said.

"Thank you, Finn," he said.

"She'll want to see you. Pete is so distraught; I'm not sure that's helping her much. We've gotta stay positive."

He followed the nurse through the double doors into a small-chambered area that had been divided up into 6 or 8 curtained rooms. She pulled back the drape from the far corner and he almost gasped out loud when he saw her. He would certainly not have recognized her had he not known it was she behind all the bandages and machines. Pete turned to look at him; his eyes were hollow and dark. He looked like he'd been crying. He was holding her hand.

The nurse asked him if he was all right with the new visitor. He stood out of his chair that had been placed at her bedside and gave Todd a big hug. Then he turned back to Piper and said, "I'll be back, kiddo. You've got another visitor. You're certainly not shy of people who love you, babe."

"Thanks Pete!" Todd concurred.

Todd stood at the side of her bed with the bouquet of sunflowers still flourishing in a vase on the other. He put his homemade CD into the Discman and adjusted the headphones around her neck. That became more of a task than what he was expecting as her head was so heavily bandaged. It was difficult to get the headset around them and close enough to her ears but with a little finagling, it was ready to go. He turned on the player and adjusted the volume. The room was filled with the sound of soft, happy tones that permeated through the cushioned ear pads.

"We'll see if that works. I recorded your favourites," he said. "I didn't ask but I figured you'd probably want our song included," as *Dancing With Tears in My Eyes* could be heard, followed by *Children*. For a normally happy-go-lucky funnyman, he looked like he was almost going to cry. Her eyes remained closed but there were a few seconds of strange 'bleeps' on the heart monitor and the breathing machine seemed to pump louder than it had but perhaps that was a figment of an overly active imagination or a sign of wishful thinking.

After seeing the concern in Pete's face and reading his body language, Todd thought that perhaps this was not the most appropriate time for him to see Piper just yet. She, as Pete mentioned, did have a host of people nearby who loved her and were showing their concern. He made it a point that this would likely be a one-time visit unless there was some change or the Browns needed some help. He really didn't want to be in the way. These kinds of crises were difficult enough for family members to endure without outside pressures, if they had felt that way about him.

"My God Piper, look what you've gone and done," Todd said to her teasingly. "You've always had a thing for shock-jocks haven't you?" That man was hilarious. I always admired the rapport the two of them shared.

"Jokes," he continued. "You're always telling me to keep it light. Isn't that the way of the Irish? They laugh in the face of adversity. You told me that as a young girl you'd be punished for giggling in the middle of a Remembrance Day service as soon as you saw the old veterans crying at the cenotaph. How dare you? You naughty girl! I'm sure Emily would've tanned your hide for that one!" That even got me laughing. Still no sign of movement in her face but Todd could've sworn that her expression had changed however marginally.

I remember a funny story that Piper had told me about Todd. He was known to keep everyone in stitches. They were in an underground parking lot together to attend some function. It was the kind of pay parking for which a machine was provided. It was clearly marked that one was supposed to flash their ticket stub in the space provided in front of a window. Todd grabbed the ticket, got out of the car and knocked on the window pretending to wait for an attendant. He scratched his head and looked pensive, just to add to the scenario. She called out the window to him to 'flash', meaning the ticket, so he raised his shirt and danced around. "Quite the card," Piper would say about him. I was thinking he seemed a little like the Brit comedian Mr. Bean at times.

If you asked him what he thought of that comparison he would have said, "No. I'm more like Ellen (Degeneres)," at which much laughter would ensue. Ellen had recently 'come out' and that, and the fact that there was a certain physical similarity, very slender with short-cropped blonde hair, simply added to his comedic bit. There was another comedy piece he'd endorse around his appearance that I heard him use once with Piper on the radio. Someone had thought Piper looked like a younger version of the famous tennis player Chrissy Evert and his response was, "Well that's good because I've been told I look like her opponent, Martina Navratilova; although, her arms are much bigger than mine!" Again, the physical similarity added to the hilarity of it all.

"Have they had Deacon in to see you yet, baby?" He asked her.

There was no significant change in her expression but he again thought there was a little colour appear in the part of her cheeks that were visible and free of bandages.

"He has an amazing affect on you and always has. He could pull you through this; I'd put money on it."

While he stared at Piper in all her wrapping he was troubled with a second thought, *"But perhaps it's not a good idea. He's just a little guy and it could spook him."*

I didn't agree but there wasn't much I could do. Kids are resilient and he's pretty mature or at least I believe he was from everything that Piper had indicated to me. I had hoped that Todd would stick with his gut instinct on that one.

"Maybe I should talk to Finn about it, eh Piper? I don't think I'll get anywhere with Richard. He's pretty old school that way and Pete is, well...you saw him. He's a bit messed up." He bent down close to her ear, lifted the headphones away and whispered, "You'll be all right, Pipes. We're here; we need you and we love you."

I wanted to cry and hold her, to never let any harm come to her and to never let her go. It sure appeared that Todd had similar sentiments.

~~

Another few days had passed and still no word about a change in condition for Piper. It had been 9 days since the accident. I had spoken to my doctor to find out just how long this coma could and should continue. He told me that after serious head trauma and surgery, physicians might want to keep the patient in an induced coma for a few days anyway, to remove the patient from any possible unnecessary pain but after that, it was anybody's prognosis. On averages, perhaps a week to 10 days, it should take a person to respond to stimuli. I began to worry.

~~

"She always claims that he has saved her from so much. I think you should try to get Richard to bring him in to see her. She hasn't even opened her eyes yet. If she senses he's nearby, she might respond," Todd pleaded with Finn.

"Okay," she said. "I'll try again and maybe this time I'll get him to bring Deacon in himself, because he wouldn't let me do it. If he was with Deacon, then he'd know whether he was handling it properly and could react accordingly."

~~

Finn called Todd the next day with the good news. Richard was going to bring Deacon in and he was to meet her at the nurses' station at the hospital at 2 o'clock. The moments just couldn't click by fast enough. My heart was racing as I waited hourly for the latest news updates.

Again Todd followed the yellow line to the intensive care unit. *What a miserable thought of feeling comfortable and familiar in this sterile environment?* He thought to himself. One could only imagine how the Brown family felt after living on this hospital floor for the past week and a half.

"They're in there now," Finn said as she hugged him. It's ironic how before last week, they may have passed each other by on the street without barely any recognition; yet now, under tragic circumstances, they were embracing one another for support.

Although it felt like hours had passed while he waited in silence, it was about 15 minutes before a nurse came out with a big wide smile. "Deacon has some really good news for you both," she beamed. "He and his dad will be out in another minute or two."

After ten days of feeling like the world had slipped off its axis, it suddenly felt right-sided again. I breathed a heavy sigh lifting the weight of Atlas from my shoulders when I heard the news. The constant stabbing I'd felt in my chest for the past week or so finally subsided and I could breathe fully and deeply again.

Deacon came out first carrying an empty gift bag. He ran towards Finn's open arms as she knelt to embrace him.

"Big hugs for Finny, thanks Deeks! So how did it go?" They were all eager to hear the news.

"Well mommy...she heard my voice when I first opened the curtain and I think I woke her up. The nurse said she's been very tired and has been sleeping. But I think she's not tired anymore because her eyes were open and she looked at me. She's not ready to play though. I brought her a stuffie football. She might still be too tired for that. She squeezed it though and felt how soft it was. She squeezed my hand too. Not too hard. I'm glad." The sentences were flying out of the little boy's mouth. His positive energy was contagious.

"Hello!" Richard said as he came through the double doors behind Deacon. He nodded to Todd, not knowing who he was exactly but trusting that he was there for the same purpose. "It's true, whatever Deacon has told you. She's conscious, hasn't spoken or really moved yet. Her eyes are responsive. She certainly recognized Deacon's voice firstly then his face, once he got closer, so she's got some of her faculties back. The nurses are doing the initial tests now. The doctor has been called in to do a further examination. We should know really soon about her state and her prognosis for recovery."

"That's such good news!" I said to myself when I heard and reminded myself to thank God for hearing my prayers.

Chapter Thirty-Two

Pain. For a simple four-letter word, it has the most extensive dictionary definition of any other. It is defined by physical, emotional or mental suffering, with synonyms of ache, throb, anguish, distress, sensation and suffering. It comes from the Latin word *"poen"* meaning punishment. It has been widely researched by masters and PHD students everywhere, and the center of focus for physiologists, doctors, biologists, and psychiatrists. It affects the trinity and all capacities: the body, the mind and the spirit. Its symptoms dominate multi-billion prescriptions a year with costs ranging exponentially more. It is one of the most intangible feelings one can ever experience; therefore it is one of the most difficult symptoms to prognosticate, find a remedy or cure. Try as we might to rid ourselves of pain, by trying to locate its source of origin, it seems inevitable and even inherent to the human condition. One could go so far as to say one cannot live without pain. It is its pure essence that indicates that we are alive. It has such a range of variable sensations, from pressure to actual distress. Does a baby cry out in pain or merely sensation? How is it that one woman can withstand the agony of childbirth without anesthetic while another cannot? Researchers are now classifying 'shadow pain' as a new form of physiological distress, thus proving that memory is so closely linked to our painful experiences and ultimately our existences. And try as we might to compensate for one's pain and suffering, to put a dollar sign on its expense, just how does one put a value on something so invaluable?

If pain were an indicator as to whether one is alive, then there would be no debate for Piper. The long weeks, months and years moving forward were a grueling testament to her strength and courage. If she had not felt the unconditional love, trust and integrity of her little boy, she claimed to me often, then she would never have been able to endure it.

~~

The Browns all took turns taking Deacon in to see and spend time with Piper in recovery. The doctors all said that her progress was much more rapid when he was around her; he was a joy to everyone who met him, in fact.

"What are we going to do without him here, the patients adore him? Such maturity for a little boy; such an old soul; doesn't he make you feel that maybe he existed in another time or place and he's only in the here and now to help us all through something?" Piper reiterated to me some of the lines she heard the nurses say about Deacon while she was in recovery.

Right from the outset her responses were acute but her ability to communicate was much slower and that caused her no end of frustration. They brought in a speech pathologist to analyze what were her key impairments in cognition then went back to square one in assembling her phonetic spectrum to aid in fluency. Her physical recovery seemed to improve in a more fluid manner. Having been a fitness instructor for many years, she already had the background knowledge of how the network of nerves to muscles, tendons, bones and ligaments were all interconnected and her general superior health leading into the accident was certainly advantageous.

Deacon was in awe of all the 'training' machines that filled the physiotherapist's room where Piper received her assisted workouts. Once the clinicians learned that he could be trusted, not the typical 4 year old running around getting into trouble, they set some of the cables up for his weight to strength ratio, so he could maneuver them himself, a true athlete in the making. He also helped the trainers put Piper into some of the seated resistance machines at first then when she was well enough to begin cardio, he would demonstrate to her what she was supposed to do on them.

"Quite the team we have here," Dr. O'Reilly said to the two of them after seeing for himself the kind of therapy that Piper was undergoing. "You're a big help to your mama. Thank you Deacon!"

Piper nodded and placed her hand on his cheek. He reached up and linked his arm around her waist the way a shorter man would embrace a taller girlfriend. "Let's meet next week, shall we? I hear you'll be going home today. I want to check in with you after you've settled in," the doctor concluded.

"Hear that mommy? You're coming home. This is kinda like my birthday only better. It's like your birthday!" Deacon exuded such energy. "So are we going to stay at dad's house or Pete's house?"

Piper looked sad as her eyes caught his. "Ppphheeeet..." She tried to say before Deacon interrupted.

"Goody. I haven't stayed with daddy Pete in a long time," he said.

~~

Piper was getting around fairly well on crutches but Pete didn't think it was wise to force her to negotiate stairs so he had a wall pulled down between his office and spare room on the main floor to convert it into a mini gym and living space for her.

She still needed a special bed, one that could raise her head and shoulders above her heart, so he had one installed before she arrived. He'd also arranged and hired for personal trainers and therapists to come to assist her as required. He was good and ready for her homecoming.

"Mom look. Pete has done all this for you. Doesn't it make you happy?" he noticed that she was weeping. Pete hugged her when he saw her in pain. Deacon joined them for a 'group' hug.

"There's a problem, though," Deacon interrupted. "What's that big boy?" Pete asked.

"Where am I gonna sleep? There's no bed in here for me."

"Well that's easy to fix," Pete replied. "We'll wheel yours in here, pronto!"

"But it's all the way upstairs?" Deacon still looked concerned.

"Isn't it going to be fun to push it down the stairs and watch it fly?" Pete teased.

Both Piper and Deacon turned quickly to catch Pete's expression, and then they all broke out into laughter.

~~

The first few days of Piper's return were relatively happy for the couple. Deacon's enthusiasm within his new environment was contagious and both Piper and Pete felt comforted in being reunited. Piper was still in a great deal of pain, though. She had a host of medications she was taking repeatedly every 4 hours, which seemed to lose their effect within 3, which meant the last hour several times a day were excruciating.

Pete seemed to be able to withstand her painful periods better while Deacon was there; he was a bit of a buffer to help, but half the time Deacon lived with Richie and thus it was just Pete alone to manage her. The guilt he felt over Piper's predicament combined with the constant suffering she was enduring, took its toll on him. He spent more and more time away from the house, hiring more and more professionals to help her and by the end of the second month after the accident, he was beside himself with grief.

"I can't do this for much longer," Piper overhead him say to their friend Ronny on the phone. "Well, I dunno. I might take the network job offer and move my studios to L.A. This is just killing me. In fact, there's nothing of me left. I can't believe she could still even be attracted to this. I feel horrible."

Ronny must have said something to the effect of, "It won't always be like this. She is improving so quickly," because Piper told me his response was, "Ya I know and moving isn't forever either but I can't get into the future like this."

Hearing this reality may have forced Piper to expedite her recovery. She worked harder with the trainers, got her doctor to increase her pain meds and began to look for a creative outlet to subsidize her depression, something that O'Reilly had suggested. She asked Pete to move a keyboard into her room so that she could spend some time playing again. Music was such good mental therapy for her and the act of manipulating her brain to hand activity would be therapeutic as well. Deacon always wanted in on the fun too when he was around. While she played, he'd start to bang away on anything in the room that made a noise so Pete decided to buy him a junior drum set on the condition that he take it seriously with music lessons.

It was about six months post surgery that Piper started to feel whole again. Her speech impediment was almost cleared up, her body was toned and gaining strength by the hour, or so it seemed, and she thought her painful times were more sporadic and managed on her own, secretly, in the wee hours of the night. She had come out of her room in the early afternoon one day, all sweaty from her workout, to find Pete sitting on the couch staring blankly into the rays of sunlight that splintered between the shutters.

"What's going on?" Piper asked. "Shouldn't you be at work?"

"I don't want to tell you this, Piper, but there's nothing else I can do. I just can't stick around here anymore. I've taken the network's offer to move my studios to Los

Angeles. My business depends on my ability to create and I can't do that while I'm watching you suffer."

"But I'm almost better. I'm not in so much pain now," Piper insisted.

"You cry out every night, baby. I hear you. I hold my pillow over my head and I still hear you. I feel so badly that it immobilizes me, paralyses me to think that I am the cause of all this suffering for you and there's nothing I can do," he said as tears streamed down his face.

"But I'll try harder. I'll try to be quieter. I'm getting better. I promise you," she begged. She moved in closer and knelt down towards him. "Please don't leave me. I need you. We need you."

They held each other and cried then found each other's lips and tongues. He placed her gently on the carpet in the sunlight while carefully lifting her sweater over her head. He continued his kisses from her mouth down her chin to her neck, her throat, and her chest. He drew his finger across her scars and kissed them as well, ever so gently. He rocked her back and forth in his arms.

"You'll be okay, Pipes," I'll see that you're looked after, never wont for anything."

"But I want you," she said through uncontrollable sobbing. He held her tighter.

"Okay. Hush, hush, slow down, breathe. Let's just take this one step at a time."

~~

In a process that took about 2 weeks, Pete moved his recording gear and his personal belongings out to a small house he bought in the Hollywood Hills. Piper and Deacon flew out to see him the week after he'd moved in. Other than his studio equipment, he was still mostly in boxes, so they spent a few days unwrapping dishes and putting his clothes on hangars. Despite the inevitable consequences of the distance between them and what the future would hold for them, they had a rather fun time together seeing the sights, meeting his neighbours and 'playing house'. It was on the 5th day on the drive back to the airport when Piper again became desperate.

"Please tell me you're only staying until this project is completed," Piper insisted.

"Okay. I'm only staying until this project is completed," he repeated devoid of any real passion.

"You're just saying this because I asked you to?" She questioned.

"Yes. Piper, Deacon, I don't know what the future holds. I'll always love you both because to me, love is forever. You mean more to me than you could ever know. But life is so complicated and I need to do this now and be here now. That's all I can promise you," Pete concluded. He pulled up to the departure entrance, got out of the car, went around to her side and opened her door. He held his hand out to her while she got out and then went to the backseat to take Deacon out of his car seat. He set their luggage on the pavement, hugged them both then watched them walk away.

It was only Deacon who turned to look at him over his shoulder then offered a little wave and smile.

Pete wasn't exactly sure what Deacon was saying due to the roar of the engines, but he felt at peace to believe that he mouthed the words, "We're going home."

BOOK FOUR

And whether or not it is clear to you
the universe is unfolding as it should
be at peace with God, whatever you conceive her (him) to be
And whatever your labours and aspirations
in the noisy confusion of life
keep peace with your soul.

Chapter Thirty-Three

Piper progressed well over the first few weeks upon her return from L.A. She immediately put herself into a routine to keep busy, following the advice of O'Reilly that, "An idle mind is the devil's pulpit." She was still suffering from physical pain and was taking heavy medication to conquer the night tremors and aches in her chest as it stiffened up while she slept. She thought she probably relied on her meds too much but didn't know what else to do. She needed to be able to function. She also needed a job.

She had been teaching fitness classes before the accident, but clearly she wasn't up to doing that just yet. Perhaps she could see if they still considered her desirable for that job once her body was ready to be put to physical work.

"Sure Piper. We're always in need of good instructors like yourself but are you sure you're ready? As you know, it's pretty rigorous, and you've been through quite an ordeal."

"I was thinking perhaps getting certified to teach yoga or pilates because that is what the physiotherapists do for my rehab anyway, so it's both better for my body and might give me a little more longevity in the business, something they're always searching for in fitness," Piper persuaded.

"That sounds good. We're not exactly hiring right now because it's halfway through the fall but we can always use you for fill-ins and by the time the new term starts in January you should be certified and ready to go with the less invasive classes. I'll make sure you have first shot at the most popular time slots then."

"Oh thanks so much," Piper said. "I really appreciate that. I need the money and I need to feel needed."

"I've got your email address now so I'll add you to the list and you should be getting calls to replace our regular instructors starting tomorrow. Good?"

"Great!" Piper agreed. It was like the manager of the fitness center said, Piper got her first call within 3 days and picked up 2 classes by week's end. It was good money per hour but teaching aerobics classes wasn't something you could really make a living from. You'd have to teach 5 or 6 classes a day to make ends meet and from a health standpoint, she couldn't even withstand 5 or 6 classes a week at this point.

~~

Piper was home alone for the third night in a row, while Deacon was with his dad. The influx of visitors and therapists she had, had traipsing through the house during her six-month recovery period were no longer needed and were long gone. She found the days to be at least, tolerable; she liked to cook and would try out new recipes. She also continued to play the piano. It was great physical therapy for the time she needed it most but she found it more mentally soothing for her, which as it turned out, was even more important. The nights alone were becoming unbearable. She went to the kitchen to pour herself a glass of wine that was becoming part of her routine. She looked at the half of bottle remaining and decided to take it with her to the couch figuring she'd probably finish it off in front of the TV. It was on such a non-particular kind of night when there was a knock on her door.

"Hi Pete!" She reached out to hug him, happy but not terribly surprised to see him.

"Oh that felt good. So great to see you again." He asked her how she was doing and if she needed money.

"Not really right now," she said, "but I'm not sure how much longer I can hold out with only making a pittance. Richie's basically covering everything for Deek and he's not terribly expensive yet, while you're covering my health-care costs. I'm thinking though, that I'd like to sell the house," she said. "What do you think?"

"That's not up to me, now" He claimed. "Because I gave it to you. I thought you'd be more comfortable in the environment you and Deacon know so well. And I am concerned about you making too many decisions and too many quick changes. It's not really good for anyone, especially yourself, who's gone through such an ordeal to lose the comfort of routine and security."

"Gawd, you sound like my doctor," she said. "It's just that there are so many memories here. It's such a big house with a lot of wasted space, especially when

Deacon is here only half the time and it's hard for me to look after it all."

"I told you I'd take care of that for you," he reminded her.

"Oh yes, you're very generous that way, always have been but I don't feel right in making you cover everything for two houses. I'd like to sell it and split the difference with you. That way perhaps I could buy a townhouse or condo for Deek and I, certainly something more manageable."

"That sounds good, Pipes. Let me know if you'll need help putting it on the market or finding a place. I'd like to be able to help you in anyway I can," he stated.

"Marry me?" She asked; he felt sure she was joking.

"One day, not so long ago, I would've married you in a heart beat." He admitted.

"So what happened? I got old and grey and undesirable from a car accident?"

"Piper, pleeeeeeease don't say that. You are so desirable, so worthy. You have no idea how special you are to me and to so many others," he assured her.

"I'm sorry. You're right. I just feel so lonely. I miss you and I miss our old life. Why can't we have it back again?" She asked as she dropped her head onto his lap. It wasn't long before sleep enveloped her and she drifted off.

"Nothing moves backwards. It's always moving forwards. Don't fear the future, Piper. Our souls are all working towards a better tomorrow. You'll see; things will settle down for you and be better than ever before. There's always a purpose. *Whether or not it is clear to you, the universe is unfolding as it should." The Desiderata*, he said soothingly so as not to disturb her; she had recited these lines to me a million times.

~~

The weeks turned into months turned into winter. It was December of 1999 when Piper sold the house and moved out to the suburbs into an apartment condo with Deacon. It was a lovely place with a beautiful lake view; even splitting the profits from the sale of the house, Piper was still able to buy something substantial that was more in keeping with her own needs and tastes.

One day just after they moved in, Piper pulled out what she had in the way of Christmas decorations and thought she'd do something special for Deacon in his new bedroom. She threaded a line of twinkling light bulbs around his 3-sided bed to give it that festive look. When Rich dropped him off for the weekend, she was so excited to show him what she'd done.

"Come in here, Deeks. Look!"

"It's so magical. I love it!" They laid on his bed in the dark, with just the lights from the bulbs twinkling all around them.

"I think we should keep your bed like this always. Why does magic just get the chance to visit on Christmas?" She asked him.

"Good point," he said. "We need magic all year round." And so the lights remained on Deacon's bed in his room for as long as they lived in that apartment.

"While we're on the topic of Christmas, what would you like Santa to bring you?" She questioned.

"Are you well enough to celebrate Christmas this year?" He asked.

"Deacon, why do you say such a thing? You worry far too much for your age. We just got a brand new place and things are fine. And besides it's Santa bringing the gifts." No matter how hard she tried to get Deacon to believe in the jolly old elf, he was far too practical and adult to ever buy into the myth.

"It's okay mom. I like believing that Santa is you because you make me happier than any big fat man in a red Santa suit could," he said with pride.

Piper couldn't hold back the tears. "Where the heck did you come from? You are an angel, my angel!"

"It's like he's got the soul of my Grandpa Taylor," she said to herself. *"Now there was a thought."*

~~

On the next visit to the doctor's office, Piper was introduced to a younger man.

"This is my son, Dr. Daniel O'Reilly," stated the aging doctor.

"Very pleased to meet you," said Piper as she held out her hand in greeting. "You must be very proud of your father. He's done such good work and he's a godsend to so many people, certainly me included. Is that what prompted you to become a doctor?"

"Absolutely, I'm walking in some mighty large shoes," he smiled and took a seat in the corner of the senior O'Reilly's office. "I'm just hoping that I don't trip."

"Isn't that our greatest fear?" She said and they chuckled in agreement.

"Do you mind if he sits in on this session today?" O'Reilly said referring to his junior.

"Not at all," Piper agreed.

"Okay then, sit down. Let's take it back to our last visit. What's been going on with you since then?"

"Well, we sold the house and Deacon and I are now living in a really nice apartment not far from here, actually. It's out of the hectic pace of the city, which I really didn't think was conducive to raising the kind of child I wanted to raise and it's closer to Richie as well, which helps with travel and expenses and everything really." Piper admitted.

"But...?" He asked.

"Did I say 'but'? She asked.

"No, but I hear one coming," he persisted.

"I'm just really down. I'm really lonely and I'm doing everything you suggest for me yet I still just don't feel like anything's working."

"You've been through so much recently, Piper. Give yourself a chance to recover, a chance to bounce back. You've endured more pain this past year than most people do in a lifetime."

"I really want a man in my life," she added and then felt embarrassed for saying this in front of the younger doctor. What had been years of speaking naturally from her heart to the older one, now seemed to make her feel vulnerable.

O'Reilly noticed her look of embarrassment and said, "It's okay. You can say whatever you wish to say, here. That's why he's here with me today. I hope that you can learn to feel comfortable around him too."

"Why is that?" Piper asked.

"Because I'm retiring and he's taking over my practice," the doctor said with reassuring confidence.

"He's what? You're what?" Piper's jaw dropped. "You're leaving me?"

"Not leaving you, certainly not right away, and I'll always care about you Piper. You can always, so long as I'm alive, book an appointment to see me. I knew when I started in this business that it meant a lifelong commitment to my patients but I need to begin my journey beyond my psychiatry. It's time and you're ready."

"You just finished telling me how I need to take the time to bounce back. I'm not ready. I can't survive the thought of someone else leaving me," she burst into tears.

"There, there," the doctor said and patted her on the shoulder. The younger O'Reilly got up and passed her the box of Kleenex.

"I'll go and get her a glass of water," he said tenderly to his father.

"Thanks son," O'Reilly said. He knew that he was leaving the room so that Piper could feel more comfortable and regain her composure.

"Piper, you'll be fine. You've got the best son around. I know because I have a good one too. Rely on him and trust him. You're worthy of that kind of relationship. Do you believe that?"

"I do, but why does this have to hurt so much?"

"It seems to me that you are the kind of person that has to hit rock bottom before you can find your way back. But you are a phoenix that will find the strength to rise above the ashes of your predecessors," he smiled at her when she recognized his reference to her favourite Irish singer. "You aren't who you used to be; you're a better, stronger and wiser version of yourself, already. You will be okay. Please trust me, trust your son and *'keep peace with yourself'*."

"*The Desiderata,*" Piper said.

"Take this time to heal, properly. You're a very creative person with so many valuable assets and these need time and freedom to flourish. Promise me you'll try to do this without a special partner in your life. You'll grow far more as a person and be better in all your relationships when you can learn how to trust yourself."

Chapter Thirty-Four

Christmas was never a holiday that sat well with Piper, the memories of Patrick in an enraged, drunken stupor reverberated through her mind and this one hadn't promised to be much better.

Although her father was long gone, she still couldn't help but feel sometimes that she was following in his footsteps. Like she had mentioned to the young O'Reilly, one's greatest fears may be about our inadequacies in living up to the expectations of our parents. Contrarily so for Piper, after years of comparison to the seemingly 'home-wrecking' man, her fears stemmed from becoming everything he was and that, she thought she'd take to her grave.

She wasn't quite in acceptance of the role he played in the development of her personality yet, but after having been through a serious accident and recovery period, she had a new perspective on his highs and lows because she suffered from them equally. She thought to herself, *"He was in such pain."* She wasn't up to forgiving him for that in the same manner that she wasn't up to forgiving herself yet, but she could at least identify the reasons behind her trigger points.

Paradoxically, she dreaded having to endure the season alone but also didn't want to let Deacon know just how miserable she was, so she made arrangements for Richie and the Sirkos' to have him for most of the holidays.

"Oh thanks Piper, but are you sure?" Richie asked.

"Quite," she said in a whisper. "I don't want to bring him down."

"He loves you and he'll want to see his mother on Christmas. Can I bring him to you after dinner then? He'll be able to show you all the neat stuff he got."

"That would be lovely, thanks!" Piper decided, however much it had disappointed her to do so.

The days leading up to Christmas were not entirely without purpose. She taught a few extra classes and popped in to visit Emily, who Piper thought was really starting to show her age. Her mother for years, had been complimented about her youthfulness; that seemed long in the past now. Her visit wasn't as uplifting as she was hoping it was going to be. She was just reminded of the damages that Patrick had left behind and her own lonely existence. She had a lunch date with Finn as well but she was so busy with her new man and burgeoning belly that the hour spent with her seemed almost inconsequential; however, it was the nights that brought forth her demons.

She'd already have taken her daily dose of painkillers by 5 pm most days and would have cracked open her first bottle of wine. When Pete was in her life, she found she liked to drink while she cooked, often infusing the flavours of the red with many of her dishes believing that it made them all more palatable but now that her cooking was just for 'one', it was more of a task to cook at all. Her dinners became more liquid than not. Some days she'd forego eating altogether, take her bottle to the couch, curl her feet up underneath her and find herself there in the morning.

It was fairly early one day just before Christmas when Finn called her and said, "Are you okay?"

"Sure, why?" Piper asked.

"Because you sounded really bizarre on the phone last night."

"I did? Um...er...you called?" Piper sounded confused.

"Yea, you don't remember? I called to see why you didn't show up at Jonny's for dinner."

"Yea sure, I remember now," she lied. "I've just got a lot on my mind and got double-booked. A friend of mine popped by unexpectedly so we stayed in."

"Okay, just checking Pipes. Have a good day, kay?" Finn's voice cracked as she tried to cover her obvious concern. None of the explanations sat well with Finn so she called Todd to find out whether he could concur.

"No, I haven't seen Piper in ages, maybe even since September? I've spoken to her on the phone a few times but haven't actually seen her."

"Hmm...maybe she meant Pete?" Finn tried to justify her sister's response. She was further concerned though, when she got a similar response from Pete too. He hadn't seen her since she helped him with his move to L.A.

Finn didn't want to include any more outsiders and at the time didn't want the guys to know of her concerns either, so she just passed them off as if there had just been a lack of communication. She phoned Dr. O'Reilly.

The female voice at the other end of the phone said, "Dr. O'Reilly senior has now retired. Would you care to speak with or make an appointment with his son? He's taken over his practice."

"Yes please. Can I come in later today? It's Finola Brown speaking. It's with regards to my sister, Piper." Finn clarified.

"Oh yes. Piper's a lovely woman. He's got a cancellation at 2; is that good for you?"

"She's the best and yes, I'll meet him then."

~~

Everyone got busy with the hustle and bustle of the holidays and I assumed that there was a reasonable explanation for Piper's odd behavior until I actually heard from her again in the New Year, in the new millennium, in fact.

She told me that she'd been drowning her sorrows, self-medicating for the past few months to help her get over Pete and the accident. She had never intended to drink her life away but as these addictions happen and alcoholism was already a familiar face in the Brown's household, she rather slipped into it. She was neither proud nor pleased with herself. She stated it calmly and honestly, the way she'd always communicated with me.

"I had been drinking and taking my meds, double-doses in fact, for the days leading up to Christmas and even right up to the time when Deacon was to visit me but I had no idea which day was what at that point; when he arrived I was completely incoherent and still to this moment, I cannot remember seeing the joy on his face nor the love in his body, as he tried to share his Christmas surprises with me," her voice faltered.

"It's okay, Piper. You don't need to continue," I tried to comfort her.

"As I said, I don't really remember what happened that night but I can piece it together by what I discovered in the morning," she went on.

"I remember thinking just how bright it seemed for a winter morning as I awoke to the blinking lights of Deacon's bed. But the ground beneath was hard and bared no resemblance to that of a mattress. I reached under me and felt the hardwood of the living room floor. Deacon was curled up beside me. He'd apparently brought out his pillows, and blankets to build a makeshift bed when I couldn't negotiate my way any further. There were piles of puke all around us and the room reeked of the vomit that permeated the air and stung the roof of my mouth. I didn't have to investigate very thoroughly to deduce that I'd gotten sick from my binging and Deacon, bless his soul, had spent the night playing nursemaid."

"Oh Piper, I'm so sorry, baby," I said.

"I sat and stared in awe of him, my child, my life, for a few minutes as he wrestled with morning; within a few moments his eyes opened by flickering, like that of all the lights that surrounded us and he said, 'Merry

Christmas mommy! I hope you're feeling better today.
Look what Santa did!'"

She couldn't continue her story but she didn't need to. I
understood the connection of a love like that. As Dr.
O'Reilly had foreshadowed, Piper had hit rock bottom
and she vowed to me that in this new year, this new
century, she was going to learn to fly like a phoenix, and
soar high above the flames that had engulfed her.

As far as I can recall, that truly was her lowest point. She
told me she was going to start the new century on the
right foot, push all the past behind her and be that
special, respected mother that Deacon so deserved.
Whatever it was going to take to eliminate all her pain
and suffering, she was ready to move past the noise and
haste.

~~

"Hi. I see you in here all the time. I guess your little guy
takes drum lessons from us?" the handsome musician-
type guy from behind the desk at the music store asked.

"Uh yes, he does," she said shyly. "He's really a bit young
and not that into it but it keeps us busy and gets us out
of the house a little."

"You're a stay-at-home mother?" He asked.

"Yes, I guess you could say that," she answered still not
comfortable with the notion.

"There's nothing wrong with that. In fact, that's really
noble. The most important jobs in the world have to do

with protecting and investing in our future." He said confidently.

Piper really liked the way he spoke. She offered her hand in greeting, "I'm Piper. Piper Brown and that's my little guy, Deacon," she added as he ran out of his lesson and towards her.

"Aw," he recognized the name. "Piper Brown the radio lady-o!" She nodded. "I thought your voice sounded hauntingly familiar."

"Oh, I'm sorry. Was I using my radio voice?" She said in a simulated deep, sexy, and sarcastic way.

"Pleased to meet you. I always find it so interesting to see the face behind the voice," he claimed.

"You used the term 'interesting'. That can't be a good thing?" She questioned.

"In your case, it's a very good thing," he reasoned.

"Well thank you!" They both giggled. "While I've got you here, I was wondering if you'd be interested in taking a part-time job with us teaching some lessons. I know your background is highly musical, piano and voice right?" He asked.

"Wow! You really did listen to me on the radio," Piper said a little embarrassed but mostly proud. She thought about it for a moment, not much longer, then said, "Well sure, thanks again, when do I start?"

"That would be up to you. Tomorrow if you like. I've got the forms for you to fill out right here. The pay's not great but the clientele and the few teachers we already have, are. I mean...I'm nice aren't I?" He batted his baby blues.

"Hmmm...this is going to be an adventure!" She thought to herself. *"And what a coincidence. Or was it?"*

Deacon piped in, "What's going on? You're going to be a teacher here? That's great mommy!"

Things were starting to look up. She was finding her wings. She now had 2 jobs, the music store and the fitness center, and she'd rejoined her friends in her running group in hopes of getting back into competitive racing. Her friends had forgotten how much they missed her quick wit and sense of humour on their early morning training runs. Piper was always the life of the party, even when the party meant 10 to 15 kilometres in the freezing cold before the sun came up.

Her final initiative was reached when she found a local yoga instructor course to sign up for. Having always believed in the high impact, 'no pain no gain', type of workouts, this was going to be something new for her but it was a time of new beginnings and so she figured she had nothing to lose. She'd also heard that all the marathoners were now stressing the importance of proper after-run cool-down stretching and recovery and many of them started to bring yoga into their training programs. She began to do some research about the way of life of a 'yogi' and started getting the itch for more knowledge, the way the old Piper was known to do. And bam! Back came her wanderlust in full throttle. Training in Tibet, the land of karma, connectedness and coincidence was now a necessity instead of a luxury for Piper Brown.

Chapter Thirty-Five

Piper booked her trip for the day after St. Patrick's Day. Being Irish and having had a father who was named after the patron saint, the Brown children always gathered together wherever they were to share a pint of green beer on March 17th. Jonny's two oldest were also now legal age so joined the rest of the clan in Brown fashion. Even Finn and David were present, although Finn was too pregnant to imbibe, David had it known that he was going to drink her share. Angela and Toni were still living in the states but told the rest that they'd be drinking 'green' in their honour.

Piper was excited to see everyone again. She couldn't recall the last time she'd seen them and even if she could remember, she hadn't been in a good place. This time around, she relished the thought of getting together. She had so much good news to tell them.

"Wow! Another trip, Pip?" Jonny teased by turning her name into a rhyme.

"To Tibet, I'm going to return with so much wisdom you won't even be able to keep up with me." Piper declared.

"Can't even do it now, babe. You look so happy. I'm proud of you, Piper," he gave her the best bear hug she'd had in eons.

~~

Her flight out of Pearson went to Gatwick in London where she had to switch planes to fly on to Beijing then stay on board but wait for another 35 minutes before the plane went on to Lhasa. She booked a few days to herself before the summit so she could get a feel for the culture first. She thought it was unlikely she'd ever have the chance to get back to the area, so she'd take the opportunity to explore. While she flew, she read through some of the travel pamphlets she had been given. She learned that Lhasa is an ancient city with "over 1400 years of history. It had been 'peacefully liberated' in 1951 and whereby in 1965, it boasted a less than 3 square kilometer downtown area in the Tibetan Autonomous Region." This capital city of Tibet was where she was going to spend a full weekend at a non-speaking Buddhist monastery, to learn the techniques and stylings from the Buddhist Zen Yogi masters.

She was very excited to take on this new venture. Some of the other fitness instructors she knew had come back from this spiritual journey over the last few years, in complete awe of the country, its citizens and the enlightened awakenings they experienced at the yogi summit.

Lhasa, she quickly discovered, is high up on the Tibetan plateau at an elevation of close to 12,000 feet above sea level. Due to the air pressure at that great height, Piper experienced a bit of altitude sickness upon arrival. She noticed dizziness and a 'thick-headed' feeling when the plane first touched down. "It's like I couldn't get my ears to pop," she mentioned to me some time afterwards. She booked into her hotel, The House of Shambala, a beautiful old authentic villa right in the centre of town, for the first few nights. She wanted a more purist approach to her adventure before meeting up with the other students at the conference, which was held at the very Americanized and elegant, St. Regis. She wasn't in her room for very long when she got the itch to run and strapped on her runners. Before she left Canada she had entertained the possibility of training for more long distance races, so that combined with the fact that she was already so high up in the sky, she figured she'd begin her altitude training. She knew lots of athletes who would fly into Denver to do their training just prior to big events.

That run was certainly much harder than she'd anticipated and she ended up doing more of a run-walk with the emphasis more on 'walk' than she wanted; there was a plus side to the pace of her training though and that was, she had a greater opportunity to take in the spectacular and breathtaking sights. She was able to get a good view of the Potala Palace, the former site of the Tibetan government as well as the winter home of the Dalai Lama. Its multi-level peaks and towering fortress walls were a memory that would last a lifetime. She was starting to feel the surge of creativity that O'Reilly had suggested that she might if she could force herself to spend more time alone. Although this yogi summit would have similar-minded people in attendance, she had registered for it solitarily, without the aid of an intimate friend.

Within a few hours she had made her way back to the hotel, showered and grabbed a quick bite at a local restaurant. She wasn't terribly hungry, still feeling the affects of jetlag and extreme altitude; she ordered herself a glass of wine, and had just had barely a sip of it when she thought she heard someone call out her name. She turned her head in its direction and there was no one around. She shook it off thinking that it was probably exhaustion that was completely overwhelming her. She put some money down for the mostly untouched food and drink that she'd ordered and went back to her room. She called down to the concierge to book her a 'lift' for a morning tour of the city and a wake-up call. She laid her head on the pillow and within what felt like milliseconds, was awakened by the hotel staff in the morning as she'd requested.

She spent a luxurious day doing whatever *'her big heart desired'* as she recalled, describing the many temples and spa-like fountains and prayer rooms. She managed to pick up a Tibetan singing bowl and gong for Deacon, in keeping with buying him musical instruments everywhere she went, for his collection. He loved the sound they made signaling the start of a yoga class. Then later that day she took a shuttle over to the St. Regis to sign in for the silent conference to be held at 5 am the following day. *"Yikes,"* she thought to herself, *"What the hell did I get myself into? A whole 2 days of no speaking and having to wake up at 4:30 each day for meditation? Good luck with that! That sounds even more grueling than a marathon."*

Bright and early she arose and donned her usual yoga attire. She packed a day bag with small towels, her digitless socks and gloves, water bottle and yoga mat. She had been told ahead of time what she'd need and what would be supplied. She then took the elevator down to the lowest level of the hotel, where she was joined by obvious other budding yogis dressed similarly. Although the summit did have some 'verbal communication areas', the fear of speaking was already foremost on the students' minds because the elevator ride was completely silent. When the doors opened, an immaculately sculpted young female yogi wearing what appeared to be the traditional robes of practice greeted them. She bowed her head and whispered softly, *'follow me'*. They were led into a rock-walled sanctuary filled with the smell of chai incense, running fountain streams, hidden among moss and vines with statues of Buddha in various poses. Meditative music was pumped through tiny speakers camouflaged by the Asian décor. The young woman then addressed the group of women in a very fluid voice. Piper was highly particular about voices, having been a broadcaster for so many years. Nothing seemed to irk her more than a nauseating sound and in a yoga class specifically, the yogi had to sound as peaceful as the postures she was creating. This woman was certainly no exception, her voice was like butter as Piper described to me, seemingly *'ethereal and weightless'*. She described the course of events that they'd experience over the next two days then asked them to take a seat cross-legged in a Buddha pose on the pillows that had been provided while she took attendance and greeted more students. From there, they were directed into the change rooms where they could leave their belongings and then they were to meet with their mats in *shavasana* in the studio, a starting posture where the participant lies on their back, legs mat width apart, arms extended at the sides with their palms facing upwards. This pose was intended for the immediate connection of the trinity: the blending of the mind, the body and the spirit. It was also a time meant to become one with one's breath, a key aspect of a yoga practitioner.

The first half of the morning included an hour meditation and two hours of actual yoga postures. The only instructions they had were visual while the tranquil music was played as background throughout. By 9:30, the students had a scheduled green tea break for a half an hour, in which they were taken to a non-silent open atrium area, where they could quietly mingle and refresh their energies. The next two hours included individual instruction and body core manipulation in a smaller group forum. The summit continued in this manner for most of the two days. Piper was in her element. She really began to understand what both the doctor had said to her and the scriptures she'd memorized from *The Desiderata, in the noisy confusion of life, Be at peace with God whatever you conceive him/her to be.* She returned to Canada feeling invigorated, inspired and most definitely at *peace with her soul.*

~~

It was several months later when Piper was in a yoga class feeling somewhat uncomfortable in not being able to find the focus she had acquired in her previous practice; her mind was moving in and out of the moment; the yogi said, "Now turn your bodies around to lay on your back with your feet facing the west wall to find your final shavasana."

She hadn't been posing for even a few minutes when she thought she noticed a familiar face. *"Hey that looks like Steve. If he's back in town why hasn't he contacted me?"* she thought. *"I'll catch up to him after class."*

The yogi continued. "Keep in mind that there are still ten minutes remaining in this class today. When you leave, make it a part of your practice; don't rush off, rather move swiftly and effortlessly so as not to disturb anyone who wishes to remain for the entire session. I do urge you to use this time to refresh, renew and regain your breath within the sanctity of the moment. The music will play for the duration and a gentle gong will sound when the time is up. 'The divine light in me honours the divine light in you, Namaste.'"

"Steve, hey Steve...wait up...it's me, Piper!" Piper called out a little breathlessly as she grabbed her yoga bag and headed out into the parking lot towards him...

~~

"Piper, Piper," she felt a soothing hand tapping her on the shoulder. "She opened her eyes to see that she was still laying in shavasana on her mat. The studio lights had been raised from their normal dimness and the classroom was empty. "You must have been in quite a Zen trance. Hope it was peaceful," her colleague grinned.

"I've been laying here the whole time?" Piper asked in bewilderment.

"Yes, love. Don't concern yourself, though. Our connectedness with the world is what is so wonderful about us as human beings," she said assuredly. "Where were you?"

"I guess I was right here all the time."

"No I mean, tell me about your journey," she said.

"I had a lovely conversation with an old friend and former boss, who I thought had been in the classroom here, doing yoga. It felt so real. He hugged me and he told me how much he missed me and that he felt so proud of the accomplishments that I'd made and the grounding I seemed to have gained since he last saw me. He also said that he thought that I looked like I had finally found the peace in my life that seemed to elude me previously and that he felt comfortable in knowing I was looked after."

"Well these are good things, aren't they?" She asked.

"Absolutely, but it didn't really happen and that makes me feel sad because I haven't made much effort to stay connected with him for many years," Piper replied, "and he didn't seem like himself. He seemed distant or not well, or something. But that's just all craziness anyway. Like I said, it never actually happened; it was all in my mind."

"But perhaps this is telling you something; that it's time you reconnect? Things happen for a reason. We're just not always sure in the moment, the reasons why." Piper smiled in full agreement.

Chapter Thirty-Six

The next few years went swiftly by for Piper and Deacon. They were like 'two peas in a pod,' she'd often say to him. She did well as a music teacher; all her students adored her, which came as no shock to anyone. She enjoyed her fitness and yoga classes alike and spent her free time playing music and running. She had a small group of good friends; her relationships with her siblings were on as solid ground as she could ever recall and were solidified particularly following her mother's death.

Emily had passed on, pretty unobtrusively. She went as quietly as she had lived following the divorce from their father. Her turbulent years were long forgotten.

"I just wished she'd found someone to love her properly," Piper said to Jonny at the funeral. "She deserved that; everyone does."

"That sounds like you're speaking from experience?" Jonny chuckled.

"Or experiences!" She exclaimed. "If there's one thing I know how to do now, it's love and be loved. Passion is such a key aspect of living fully, whether it be a passion for your career, or kids or lover; how can one really feel alive unless they experience this kind of enlightenment?"

"You sure sound like someone I used to know." Jonny said beaming.

"And who's that?" Piper winked.

~~

Piper had competed in three marathons improving her time on each and decided that she'd do one more with the intent to qualify for Boston. She was already so close to the mark.

"What do I need to do?" She asked her running mates.

"Well, do the Corning Glass Marathon in New York State with us this fall. It's a flat to gently rolling course, at a time of year where the temperature is most moderate. There are a fair number of local runners who head over the border to compete in that one who end up with their best times ever."

"That sounds good. I'm 39 now so my qualifying time is 3:45. I'm only about 6 minutes off so with a little extra conscientious training, I should be able to do it."

She set about getting a training log and scheduling in her long runs and fitness regimen the way Richie had taught her so many years previously. When fall arrived that year, her spirit was as colourful as the scenic Appalachian forests that wound around the Finger Lakes. Everything felt right. She was in perfect harmony and health with the nature around her.

She had her fastest time at the halfway mark, then slowed her pace a little to the 18-mile water station but still was ahead of her target. Her goal was to try to keep just behind the 3:45 pace bunny so she could slide into the finish at her desired goal.
The last few minutes she seemed to hit 'the wall' that runners spoke of but she'd never experienced herself.

Several runners passed her at that point and she started to lose confidence.

She used the familiar sounds of runners and fans encouragement as she struggled to regain her last few kilometres into the finish. As she crossed the line, she noticed the time on the clock read, '3:48:56'. "Damn it!" she said out loud knowing she had missed her Boston target mark by close to three minutes.

"You did great!" said her running buddy who came in just ahead of her.

"Not great enough. I needed a 3:45 to qualify for Boston," she said disappointedly, "and the problem is, I really don't think I could run much faster than that." She left Corning, N.Y., with a heavy glass medal around her neck and an even heavier weight in her heart.

Her friends advised her to check the Boston website to see if they had changed the requirements or they allowed for any exceptions to the timing restrictions, as sometimes the marathon committee would do. She thought it was a long shot but she took their advice once she arrived back home to her computer.

"Let's see here," she said to herself as she browsed through the site.

"Awesome!" She proclaimed out loud.

"What's awesome, mom?" Deacon asked. Even at the age of 9 he was never far from his mother's side.

"We're going to Boston. I've qualified for the oldest and most prestigious race in North America."

As it had always been her goal to run Boston by the age of 40, she thought that her age at the time of her qualifier was what was supposed to match the standard in Boston, but as it turned out, Boston takes your age at the time you run their race. She had been training and hoping to run the 39-year-old pace in Corning as a qualifier, which was a 3:45, but in effect, since she was turning 40 by Boston's race day, it was a 3:50 time that should have been her goal. Her 3:48 then, was a bonafide Boston qualifying time. She did it, no exceptions required!

~~

Piper and Deacon were up early with their bags packed and ready to go when Jonny arrived to drive them to the airport. They were going to meet Angela at Logan International when they landed. Toni was at a medical convention in Texas and their kids were all old enough to stay home alone, so Angela thought she'd take a little break from them and go and cheer Piper on in the race. Her purpose for going was twofold; someone pretty much had to stay at the finish line with Deacon anyway.

"Don't you just love the feel of the airport?" Piper said to Deacon, as she squeezed his hand in the excitement. "There are just so many people, coming and going, and so many adventures in the air," she continued to share her secret passions with him.

His eyes lit up. "And look at that big plane. Is that the one that will be taking us to Boston?" Piper nodded in agreement.

They touched down at Logan and easily met up with Angela, who went to bend down to pick him and then realized that he was almost as tall as she was and certainly would be too heavy to lift.

"Wow! You've gotten to be such a big kid. Mom's feeding you well, I see," she noticed.

"Hi Angie!" Piper and Deacon said in unison and took turns giving her hugs.

"This sure is exciting! You amaze me Piper. Maybe next 40th, I'll run this with you?" They laughed.

They walked around the city a little the day before the race and went shopping in the runner's mall making sure they all bought sufficient souvenirs to com-memorate such a monumental occasion.

"We've got to make sure that we eat properly tonight and get a good night's sleep," Piper said. "I realize that I'll be too excited to sleep well but good rest and keeping my legs above my heart for as long as possible are pretty vital aspects."

"What do you think your time will be?" Angie asked.

"I'm not doing this to break any records. Everyone says that the goal is just qualifying. The rewards are in the race itself, making it here, being considered the top marathoners in the world," Piper said with modest pride.

"You rock our world, Piper! Mom and dad would both be so proud of you!"

~~

The race wasn't set to begin until noon which Piper then figured out, would have her finishing up by 4 to 4:30 that afternoon. Angela and Deacon would try to meet up with her at various points during the race but as they weren't that familiar with the course and city, they weren't entirely sure whether they'd be able to; however, they were definitely set to be at the finish line to see her cross. Piper hugged them through teary-eyes as she boarded the athletes' bus from in front of their hotel.

"Go mom go!" Deacon waved as she read his lips through the bus windows.

It was an uncharacteristically hot day in April in Boston and waiting all morning just seemed to make it that much more overwhelming for her. That, and the big, familiar fireball in Piper's chest made her feel like she was in over her head. She was corralled into her qualifying time gate, an area where she was going to start with other runners that ran relatively at her same pace.

Just to add to the exhilaration was all the pomp and circumstance that big American events attract. F-18 jet fighter planes took off from a nearby landing pad while a fireworks display lit up the sky all before the gun went off signaling the start of the race. Piper could barely breathe not just because they were squeezed in so tightly but because she felt so emotional about having achieved a lifelong dream. *"Pinch me, am I really here?"* she said to herself as she could hear similar sentiments echoed by others around her.

The course was lined by 3 or 4 supporters deep, the entire 26.2 mile route and as Piper recalled on many occasions thereafter, there were too many amazing stories to tell that developed and that she'd experienced herself and by others along the way.

As she predicted, there was no record-breaking gold medal time to carry her across the finish line but seeing her 9-year-old son there to cheer her on as she fell from exhaustion into his open arms, was more golden than she could ever possibly desire.

~~

Back at home, the thrill of her accomplishment stayed with her for quite awhile. She was congratulated seemingly everywhere she went, from her music students to her yoga practitioners. It was one day about a week later that I finally broke down and called her after all those years.

"Hey kiddo, congratulations!" I said.

"Steve, wow! I thought you'd dropped off the face of the earth? Uh...thanks by the way! Yes that was something else, a big deal. I'm a big deal," she said rather coyly and uncharacteristically proud.

"You done good, Piper, and you should be proud," I said and heaved a big, pregnant sigh.

"What was that about?" She asked. "You don't really sound good. I mean...I didn't mean that to come out the way it did. You just sound... Are you okay?"

"I'm fine. I guess I just miss hearing your voice," I said very honestly but trying to withhold the real reason why I wasn't sounding like myself. I had been diagnosed with lymphatic cancer following a tumour that was found in my lung a few years previously and at that point the doctors had given me just a little while longer. I knew it would be the last time I'd speak to her.

Piper recalled her deja-vu, "Hey! Do you ever do yoga? I could've sworn that I...nevermind," she said, remembering that the whole scene had only been played out in her mind, having reached that Zen state.

~~

A few months later...

"Am I speaking with Ms. Piper Brown?" the man at the other end of the phone line asked.

"Yes, this is she," replied Piper.

"I'm Robert Henry from Williamson and Associates. I'm an estate lawyer calling on behalf of Steven Anderson," Piper let out a gasp and he continued. "I'm sorry Ms. Brown," he paused. "Yes, Mr. Anderson passed away after a long battle with cancer."

Piper's mind began racing through all the memories she'd had with and of him. He always seemed to be present in her thoughts, in her times of greatest need and she felt devastated that she hadn't been able to connect with him more often over the years. Had she remembered him standing over her with tears streaming down his face while she was unable to communicate during her days in a coma? And why does her dream about him a few years ago, where she thought he had told her that he wasn't well, remain so acutely in her mind? Why didn't she listen to those voices in her head? Why hadn't she stayed connected?

"Mr. Anderson has left a manuscript with your name on it. He really wanted you to have it. If you could please give me your address, I'll mail it to you."

"Yes, of course, thank you," Piper said.

"So sorry for your loss Ms. Brown. He spoke very highly of you."

EPILOGUE
Chapter Thirty-Seven

With all its sham, drudgery and broken dreams
It is still a beautiful world. Be cheerful. Strive to be happy.

~~

It's been some thirty years since I'd met with her and was able to wrap my arms around her; despite the fact that her hair is grey and her skin is old and wrinkled, the energy around her still seems to carry a certain youthful glow. Ever since I first laid eyes on her I have known some deeper connection. I await her with the same intrepid anticipation I always have.

We've always had this odd connection, like we were one and the same, two bodies sharing the same soul. I knew her better now than I ever would.

She did not hop towards me with a girlish burst or waddle towards me with a weighted belly, rather she moved as if being guided by angels, her arms open wide yet not wider than her bright white smile that dimpled her face when she laughed. As she leaned in towards me I could smell that same familiar sweetness and warmth that always surrounded me and so naturally guided me into the endearing caverns of her soul. "I am home," I thought. This was always the way it felt when I was with her.

~~

"Deacon, it's Brian. I think you should come here as swiftly as possible; the doctors aren't sure how much time she has." Piper's husband of twenty some odd years, said with a tender urgency.

"Is she conscious?" Deacon asked.

"She has moments of lucidity when her eyes are open."

"Has she said anything about the airport?" Deacon questioned.

"That's where they found her but she hasn't said anything; she slips in and out of consciousness. Apparently, she's had a stroke."

"I'll be there as soon as I can," Deacon said.

When Deacon arrived he was holding a remote control for an electronic model airplane. He pushed the power switch to the 'on' position and raised the aircraft into the air in view from Piper's bed. It twirled and swirled over-head and remained suspended just out of reach while he bent down to kiss her cheek. She sensed his presence and opened her eyes with his touch. Although her face didn't move, there was a certain creasing around her eyes, when she saw him, which made it look like she was smiling. Her eyes moved slowly and intently back and forth from the plane to Deacon. He drew in closer so that his ear was within inches from her lips.

"I am home," she whispered and then closed her eyes for the last time.

~~

Brian invited Deacon back to the house that he'd shared with Piper over the past few decades and asked him to help himself in going through her personal affects.

He had constructed a beautiful memory box for her on their first anniversary, knowing just how much she valued special photos, trinkets and other keepsakes. Although he had been a certified electrician before his retirement, he had always maintained his 'jack-of-all-trades and master of none' status, in the same way that Piper would tease about her grandfather, Stanley. The box was clearly hand carved with delicate lettering engraved right into the root and shafts of the wood. It was a 3 by 4 foot box, 2 feet deep with antique hinges and latch. When Deacon opened it, the creaking sound reverberated across the room with an air of mystery and intrigue. Combined with the fresh scent of pine and cedar was the smell of Piper, patchouli and sunflowers. He swallowed back the tears of his mother as he scanned the contents of the container full of the loving memories that she had shared with so many people. He brushed aside a few of the petals from the dried bouquets of flowers that she had kept from her days in a coma and discovered the manuscript that was addressed to her from so many years ago. He opened the large manila envelope and read the enclosed letter.

> Dear Piper:
>   I really hadn't intended on giving you this manuscript in this way. I had hoped to be alive and well, to see you read it and have you share it with me, its author. But as is the nature of this strange existence we lead, no one ever really knows for sure what is to be his fate.
>   This is the story of your life, your unique, amazing, wonderful, ever-perpetually changing life. You have meant so many things to so many people; we are all better for having a little part of you in all of us. And it is by no means, all of who you are; only you can truly fill in the gaps but it

is a good start to a wonderful journey. Perhaps one day you and Deacon can continue where I have had to leave off in this physical incarnation.

Eternally,
Steve Anderson

Deacon read the entire typewritten manuscript from start to finish and noticed that Piper had added in pen, some finer details when the author's description seemed inadequate, cloudy, or sparse. So much was familiar to him, as he'd shared such a close relationship with his mother over the years; some of it had come as no surprise to him, yet some, was entirely new. There were also adjuncts to the original manuscript that included a page of handwritten notes by Piper appearing to have been transcribed from a conversation she'd had with her sister, Finn. It seemed to explain a few of the uncertainties that his mother had worried about in her younger years.

Finn had visited with the O'Reilly's when Piper was at her lowest point. Although they couldn't reveal everything that had transpired during Piper's visits to them, due to doctor-patient confidentiality, they were able to help Finn come to terms with some of Piper's eccentricities and it was really the younger O'Reilly that put some of the puzzle pieces together.

Dr. O'Reilly Junior had been Piper's psychiatrist for the 30 some odd years after his father's retirement. Deacon had always been aware of the bipolar diagnosis from her former years but hadn't been aware of the research they had been doing with her on split personalities and mild schizophrenia until he read her accounts in the manuscript. They used her research from her discoveries about her heritage in Ireland and her near-death coma experiences to pave the way for further studies in the theory of the eternal soul and 'spirit passaging'; whereby one's soul was linked or connected to several others, in their physical forms, creating a sanctity of oneness. There had been no affirmative diagnosis in Piper's case, as each of her 'episodes' could have had a viable reason for their occurrence, if even to chalk them all up to merely coincidence. However, her psychiatrist believed, that it was a combination of her ancestry, experiences and her unique personality that provided her with these seemingly innate and extraordinary capabilities.

Deacon learned that his mother had such an intense imaginative perception on reality that given certain circumstances, she believed she could see, in her mind's eye, situations that were about to arise; in the same vein, she thought she could hear voices that would guide her in making the right choices about herself and those people for whom she cared. Where some people with this particular affliction might subscribe to these possibilities as being frightening and would refuse themselves of the benefits, Piper embraced her spirit's uniqueness and cherished the moments she perceived to be real, as a gift and a blessing.

~~

Deacon pulled his car up along the same service road leading into the airport, that he'd pulled into on so many previous occasions. He turned off the car's engine and pushed the electric-powered seat back to a greater reclined position. He reached his arm over and brought Sarah in closer to him. He loved the smell of her freshly washed hair and the touch of her soft cheek against his.

"Where are we going this time?" She asked.

"We're not going anywhere, darling. We are home."

~The End~

~The Desiderata~

Go placidly amid the noise and haste
Remember what peace there may be in silence
As far as possible, without surrender, be on good terms
with all people,
Speak your truth clearly and listen to others
Even the dull and ignorant have their story.

Avoid the loud and aggressive; they are vexatious to the
spirit.
If you compare yourself with others, you may become
vain or bitter
For always there will be greater and lesser than
yourself.

Enjoy your achievements as well as your plans
Keep interested in your career,
It is a possession in the changing fortunes of time,
Exercise caution in your affairs for the world is full of
trickery.
But let this not blind you to what virtue there is,
Strive for high ideals; everywhere there is heroism.

Be yourself and do not feign affection,
Be not cynical about love for it is as perennial as the
grass,
Take kindly the counsel of the years; gracefully
surrender the things of youth,
Nurture strength of spirit to shield you and do not
distress yourself with dark imaginings.

Fears are born of fatigue and loneliness,
Beyond a wholesome discipline be gentle with yourself,

You are a child of the universe, no less than the trees
and stars,
You have a right to be here.

And whether or not it is clear to you,
The universe is unfolding as it should, so
Be at peace with God, whatever you conceive her (him)
to be.

And whatever your labours and aspirations
In the noisy confusion of life
Keep peace with your soul,
With all its sham, drudgery and broken dreams,
It is still a beautiful world.
Be cheerful. Strive to be happy.

~~

Acknowledgements:

Max Ehrmann for his copyright © 1952 of *The Desiderata* for which this story is founded.

My Lucky Seven:

1) Jeff, Conor, and Kiki...very supportive despite not getting fed, watered or walked for the duration
2) Music companies/interviewees...who helped maintain the story's authenticity
3) Radio DJs and other characters and 'ex's for providing the 'colour', conflict and charisma
4) The Scot(t)s in my life...best friends who have provided me with the inspiration for this story and through which my spirit continually soars
5) Kirk...'my Captain'...who encouraged me to stick with my gut
6) My sisters (including Lu!)...reminding me that I have a gift and jumped on board very early and quickly in this project!
7) And last but not least, my son Eli...wherever I am and whoever I become, he always guides me back home.

Made in the USA
Charleston, SC
07 June 2014